The Corpse Wore Stilettos

MJ O'Neill

The Corpse Wore Stilettos
Red Adept Publishing, LLC
104 Bugenfield Court
Garner, NC 27529
http://RedAdeptPublishing.com/

For Brian, who never stopped believing

"Over the years I have learned that what is important in a dress is the woman who is wearing it." – Yves Saint Laurent

Chapter 1

In the four months since my dad's unexpected trip to the slammer had plunged my family into poverty and me into desperate employment at the county morgue in St. Louis, Missouri, I'd learned to accept a lot of things. I'd stopped lamenting that the color of the blood clashed with my lipstick. While I still considered shoe booties fashion suicide, I had grown to appreciate their practicality in maintaining the pristine condition of my Jimmy Choos. For the most part, I had become acclimated to the gore, although I still reserved the right to call certain things icky. I'd come to terms with my every move being tracked by a time clock and with taking orders instead of giving them to maids and cooks. And I'd mostly accepted becoming a peer of people who thought wine from a box was an innovation and that a gourmet meal could be cooked in a microwave.

But one morgue situation still astonished me.

"Ahemmm." I cleared my throat, hoping Miss Skinny Thing, squished like a pancake between Big Max and the steel autopsy table, would realize the two of them weren't alone in the morgue. Why people thought sex in a morgue was some arousal-heightening, must-have experience was beyond me. The cold stainless steel tables would give anyone's ass frostbite, the place reeked of a combination of spoiled milk and formaldehyde, and the lighting was more suited to interrogations than romance. Yet since starting at the morgue, at least twice a week, I'd had the lucky job of chasing away lusty lovers from the hospital above us.

This was the last thing I needed tonight. A girl couldn't even find a secluded place next to a dead body to lament her broken heart without being reminded of all the happy people in the world.

Martin and I would never know necromantic love like this. Not that *the* Martin Eldridge would ever be caught dead in a place like this doing that. But still. He was gone. We had broken up months ago, right after my dad's arrest, but nothing had made it seem permanent like receiving the box of my leftover belongings from his apartment.

Fighting back my irritation, I focused on tonight's winning couple in the game of "morgue make-out." Big Max was the large LPN from pediatrics, and Miss Skinny Thing was a candy-striper bimbo who'd probably had zero intentions of shagging Big Max until she found herself all revved up on a combination of the forbidden and the macabre. Oblivious to my presence, they started rounding second base. Her dress hung crookedly from the X-ray viewer mounted on the wall.

"Max," I said in a fairly audible tone. I was trying not to startle them into flying off the autopsy table but needed to speak loudly enough that they would get the hint before he started to "show me something beautiful, baby," as Miss Skinny Thing put it.

I would have thought that with something as serious as dead people, the county would spring for a decent security system, but for some reason, it never made the "necessities" list in the budget. The hospital's living people tended to get all the money. While entering through the morgue's main intake door required a badge, anyone with half a wit who knew their way around the hospital could make it down here through what had affectionately become known as the "sexavator," the unmonitored service elevator used for transporting bodies from the hospital's main wings to the morgue.

"Max!" I yelled, startling both of them.

Miss Skinny Thing let out a tweet like a crushed bird. Max flew off the table and landed with a loud crunch on what might have been his knee. The instrument table next to him toppled over, metal clanking with a shrill clatter as it hit the institutional linoleum. Max scrambled to find something to cover all God had given him.

"Sweet Lord Jesus!" he yelled.

"I don't think he's going to help you today, Max," I said.

Miss Skinny Thing scrambled for her clothes and flew out the door. As I helped Max to the emergency room to get his knee looked at, I tried to provide comfort by reminding him that the average male would have seven sexual partners in his lifetime. I followed with the story of a Moroccan emperor who had held the Guinness World Record for siring at least 867 offspring. Before I rattled off some additional useless fact about the resilience of knees —I had a habit of spouting trivial facts when I got nervous—we arrived at the ER.

The triage nurse asked what had happened. Max looked at me like an eight-year-old boy who had just been busted by his mom for stealing cookies.

"Max was helping me. We were... moving morgue equipment," I said in a thinly veiled rescue attempt, grasping for the first explanation that made sense. No one deserved Nurse Nancy's wrath. "I'm so sorry you were hurt, Max."

Relief flashed across his face. "Uh, it's all right. It was my own fault."

I left Max to the nurse and headed for the cafeteria. Between the text from Martin and that ordeal, I needed ice cream. Despite how often I had to play sex police in my new career, I still found it surreal that anyone would want to do *that* in a morgue. I was pretty sure Max now regretted the decision. I would be pissed if he filed for workers' comp and I had to do the paperwork.

The cafeteria generated customers for the hospital as much as it provided a service to families and employees. On most days, the main entrée looked unrecognizable, and brown gravy covered everything. Despite the questionable nature of the other food in the cafeteria, though, I could always count on the ice cream machine. I grabbed my cup of vanilla, heaped on some Oreo cookies as an extra treat, and headed for checkout.

"I'm sorry, miss, but this card has been declined."

"Seriously?" I asked the cashier to try it again, but I knew what the result would be.

Since my dad's arrest on racketeering and money-laundering charges, every day brought a new reminder that my life had turned into a Shakespearean tragedy. Or maybe a comedy. Six months ago, I wouldn't have thought twice about spending thousands of dollars on a beautiful new Louis Vuitton handbag. Now, even scraping together change for ice cream from the hospital cafeteria proved challenging.

When the police had arrested my dad, they froze all of our assets—bank accounts, credit cards, investment funds. They seized our house, leaving my mom and grandmother, Grand, homeless. We'd blown through my meager savings in the first few weeks after I'd moved home from Boston to help my family in the wake of my father's arrest.

If I didn't want my mom, Grand, and me out on the streets and eating cat food, I needed a job. Luckily, Grand's boyfriend, Claude, had some connections with county law enforcement. When he offered to put in a good word to help me land something, I was thrilled. I pictured myself as a receptionist at the police station or an assistant at the courthouse. But all he could get me was a job in the morgue, and it was better than nothing. While morgue work didn't have much call for Art History, my minor in biology—along with my beauty pageant award for outstanding makeup—was good enough to land me here.

My parents didn't like to acknowledge my employment at all. They took every opportunity to insult my new job as being beneath me, asking when I would return to my more respectable job at a museum in Boston. As if I could. When Daddy was first arrested and I flew home to help Mom, I took one look at them and knew I was home to stay. I'd never seen my larger-than-life mother look so small and shaken. I didn't understand how the people who'd raised me could seriously believe I'd be fine back in my cushy apartment while Grand sweated about whether mattresses in shelters could be Febrezed. Waters women stuck together. Waters women took care of their own.

So now I worked at the morgue, waiting for the misunderstanding with my dad to be cleared. Because it *was* a misunderstanding. As if bean-counting Clarke Waters could be part of the mob.

But my job barely paid enough to cover rent and an occasional Oreo ice cream splurge. The ice cream was supposed to be salve for my romantic soul. Before I'd interrupted Big Max, I'd been looking for a place to recover from the news that I was no longer going to be Mrs. Martin Eldridge of the Boston Eldridges.

I turned from the cafeteria and headed to the morgue office, contemplating that my relationship was officially a casualty of my dad's wrongful arrest. I was amazed that one misunderstanding could have wreaked so much havoc.

As soon as I left Boston, Martin—or in my opinion, Martin's mother—had concluded that with me in St. Louis, maybe it was best for us to "take a break." He texted that the break would free me to focus on my family situation. Never mind that it had the added bonus of also delinking the Eldridges from a mob scandal. As soon as my dad was cleared, Martin and I would be back together. But looking at the Gucci hatpin and Michael Aram cheese board staring up at me from the box of exiled things I had received in the mail today, I had my doubts.

I was shaken from my reverie by the morgue phone ringing down the hall, and I made a mad dash for it.

"County morgue, Kat speaking. How may I assist you?" I managed to get out between gasps of air.

"Oh, Katherine, there you are. For a moment, I thought maybe no one was there," said the raspy voice at the other end of the line.

"Sorry, Dr. Hawthorne. I was taking care of a problem with the elevator."

"If we could charge room fees for every time that happened, we might get enough money to upgrade some of our equipment." Dr. Hawthorne, the medical examiner, was like a favorite high school science teacher—old and frumpy but kind of cool.

I thought perhaps he'd hired me so he could brag about having a Harvard grad on staff, but he seemed to like me.

"We have a murder victim on her way to you. I'm finishing some things up here with the detectives and folks from the mayor's office."

"The mayor's office?"

"Yes, lots of eyes on this one, Katherine. We'll need to be on our toes. Go ahead and start processing her. I'll see you soon."

The county hospital morgue acted as overflow for the county medical examiner's main office up the street. In my short stint at the morgue, I'd processed only one other murder. Male, black, twenty-two, allegedly killed by his brother for sleeping with his brother's wife and stealing his power tools. I would have guessed a chain saw would slice clean through the man's head, but there they were, the gurney and the body with the protruding chain saw, all rolling along.

Curating bodies wasn't much different from curating art, which had been my job at the museum in Boston. First came authentication to confirm that the art—or in this case, the body— was who it was claimed to be. Then came investigation of the story. The most valuable art pieces had interesting, verifiable stories. The most valuable autopsies were the ones that told the story the victim could no longer tell.

Autopsies were broken into two phases, the external examination and the internal. As a *diener*—a German word for "servant" and, thankfully, one that sounded way fancier than "corpse washer" for when my mom talked to people at her bridge club—I had responsibility for the external exam and helping Dr. Hawthorne with the internal.

I put on my gown, gloves, and shoe booties and found the voice recorder. Pulling my mop of wavy honey-brown hair into a ponytail, I flipped through my iPod for music to get me in the right mood and cranked up some Florence + the Machine. The paramedics pushed through the doors with the murder victim.

My biology minor hadn't been a total waste. When I looked at dead bodies, I rarely found them alarming. They almost looked like large rubber dolls. The blood drained and pooled at the body's lowest point. If they were left lying on their backs, all the blood pooled there, or wherever gravity took it, giving the face a white rubbery appearance.

I signed for the body and wheeled her to the autopsy room. The walls were a murky brown color probably called Morgue Drab. Two X-ray readers from the 1970s hung on the back wall, next to an enormous walk-in refrigerator that looked like it belonged in a Burger King. No fancy sliding drawers. Instead, bodies were placed like bags of lettuce on the shelves. Our facility could use an Extreme Makeover: Morgue Edition.

Two steel exam tables with built-in sinks sat in front of the fridge. To the right was the sexavator. The wall to the left had a large floor scale and a table where the body could be processed. I rolled her over to the scale for weighing and transferred her to the mobile gurney. People would be surprised how easily someone could be moved when their comfort wasn't a concern.

The main way I knew the corpses weren't dolls was by the smell. This woman had been dead longer than a few days. Within a couple

of days of death, the bacteria that normally existed in the body started to eat the contents of the intestine, then the intestine itself. The
bacteria were well on their way with this woman.

Holding my nose, I glanced over her. Something didn't seem
quite right, but I couldn't put my finger on it. It wasn't just that her
face was covered with blood and numerous contusions. Underneath
all that, she was beautiful. She wore what Grand would refer to as
"hoochie mama" clothing—fishnets, thigh-high miniskirt, and low-
cut blouse. A simple gold cross hung from her neck. Her hands were
in bags, standard procedure for foul play. But her shoes made me
gasp—gorgeous Valentino Rockstud caged stilettos worth close to a
grand at Barneys.

After leaving the autopsy room, I headed up the hallway and
opened the door to what I loosely termed the evidence room, home
of bad wigs, cheap costume jewelry, a surprising number of rubber
blow-up devices, and evidence bags. Here, in various states of aban-
donment, were autopsy remains not needed in criminal cases but not
claimed by family members after the case closed. Once I'd grabbed
a couple of evidence bags from the back file cabinet, I returned to
the autopsy room. I put all the jewelry into a bag and labeled it "Jane
Doe."

Before beginning the inspection, I turned on the voice recorder.

"Female Jane Doe, approximately nineteen or twenty, white,
brown hair, brown eyes," I began as a brisk slamming of the door interrupted me. At first, I thought Dr. Hawthorne had arrived sooner
than expected. Then I heard a deep, silky voice I didn't recognize.

"What the hell kind of music is that, DC? Some new phase
you're in? Your phone's off again. We're only about ten minutes
ahead of old man Hawthorne, so we have to work—"

As I rounded the corner from the exam room, the man stopped
talking and walking, apparently realizing I wasn't who he'd expected.
For a moment, I thought I'd walked onto the set of *Extreme Loggers*.

He wasn't a pretty man but was naturally rugged, his sharp jaw with a slight five o'clock shadow. He had coal-black, tousled, curly hair and deep, dark eyes and wore perfectly cut blue jeans and a slightly rumpled flannel shirt. He looked momentarily startled, then a cool mask slipped over his features. He stood tall, his posture locked tight, his eyes searching.

"You're not DC," he said.

"Is it the white skin that gives it away or the ponytail?" I replied, staring at him.

He looked me over, his eyes narrowing with intense scrutiny, but he didn't respond.

Daryl Claiborne, DC to his friends, was a Southern black man and fellow morgue assistant. He was also my best friend. "He had to take his cat to the pet psychologist, so I'm covering for him. May I help you?"

"Pet psychologist?" The man said the words quickly and began looking all around as if searching for something. His anxiousness reminded me that I was alone with a stranger.

"Yes, it's a growing profession. Americans spend forty-one billion dollars a year on their pets, more than the gross domestic product of all but sixty-four countries in the world." And there it was. I couldn't stop it. A nervous blurt with no other purpose than to make me look like a complete idiot. "I'm sorry, Mr...."

"McPhee, Burns McPhee."

"Mr. McPhee. I have a lot of work to do. I'll let DC know you came by."

He didn't reply. He didn't turn to go. He stood there as if sizing up the situation and what to do next.

"This is a delicate situation, Miss"—he poked at my badge—"Katherine Waters. You see, I believe they brought my sister here tonight, and I hoped to spend one last private moment with her before she's so violently cut open."

Burns McPhee had obviously sized me up as a naïve dimwit. He was about as related to that woman on the table as I was.

"Oh, then you can be of some help to me, Mr. McPhee. Tell me about your sister. What's her name? Do you know when she ate last, and did she have any particular personal effects with her that I should be looking for, like a necklace or watch?" I asked, hoping the barrage of questions would cause him to backtrack.

He took another look at me, scanning every inch as if trying to figure out what he had missed. "Okay. Maybe she's not really my sister. But I do need to see her." He started moving to the back of the morgue, obviously familiar with where we kept the bodies.

I stepped in front of him, holding out my hand to halt his momentum. "Why would I let you do that?"

He stopped. "DC would let me if he were here."

"I don't know that. We're very close, and he's never mentioned you before. And given that you just lied to me about being her brother, for all I know, you've never even met DC."

The corners of his mouth turned up into a small smile. "Hmm. Maybe you aren't that close if he's never mentioned me. I've found that it's usually difficult to get DC to shut up."

That was true. DC was a talker. Maybe he did know him, but that didn't mean I was going to let him peek at my Jane Doe. Before I could tell him that, he said, "He helps me with my kids."

"You have kids?" I asked, wondering if that meant he wasn't single and questioning his intelligence since he was asking DC for help with children. I loved DC, but using him for childcare was like letting the animals run the zoo.

"Not that kind of kids. One of my businesses takes care of Afghan and Iraqi orphans."

Oh. So this was the larger-than-life Army guy DC was always going on about. DC worked with local businesses to get supplies donated then shipped to the orphanages overseas. He and this guy had a history, but I never knew his name or what their story was.

"Ah. Even so, Mr. McPhee, I still can't let you near the body. Why do you want to see her, anyway? She came in as a Jane Doe. Did you know her?"

He grew quiet again, those dark eyes of his trying to look through me. He seemed to struggle with how to answer the question. Finally, he sighed, slumping his shoulders, his eyes dropping to a spot on the floor.

In a soft voice, he said, "I think her death is connected to the death of my best friend, but to be certain, I need to look at her wounds."

I looked at him, pondering whether I could trust him. He looked sincere, almost tragic, when he said it, but he had lied to me before. Maybe this was just another lie.

"What's taking so damn long, McPhee?" yelled a large, burly man as he barged through the door, entry pass in hand. The man looked nothing like McPhee. He was shorter yet looked substantial, like if someone ran into him, they would bounce off into space. His silhouette looked cartoonish, with great big muscles bulging on top and a skinny waist and legs. His straggly, sandy hair needed a cut, and he looked as if he'd slept in his clothes.

McPhee jerked around to the man at the door and watched him move forward. "Flynn. I was... explaining to this lovely woman who is filling in for DC tonight why we would need to see the body that was put into her care."

"Oh," Flynn said. He began slowly backing up, appearing to assess the situation. He moved strategically between McPhee's left side and the door. I felt maneuvered across the room.

Despite my self-defense training, I couldn't have taken out either of them, given their well-built physiques and advantage in number.

My only hope of keeping them away from the body was to convince them that I would not be alone for very long.

"If by 'explaining' you mean trying to con me, I'd agree," I said, moving into a frantic but confident speech pattern, even as my insides shook. "He started off by lying to me, then tried to play on my friendship with DC, and then went for a pity play. While I understand that you had a different expectation about how your trip here would go tonight, as you aptly pointed out when you barged into my lab, Mr. McPhee, *old man Hawthorne* will be here any moment."

Then I fell silent and stared at the door, holding my breath, as if my concentration could actually produce Dr. Hawthorne, and prayed they bought my act.

Both of the men tensed as the quiet in the room grew heavy.

"Well, she's a tight ass, isn't she," Flynn finally said.

A smile flashed into McPhee's eyes as he started to speak, but before he could, we all jumped at the loud clang from the examination room.

"Is that another one of your men, Mr. McPhee?" I asked, my nerves obviously showing. I had no idea who was in the next room.

Neither did they, it seemed. Both McPhee and Flynn pulled guns from behind their backs and pushed me down and behind them. I gasped, wondering why they would bring guns to a hospital if they were just going to look at a murder victim.

"Stay here. Stay safe," McPhee said as he and Flynn began moving cautiously toward the room, in a flanking position.

Safe? What in the world is going on here?

Crouched on the floor and behind a cabinet, I saw the wheels of the gurney rolling into the sexavator. I stood up to get a better look. The man pushing the gurney caught a glimpse of me out of the corner of his eye and froze. He turned, his eyes fixated on mine with an eerie intensity.

He was fairly ordinary—average height and build, sandy hair that reminded me of beige carpet. He was dressed all in black and seemed wired, his twitchy mannerisms resembling an animal that had been caged for too long. Finally, after what seemed like minutes but I'm sure was only seconds, he smiled at me. His was not a happy smile but an evil grin, making me shiver reflexively from the coldness.

"He's taking the body into the elevator," I yelled to McPhee and Flynn.

When my words registered, they bolted into the room just as the door to the sexavator slammed down.

"Damn it all," Flynn cursed.

"Where does this elevator go?" McPhee asked.

"It's a transport elevator. It goes up to every floor," I answered.

They quickly backtracked to the lab door, me following. The three of us ran toward the stairs.

"I'll cover the floors. You hit the parking lot. It's a guy with a body. He'll be looking for a way out, and he won't care how conspicuous he looks. Radio Neutron to pull the truck," McPhee yelled to Flynn.

Without question, Flynn changed his trajectory and disappeared.

McPhee and I continued running, hitting the stairwell, and I thanked God for my recent diligence with my aerobics DVD. McPhee's moves were swift, practiced, as if he knew how to make the most forward gains with his movements while expending the least amount of energy. At the top of the stairs, he threw the doors open wide, obviously aware of me still behind him.

I ran through the stairwell after him, trying to evaluate everything happening. I asked myself why I should run with him at all. Five minutes earlier, McPhee and Flynn had eagerly tried to do the same thing as the man I was now chasing—get to my Jane Doe. Even if we successfully apprehended the man with the body, I would be in the exact same predicament as now, only I'd be chasing McPhee and Flynn instead. But no other options sprang to mind. So I ran.

We jogged through the hallway, weaving around nurses' carts and wheelchairs, until we arrived at the sexavator. It was shut, the floor indicator light showing it stopped on our floor. McPhee took out his gun again. Pointing it at the elevator, he signaled for me to push the button to open the door.

"Maybe we should wait for security," I said.

"No time. If you want to see that body again, push the button."

I did. The door opened, and I momentarily breathed relief only to quickly realize that, while the gurney was there, the body wasn't. McPhee put his gun away and circled around.

"Where are the other exits on this floor?" he asked.

Before I could answer, a loud commotion erupted behind us. A nursing cart had flipped over, and supplies spilled to the ground. The man in black, struggling with the weight of Jane Doe over his shoulder, bounded down the hall and toward the exit door. Security was coming from the other way.

McPhee and I ran after the man.

"Stop him!" I yelled to the various bystanders as McPhee and I sprinted through the hall.

The man took off through the exit door. As we passed through it, tires screeched ahead. A cargo van came roaring up. The door slid open. The man and the body disappeared inside. The door slid closed as the van screeched again and drove off.

By the time I caught up with him, McPhee stood hunched over, trying to get his breath. In a whisper, he repeated the license plate number of the van over and over. As I approached him, a black hybrid Escalade whipped around the corner. McPhee sprinted for it, waving his hand above his head at me, yelling, "I'm sorrrryyyy" as he disappeared into the truck that took off following the cargo van.

I stood at the front of the hospital entrance, stunned. Then the coroner's vehicle drove up, and I knew my night was about to get even worse.

Chapter 2

Despite the common notion that an understanding of fashion was more likely to indicate frivolity than seriousness, I had learned that a person's fashion choices were usually deliberate. If someone chose sensible shoes with tassels, they were telling the world that they were secretly hiding a party animal inside. A wild tattoo hidden in a less than obvious place tended to indicate the opposite—the partying conservative. When *Vogue*, Princess Di, and Sherlock Holmes all agreed on something, it was usually worth paying attention—a person's fashion spoke volumes about them.

I probably shouldn't have expected someone dressed in a baby-blue button-down and khaki pants, most likely purchased from his local Sears while on a tool run, to have grasped that tip. Even if he was a detective.

"So you believe the man who stole the body from the morgue was with the mob, more specifically the Russian mob, because of his shoes?" Detective Driscol asked me again, scribbling in his notebook.

"Yes, as I've already said. If he were Italian Mafia, surely he would have been wearing Berlutis or Testonis, if he could find them. There's a shortage."

In addition to his unremarkable apparel, Detective Driscol had short brown hair and a skinny build, and he wore a blue-striped tie. Because of my dad's situation, I had recently spent my fair share of time with police detectives. They all owned that same ugly blue-striped tie. Maybe it was part of a departmental Christmas giveaway.

Next year, they should use a personal shopper instead. I'd make a mental note to suggest that.

I couldn't quite understand the detective's reaction. Sure, my family had had some recent unpleasantness with the police, but all of that was a misunderstanding. Right now, all I wanted was to help them recover that poor girl's body. But they seemed completely skeptical about any information I shared.

"Or maybe the Ferragamo Pythons if he were into snakeskin and looking for something a little more affordable. The man who ran off with the body clearly wore brown New & Lingwoods. I remember it distinctly because they didn't match the rest of him, which was clad in black from head to ankle." Detective Driscol continued to stare at me with a blank look. "New & Lingwoods are Russian calf shoes and the second most expensive men's shoes on the planet. Who else would wear them to steal a body but the Russian mob?"

I wondered how they could not understand this. These were the most legendary shoes on the planet, first made famous by Prince Charles and fashioned from reindeer leather found in a shipwreck, the markings distinctive.

Maybell, my pet pig, snorted from the corner of the room and tried to stretch. Poor Maybell. The police had quickly stuffed us in the morgue's conference room to await questioning. I had tried to make her comfortable by putting down her favorite pink cashmere blanket, but the cold, grimy floor seeped through, making her bones stiff.

"Why do you have a pig with you?" Detective Lambert asked. Unlike Driscol, Lambert was slightly heavyset and muscular. She gave the impression she could break me in half if I provoked her. She wore a navy-blue pantsuit that tried to be stylish through the addition of fake crystal buttons. Her short black bob was a great choice to frame her pear-shaped face. Although I didn't think Detective Driscol quite understood it, between the two of them, Detective Lambert was the badass cop.

"My pig sitter was only scheduled to watch her until ten, and my grand is on a date with her boyfriend." I had swapped a course in biker chic makeup with a lady in our building in exchange for the pig-sitting time. She was having issues with her makeup running under the humidity caused by her helmet. A few quick changes to her routine and she was all set.

"It's your pet?" Lambert shifted in her chair across the table from me and gazed at Maybell as if considering the idea.

Maybell snorted at the offending comment and wandered over to get some much-deserved reassurance. I wondered why on earth they cared about my pig when there was a body to find. I supposed Maybell was unique, though, so maybe if we dealt with their curiosity, we could get on with more important matters.

"First, Maybell is a 'she,' not an 'it.' As indicated by the rhinestone collar and pink tutu." I bent down and lifted the front hoofs of the light-pink-and-black-spotted, potbellied Maybell onto the table so the detectives could see her better.

She poked her snout at them.

"Second, pigs are smarter than most average human three-year-olds, much smarter than a dog or cat." I set her down, petting her as I did. "Third, Maybell is family."

Seeming satisfied, Maybell waddled back to her blanket.

"Despite their reputation, they're freakishly clean." I folded my hands on the table.

"Ms. Waters, may I call you Katherine?" Driscol asked.

"Only if you're related to my mother. Otherwise it's Kat, please." I took a drink of water from the small Styrofoam cup. After the sprint through the hospital, I felt parched, and the thought that I was sitting in yet another police interrogation made my throat go tight.

"Okay, Kat, why don't we start at the beginning? How long have you been working at the morgue?" Driscol asked.

"About four months."

I told them how Grand's boyfriend, Claude, had helped me get the job. He had connections on the hospital board.

"If you don't mind me saying, Ms. Waters, you don't seem particularly suited to this line of work," Lambert said.

The fact that the morgue was not a dream career move for me was fairly obvious. However, I'd come to realize one could be good at something even if the job wasn't an obvious match. The autopsies were actually fascinating once I tricked my brain into forgetting they were dead people. And the bodies all had a story to tell. I liked that I could help the people who loved them find some understanding in their loss. After all, with my situation these days, I'd had plenty of experience with loss.

"Actually, Detective Lambert, with a minor in biology, and as a two-time Miss Missouri winner in the best makeup category, I think I have a unique skill set to offer the fine office of the St. Louis County coroner." I smiled and flipped my ponytail in a well-practiced move usually reserved for the final-question round of a pageant.

She sat expressionless, not looking convinced. "Why don't you start from the top and take us through what happened?"

If it meant helping to find the missing girl's body, I wanted to be a good sport about all the endless questioning. I couldn't help being nervous with everything else going on with my family. We didn't need more police attention. Something must have been terribly misaligned with my karma for a body to go missing on my shift. The pleather conference room chair had ceased being comfortable almost the moment I sat in it.

Sensing my upset, Maybell snorted in agreement and waddled over. I gave her some water from my cup as I took the officers through my afternoon.

"And did you notice anything unusual about the victim during this process?" Lambert sat more upright in her chair, leaning in on the table, looking at me as if I finally might say something important.

"I'm paid to be a keen observer, Detective. I noticed several things. First, she smelled."

Driscol smirked as if trying to hold in a laugh. "With due respect to your keen observation skills, Kat, dead bodies tend to smell."

He was being smug. I was beginning to develop a healthy respect for Lambert for managing not to punch Driscol in his smug face on a regular basis.

Maybell began snorting. I patted her to settle her nerves. "It might surprise you to know that dead bodies *don't* smell right away. That takes time. The bacteria that normally exist in the intestine had begun to decompose the body enough that she had a palpable smell, in a food-left-sitting-out-on-the-counter-overnight sort of way, indicating that this body had been dead longer than a few days." I wrinkled my nose at the memory of the sticky-sweet smell that floated in the air.

Driscol's smile faded.

"Isn't it kind of cool the way nature takes care of itself?" I asked.

This time, Lambert smiled, clearly pleased with my jab at her partner. "What else did you notice about the victim?"

"She was pretty. I mean, despite the blood and bruises that dotted her beaten face." I closed my eyes to remember her, trying to shut out Driscol and Lambert so I could feel my way past my sadness and better recall how her body had confused me when I first saw it. She had looked so delicate lying on the table. Everything about her seemed like a contradiction. "She had meticulously styled hair that made her look like she'd come straight from Ted Gibson's salon. Despite the circumstances her body was found in, her hair appeared to have been well taken care of on an ongoing basis. And she had a beautiful manicure. Chipped nails, but the expensive French polish

job was still apparent." Before opening my eyes, I smiled, remembering the shimmering little butterflies on each finger, visible through
the plastic bag. "That was no budget job. I heard some of the other
policemen say they thought she was a prostitute, which seemed to
match her clothing choice, but those clothes didn't seem to fit the
rest of her. Neither did the cheap plastic-coated glitter bracelets dangling from her wrist while an expensive gold cross hung from her
neck."

I reached up to my own neck and sighed at the missing diamond
cross. I'd sold it to cover Grand's insurance. "And those shoes!" I
closed my eyes, remembering them. "Stilettos to die for."

They were glaring at me when I looked up.

"Oh. Poor choice of words. Anyway, that's when they arrived, the
men. Right as I began recording the information on her external examination, the door slammed. At first I thought Dr. Hawthorne had
arrived sooner than I had expected, until I heard the voice."

"How did they get in?" Driscol asked.

"He must have had a badge. They came in through the badge-
controlled door."

"So you didn't let them in?" Driscol asked again.

"No. I wouldn't have let some strange men into the morgue
while I was there alone."

"So you didn't know this man?" Lambert followed up this time.
Conversations like this were why people thought their tax dollars
were being poorly used. The repetition was becoming annoying. If
they had a point, I wished they'd get to it. With every minute that
went by, the trail to the girl was getting colder.

"No, as I've said, I didn't know him."

"Can you describe the man?" Lambert leaned back again, her
posture slumping. Apparently, my moment for saying anything worthy had passed.

My mind wandered to the thought of him, how intense yet casual he looked, all wrapped up in a rugged package. And those sad eyes when he talked about his dead friend. "He said he was military, and his sharp looks and efficient movements seemed to back that up. Although, he's been out for a bit, I'd guess, with the handsome North Face vibe he had going."

"You thought he was handsome?" Lambert asked.

"That doesn't mean anything. You asked me to describe him. That's what he looked like."

"Did he say who they were?" Driscol had gone back to furiously writing notes in his notebook, not looking up as he asked questions.

"Yes, the first man who came in said his name was Burns McPhee."

"McPhee?" Driscol snapped his head up, his eyes growing wide at the name, as if he knew who I was talking about but wasn't exactly happy to hear it.

"He said the victim was his sister."

"His sister?" Driscol looked puzzled.

"Yes, he said he wanted to say goodbye to his sister."

Driscol whispered something to Lambert and, without saying anything to me, left the room.

"Sorry," Lambert said to cover her partner's rudeness. "Please continue."

"Well, he was lying," I said, returning my thoughts to the detectives.

"How did you know?" With Driscol gone, Lambert had taken to writing in his notebook.

"He wasn't very good at it. Slow speech, repeating questions, lack of contractions. Or maybe he was, and I'm good at spotting liars. I can't decide in my current state. I'm sorry." I laid my head down in my hands.

I was not the world's best decision maker. My trip through fifteen different college majors and a host of minors was a testament to that, and my decision-making impairment tended to get exacerbated when I was tired, and the interviews were dragging on. The room had no windows. I wondered if it were morning yet. Maybell had fallen asleep, and she snored under the table next to my feet. "Anyway, that's when he told me about the death of his friend, but before I could figure out if that was more of his con game, the second man I told you about came in. Flynn."

Lambert didn't blink at the mention of McPhee's dead friend, which puzzled me. It seemed as though everyone knew more about what was going on than I did.

"It's pretty brazen, don't you think, to come to the morgue and lie to an attendant to try to get access to a body that's part of a murder investigation," Lambert said.

"Look, why are we dwelling on this? I have no idea why Mr. McPhee thought he could stroll into a morgue and have his way with a body. You seem to know him, so why don't you call him and ask?"

"We did," Driscol said as he reentered the room.

Maybell startled awake at the sound of the door and padded over.

"Great, finally some progress. So why did he say he was here?" I asked.

"He's unable to corroborate your story."

"What does that mean?" I flipped the phrase around in my head. It sounded like detective speak. "Unable to corroborate my story." Of course he could corroborate it. He was there. Neither of them answered. "What does that mean?" I asked again, looking from one to the other of them.

"Mr. McPhee has an alibi for the whole evening." Driscol leaned against the wall.

"He's lying." My heart sank as I racked my brain to figure out why McPhee wouldn't admit he had been there.

"And you can tell?" Lambert asked.

"Yes." I petted Maybell for comfort. She wouldn't abandon me.

"Because he's bad at it?" Lambert was mocking me at this point.

"That probably wasn't even his real name. The tall, dark lumberjack was probably in on it from the start, and I played right into it." I took a deep breath. If I were going to avoid ending up on the front page of the paper for body snatching, I was going to have to change directions. "I'm sure the surveillance video will back up my story."

"There has apparently been some issue with the surveillance system tonight." Driscol ran his hand across the back of his neck, squeezing as he went. Since returning from checking out my alibi with Burns McPhee, he was noticeably crankier.

"What do you mean 'some issue'?" That video was my one ace for getting out of this mess. There was no way it could be an issue.

"It appears the footage has been tampered with," he said matter-of-factly, as though he hadn't dealt my world another strong blow.

"What do you mean 'tampered with'?"

"I'm not at liberty to say."

"Not at liberty? This is my life we're talking about here!" I took a deep breath and tried to concentrate on my inner calm.

"The video from Billy Idol's song 'Body Snatcher' plays in a continuous loop for the entire time period the body was stolen." Driscol's face twisted in disbelief at what he had just said.

Lambert glared at him for giving away the information. Surely they would now see the absurdity of my being involved in this.

"McPhee didn't steal the body, anyway, so really, I guess it doesn't matter that he's denying involvement," I said.

"The other man, Flynn, did?" Lambert asked.

"No. As I said at the very beginning, the creepy Russian mobster with great shoes did." I took them through the whole hospital chase and how I had watched as the mobster disappeared with the body and then McPhee disappeared.

"And it didn't occur to you that these alleged three men may have been playing you for a sucker?"

Her snippy tone on "alleged" snapped me back from my memory of the chase to the cold reception in the dank room and Lambert's questions. "No."

"Let's try a different angle, Ms. Waters. Would you like to tell us how much you were paid to help whoever took the body?" Lambert sat up tall in her chair again.

"Excuse me?" I accidentally crushed my cup in my hand. Maybell snorted. So this was it, the reason for all the skepticism and tough questioning.

"A tip was called in to Dr. Hawthorne while he was on his way from the crime scene, alerting him to the fact that you had been paid off to help steal the body."

"That's preposterous! Who would make such an accusation?" I stood up from my chair.

"We aren't at liberty to say," Driscol said, becoming alert from where he leaned on the wall.

Of course they weren't. First the mess with my dad, and now this. "Here's what I think, Detectives. If you actually had a clue about who called in the outlandish accusation, you would have already arrested me. Further, you"—I pointed at Driscol—"don't believe I'm smart enough to have pulled off this whole insane scenario from planting Billy Idol songs to snatching bodies out of the hospital."

Driscol lowered his gaze.

"And you"—I pointed at Lambert—"know that I'm too smart to have concocted such an outlandish story."

"A young girl has been murdered, and her body is now missing, and somehow you're involved in all of this. We're just doing our job, Ms. Waters," Lambert said.

"I know you are, Detective. Now, I've tried to cooperate because I really do want you to find that poor girl. But I'm tired, and Maybell is hungry. So unless you're going to arrest me, I'm going home."

When neither of them said anything, I walked out of the room, Maybell following.

ON MY WAY OUT THE MORGUE doors, I met Dr. Hawthorne, the coroner. His green tweed jacket with its large brown patches bulged at the elbows and opened to reveal the white band where the rim of his brown slacks had folded down under his slightly portly belly. His shaggy gray hair poked out from beneath the temples of his wire-rimmed glasses. The bags under his eyes were puffier than usual, perhaps from his lack of sleep, but he forced a smile when he saw me.

Dr. Hawthorne had been working at the St. Louis County morgue for most of his career, some twenty-five years, and was counting the days to retirement. From my first day, he'd taken me under his wing, spending a large amount of time teaching me about autopsies. Even though I'd been there only a few months, he allowed me to do more internal work than other attendants who had been there longer. I found his presence reassuring, and I really did appreciate being taught.

He looked pained as he explained that I was being referred for disciplinary action—on probation for body snatching. I could end up being suspended without pay or even fired. I hadn't believed this night could get any worse, and now it had. He knew how important the paycheck was to me, that my morgue income was the only thing standing between Grandma Waters and me dining at the soup kitchen.

"I'm sorry, Katherine. I know what a shock this is for you," Dr. Hawthorne said. He rubbed his hand up and down my arm.

"I swear I didn't have anything to do with this."

"I don't believe that you did, but I also don't know why someone would call and say that you did either. The best way to sort it out is to keep talking to people who can help us."

"You mean the police?"

"Yes, of course."

"Because they've been so helpful to my family lately."

"Well, I wouldn't necessarily share that point of view with them. The goal is to get you out of trouble, not get you in deeper. At least there's going to be a hearing. That gives us some time. I'm sure we'll be able to clear all of this up."

He left me standing in silence and went and yelled at one of the detectives who was trying to put crime scene tape over the instrument cabinet. I was alone for the first time since before I'd met Burns McPhee, and my body reminded me how exhausted I was. All I wanted to do was go home and climb into bed.

I buckled Maybell into her seat belt and climbed into my beater 1997 Ford Escort with a quick pang of desire for my hybrid. That was another thing I had lost when Dad was arrested. The repo man was at least nice and gave me a lift to my apartment before he took my car. I had bought this one off the internet, sight unseen, after my research revealed the Escort as one of the top ten best beater cars to buy. That there was a list, I found amazing. The man asked if I wanted to look at it, as if I would have had any idea whether it was the best car ever or, alternately, if it were going to spontaneously burst into flames the next time I turned it over. True to its hype, the little red car with the dented-in fender managed to get me from Boston to St. Louis with few complications. Occasionally it had issues starting and, depending on its mood, required me to either talk nice to it or open the hood and bang on the battery wires. Today, though, it started on the first try.

For a moment, I sat there trying to absorb it all, wondering how this could be happening. I didn't think it was possible for things to get worse. If I thought about it too much, I was going to cry. If I started, I might not stop. So crying was not allowed. Instead, I beat the steering wheel hard while shaking my head like a wild banshee and shouting expletives. Maybell hid her snout under her hooves. My hand hurt, but the rest of me felt better.

I eased the car into Drive and headed home. Over ninety cities divided St. Louis County into four main sections—North County, West County, South County, and Mid County. Southerners never ventured north for anything and vice versa. West County folks had everything delivered, and in the Mid County, they "borrowed" what they needed. The morgue operated in a transitional neighborhood in North County, still more blue collar than white.

When my mom was thrown out of our house in the better-off burbs of West County, Grand's boyfriend, Claude, hooked us up with a flat in Mid County, specifically in University City. The move from West County to U City felt the way I imagined it would feel to move to a foreign country. We'd gone from gated communities with impeccably manicured lawns—where status was determined by the number of maids employed and who installed the security system—to one of Literary St. Louis's Top 100 Places for Small Houses, where security was determined by the number of pit bulls in the living room and guns in the cookie jar.

At first, Mom was in denial about what was happening. Never having rented an apartment before, she had no clue how little my salary could afford. Thankfully, Claude was willing to help out, and I was able to swap my time as a personal stylist to the landlord's wife for some of the rent. Even then, getting Mom and Grand to go look at the place was a feat. The only time either of them had previously ventured out of richburbia was to attend the symphony downtown.

But when they learned that U City was founded in 1903 by the owner and publisher of the *Women's Magazine* and *Woman's Farm Journal*, Edward Lewis, they agreed to go look at the place Claude offered to sublet to us—at a cost to him, I was sure. Lewis had constructed many buildings to support his growing publishing empire that still stood today. Mom and Grand had screwed up their courage to follow in the footsteps of the founder of the American Women's League.

U City was now culturally diverse, and it was home to a mini Chinatown. The main drag in town was the Delmar Loop, a name left over from when it marked the end of the streetcar line that originally anchored the city. There was something cosmic about a place that once nurtured both Tennessee Williams and rapper Nelly.

I'd done the drive enough times that my mind was on autopilot. That allowed me to think about the night's events.

First Martin and now this. The realization that I could be fired was overwhelming. In a strange way, I would miss the morgue. It had become routine. The assembly of odd characters there kept mostly to themselves and ignored the sensationalism of my situation. No one asked too many questions. Especially the ones on the exam table.

I couldn't lose my job. Not only was this the only way I could see to get closer to the evidence the police had against my dad, but also we desperately needed the money. Mom was trying to find work, but for a fifty-something woman who had never held a job before, finding someone to hire her, and somewhere she would find acceptable, was slow going. To keep Mom and Grand calm, I'd have to look for something else quickly and quietly, but that would mean a setback in helping Dad's lawyers clear up this whole mess.

Although I was quite sure Mom would celebrate my morgue exit, she would be apoplectic at the news of my canceled engagement to Martin, the coming nuptials viewed as the last bastion of respect for my station. Maybe it would slip my mind to tell her we were on a break.

I switched gears. I had to keep this job, and the only way I could do that was to do everything in my power to get to the bottom of things and prove my innocence.

First, I had to deal with the possibility that someone in the morgue had not only set me up but also ratted me out. Only someone with access to the morgue schedules could have known that I would be at the morgue last night instead of DC. They'd used my name specifically when calling Dr. Hawthorne and the police about my supposed involvement in the corpse-napping.

It could have been Burns McPhee and that Flynn, whoever they were. But I was at a loss about why they would have set me up. I would not start believing that my social radar was malfunctioning. McPhee had seemed sincere when he talked about the death of his friend being somehow connected to this body. Plus, they appeared genuinely surprised by the man who stole the body. And who was he, anyway? None of this made sense.

Flynn had addressed him by name. "McPhee," he'd called him. That must have been his real name. And he was there looking for DC. Hopefully, DC would have answers to some of these questions.

The only option was to find McPhee and get him to corroborate my story so I could get off probation. DC would know where to find McPhee. That meant that instead of a good cry and a date with my lovely bed, I'd be doing a quick turnaround.

I pulled into a curbside parking spot and unbuckled Maybell. Seventy-five percent of all houses in the city had been built before 1959, and most of them, including ours, were tiny, coming in at less than nine hundred square feet. The little brick structure with concrete steps was shaped like a tiny Monopoly house with its pointy roof and perfectly centered door, flanked by tiny square windows on each side. Unfortunately for us, there was no trading up to a hotel. The whole neighborhood had undergone a resurgence before the recession. Even with the economy starting to bounce back, St. Louis still wasn't faring great, and many half-renovated buildings sat empty or in foreclosure.

I put my key in the first of several locks and took a minute to brace for what was about to ensue. To keep from panicking my mom and Grand about my predicament, I would pretend that everything was perfectly fine. Our small apartment already held too many people with too many problems. Catholic guilt settled in my stomach. Under no circumstances could I add to the problems.

As I walked through the door of our tiny apartment, the first thing that hit me was the smell of brewing coffee. This was unusual because coffee was a casualty of our current financial situation. Coffee brewing meant company. Important company. After the night I'd had, company was the last thing I was in the mood for.

Chapter 3

I quickly scanned the room. Our house had no couch, but it sported a lovely antique Tiffany lamp and several other nonfunctional but expensive sentimental pieces that Grand couldn't part with. Grand was playing cards with Claude at the table I'd picked up at the secondhand store, dirt cheap. It was missing a leg, but we'd stuck Grand's antique side table under it.

"There you are," Grand said, putting down her cards and jumping up to meet me. Grandma Waters was a small woman, five four at best. She claimed she used to be taller and that she was shrinking. She had shoulder-length pure-white hair with an abundance of natural waves, a welcome trait she'd passed on to me. She always coordinated her outfit with matching shoes and purse, and lately she'd taken to wearing sun-visor-like hats without a top to them. Some were made of foam with pictures on them and others of canvas, but she almost always wore one now, even indoors. She said it made her look more like a true detective. Since Dad's arrest, she'd turned into a geriatric Nancy Drew. Not a day went by that she wasn't following up some lead or angle that might help get him out of prison. Today's hat was lime green with pink flamingos. It matched her lime-green jogging suit and pink purse.

"Did you really steal a corpse?" she asked eagerly in her gruff voice. She quit smoking when Grandpa got sick, but her voice never quite stopped sounding like she'd swallowed a bullfrog. Now she toked on a fake plastic cigarette whenever she became nervous or agitated about her memory.

"How did you know about..." As I began to answer her, a tall, good-looking man with an easy gait strolled out of the kitchen, carrying a cup of coffee.

Staring at him, I let Maybell off her harness. She immediately made a beeline for her bed in the back of the apartment. The man didn't even flinch as she waddled past him.

"You must be Katherine Waters," the man said, blowing on his hot coffee and eyeing me over the edge of the cup.

"Yes, and who are you?" I'd had enough surprises for a while. I was tired, I smelled like two-day-old corpse, and I wasn't interested in meeting any more new mystery men.

"Katherine, this is Fletcher Reid, from the *Post*," my mom said, following him out of the kitchen.

"Fletcher Reid," I repeated, taking a moment before the significance of the name came to me. "Misinformed truth-butchering crime beat reporter Fletcher Reid?"

Mom glared at me over my lack of verbal filter, the exhaustion of the previous day overwhelming me.

Since Dad's arrest, one outlandish article after another had appeared in the paper under the byline of Fletcher Reid. Most claimed Dad was as big as Gotti. As if Clarke Waters, a man entertained by actuarial tables, could seriously be a mobster.

"That's him. A lot easier on the eyes than you'd expect for a two-bit hack, huh?" Grand asked.

"Mother!" my mom cried.

Grandma Waters was a chameleon. To most, she came off as the picture of a cranky old person. Underneath the gruff exterior, though, was a sweet old lady and then probably another layer of cranky that I wasn't convinced had anything to do with being old. Much to my mother's dismay, Grand's crankiness seemed to be on full display.

Mr. Reid looked amused. "Yes, that would be me," he replied. A big, easy smile came over his face. His blue eyes almost twinkled in the light of the Tiffany lamp.

"Why did you let him in here?" I asked, raising my voice more than I should have.

"I didn't exactly," Mom said.

"Claude and I couldn't get the chair through the door without help."

When the cops confiscated someone's house, it was supposed to be off-limits. The homeowners weren't supposed to take things from it. Every time I came home, though, another object from our old life had reappeared. Once Grand figured out that no one actually watched the old house, she started making "shopping" runs. Sometimes Claude drove. Other times, they took an Uber. How they convinced a driver to wait for them at no charge, while they essentially broke into our house and pilfered some large object, was beyond me, but they managed.

Today's addition was a doozy—an antique pink Queen Anne armchair that almost looked like a throne. Selling these things would help cover rent, but I didn't have the heart. They were Grand's only link to her history. Plus, they weren't even supposed to be here. The last thing we needed was an arrest for selling stolen property or, worse, tampering with evidence.

"That was very nice of you to help, Mr. Reid, but I think you should be going," I said. We were not giving an interview about my alleged corpse-napping to someone with a history of passing off trumped-up gossip as news.

"Rule number thirteen," Mom said calmly, glaring at me intently. For as long as I could remember, my mom had a rule for almost everything. Not normal kid rules like "Look both ways before crossing the street." These were life rules, like "Don't cross the street with someone you don't trust." They'd become so engrained, I often repeated them, either out loud or in my head. Given my indecisiveness, they were comfortable go-tos. They were also good for times like this when she wanted to communicate something subtly: *Rule number thirteen—Perceptions are everything.*

"What's rule number thirteen?" Reid asked, looking confused.

"It's a coded reminder for me to always ask how a guest takes his coffee," I replied.

Mom beamed a smile at him and handed me the sugar jar.

"I understand you had some misfortune last night?" Reid pushed.

"That would be one way to put it."

Fletcher Reid was so tall he was gangly. He looked like a grown-up surfer—thin with slight muscles, nice tan, floppy dishwater-blond hair, brilliant-blue eyes, and a smile that wouldn't quit. His clothes were standard beat reporter: slacks, a casual button-down shirt, and what looked like well-worn comfortable shoes. Nothing pretentious, casual but polished, like a Land's End model. I wasn't sure if it was his actual persona or the reporter in him. He seemed to put everyone in the room at ease with his casual conversation and hundred-watt smile.

"The tip I got said you were paid off to help boost the body."

"A 1992 study in the *Canadian Journal of Communications* proved that anonymous crime tips are of little value and that the offering of rewards may serve as a crime starter, with anonymous tipsters entrapping people to commit crimes so that the tipster can collect the reward," I recited almost completely without taking a breath. I wasn't at all put at ease by him and his boyish "Let's go lock lips in the stairwell" smile.

Fletcher Reid looked amused. "So you're the victim of a planted tip to extort reward money?"

"Look, Mr. Reid." I attempted to change the subject.

"Fletcher, please," he interrupted before sipping his coffee slowly.

"Mr. Reid," I continued, putting down my bag, "I'm not at liberty to discuss the ongoing investigation, but perhaps you might ask yourself why, if I were in it for the money, I would have been stupid enough to let myself get caught. I'm now on probation, pending a hearing that could end with me losing my job."

"Probation?" Mom asked with only a slight inflection in her normal monotone, indicating her panic. The blurted mention of my probation starkly conflicted with her "nothing to see here" effort.

"Oh boy. Homeless shelter, here we come. Do you know what they do to old people on the streets?" Grand added.

Before the arrest, she'd resided in an assisted living home not far from my parents, having been diagnosed with early stages of Alzheimer's. Equally important, she was suffering from a broken heart after the loss of her husband of forty years several months before. The staff at the home and the passage of time had worked some magic on her. She'd met Claude Pederski, an adorable, bow-tie-wearing man who regularly brought her flowers and didn't mind her bingo obsession. Of course, we couldn't afford the home now, so she had moved in with us.

"I'm sure your Harvard degree will have you in a new job soon enough," Mom said, her tone breezy. "She was top of her class, Mr. Reid. Did you know that?"

I glared at her. We had been through this countless times. My mother refused to understand that Art History majors weren't rolling in job offers. The morgue was a good job. Plus, Mom didn't like to talk about the *real* reason I was working at the morgue. Now wasn't the time for another round of that fight, though.

"Can't you just give the body back?" Grand asked.

"I didn't take the body. It's just a misunderstanding."

"Like with her father, you see, Mr. Reid," Mom said. "Our family has been the unfortunate victims of a series of misunderstandings.

I'm sure Katherine will get it all straightened out soon." She beamed at him as if she were having her photo taken for *Housewife Monthly*.

Apparently amused at the glimpse of family drama, Reid changed the subject. "Anything you'd like to share about your father's investigation, since I'm here?"

At that, both my mom and I cringed. The invitation to talk about Dad's investigation launched Grand into attack mode.

"Now look here, you surf shop reject. My son is being framed," she yelled from the far side of the room. "If you really want to do some decent investigative reporting, you'd follow up on one of the many leads I've generously sent your two-bit hack paper," she said.

"I'd love to hear whatever you have to say," he said as he took out a small notebook.

A glint appeared in Grand's eyes. "Claude, get the scrapbook." Grand smelled opportunity.

"I apologize, Mr. Reid. I'm not sure you realize what you've just done," Mom said, effortlessly intervening in what was shaping up to be another headline-grabbing story in tomorrow morning's paper. That was the exact opposite of what my mom had planned when she let Fletcher Reid in the house.

"Look, look right here. Fletcher, is it?" my grandmother began, smiling up at him. Putting on her doting-grandmother act, she took his hand and led him to the table where Claude sat with the book.

The scrapbook that Grand and Claude had put together was truly a monumental achievement. They'd included every article, picture, and useless fact that had been written about my dad's case. Grand had also managed to link the crime to numerous other people and points of interest, from the real mob to a conspiracy involving NASA and extraterrestrials. For weeks, she'd been trying to get Dad's lawyer, the prosecutor, the newspaper—really anyone—to listen to her, all to no avail.

Now that she had Fletcher Reid in her sights, I figured I was safely off the hook on the missing-body issue. Grand smelled opportunity, and Mom would be busy mediating. As he was being sucked further into Grand's world, I slipped around them and escaped into the bedroom. I needed a shower, some coffee, and a long nap. I turned on the shower and waited for the hot water to come.

In our old house, I would have been slipping into the whirlpool tub. It was the one luxury that I truly, unequivocally missed. Well, that and the stylist I could no longer afford—Stan the hair man. For a couple of weeks following the arrest, he'd given me pity 'dos. Once it looked as if our circumstances might become more permanent, he'd suggested I find an alternative. Since I was unable to decide on a new, more affordable stylist, my hair became more unmanageable every day. Usually I wore it up, but ponytails gave me a headache.

I showered quickly and scanned my wardrobe for something appropriate, pondering what exactly one should wear to hunt down a body. After several minutes of indecision, I put something on, stuffed my thick, curly locks into a pony, and selected a nice pair of Chloé wedges. In the event that I had to do any more running, they were a lovely choice. Yet I cringed as I caught a glimpse of my chipped nail polish on toes in desperate need of a pedi that I couldn't afford.

There would be time enough to mope about my circumstances later. If I had any chance of holding on to my job, I needed to figure out who at the morgue had it in for me, where that body was, and why McPhee had lied. He had been there to see DC, so that was my starting point. As Master Tahkaswami, my former spiritual advisor, said, overcoming adversity required action.

Which meant that rather than taking the nap I so desperately craved, I instead had to find DC and the elusive Burns McPhee. I grabbed my backpack and threw in a few supplies—granola bar, which would be breakfast and lunch today, mace because it was a habit, and Grand's *Private Investigation for Dummies* book, in case finding Burns McPhee or the missing body ended up being harder than anticipated.

Mentally focusing on my new plan and visualizing my success, I marched out of the only bathroom in the apartment and crashed squarely into the chest of Fletcher Reid. In my wallowing, I'd totally forgotten him. He knocked against the wall, and I hurtled straight to the floor.

He reached down and plucked me to my feet and gave me a once-over.

"I thought you'd be long gone," I said, putting some distance between us.

"Your grandmother held me hostage, taking me through each of her theories on your dad's case." He didn't look annoyed as I had expected, more like amused.

"She means well. She only wants to help, and that's her way. Plus, I think all the pictures and stories help her remember what's going on. It was very difficult for her when we first moved. With her condition, she doesn't always remember where she is or why we're here."

I didn't know why I was going on about it like that. Maybe I was trying to invoke sympathy or keep him from returning to the questions about the missing body.

He grinned. "It's okay, really. Underneath that shark attitude, she's very sweet. And it gives me more time to get to know you better," he said, flashing a Cheshire cat grin.

"Did you know that while all other leading causes of death have decreased precipitously, Alzheimer's deaths have actually increased forty-six percent since 2006?"

He looked confused, as if he wasn't sure whether he should answer the question.

"In other words, she's very fragile. So stay away from her. Stay away from all of us, Mr. Reid," I said in an attempt to end the conversation.

He leaned back against the wall as if getting comfortable for a long chat. "So what are you going to do about your probation?"

"Why don't you tell me who told you and the police I was in on the body snatch?"

His practiced smile returned. "We're like priests," he said, a big smile coming to his face."

"You don't have sex, and you look terrible in black?" I smirked.

"Funny, but no. We can't give away our sources."

Not many people knew that I had been working at the morgue last night. Only my coworkers and a few of the hospital administrators could have accessed the online schedule. On my first day, I'd brought them all baked goods. Sure, they weren't from Michelle's, known for their insanely expensive but incredibly delicious pastries, but they were still good. I didn't know what someone could have against me.

"Was it Burns McPhee?" I asked. Maybe the journalist could give me some answers.

"McPhee? How is he involved?"

I jerked my head up to look at him. His face was scrunched, and he wore a scowl. For the first time since I'd met him, he didn't look happy.

"Why does everyone have that reaction when I mention his name?"

"He has that effect on people. I'm sorry. I have to be going." With his long legs, he cleared our small hallway and was across the room in only a few strides. I had to run to keep up with him, thanking the deities for my wedges and desperately wondering how Reid knew McPhee.

"Wait, Mr. Reid," I said when I finally caught up.

"It's Fletcher. I do hope we meet again, Kat." On his way out, he stopped and warmly shook Grand's hand, giving her a wink.

"Woo-hoo, you better be careful, Claude. He's got eyes for me," she said, blushing as Fletcher left.

"Where are you off to, honey?" my mom asked as I cruised out of the bedroom toward the door.

"To make sure I keep my job," I answered.

My mom looked slightly relieved. While she hated the morgue, she hated the thought of a homeless shelter even more. "Katherine, I hate to ask, but Grand is going to need more medicine."

She said it all very casually, with that almost-always-present cheerful smile. She knew perfectly well that the request wasn't casual, because as she said it, she handed me a chocolate bar.

Rule number four, I thought as I opened the wrapper, *chocolate makes everything go down easier*. In this case, I was steadying for a trip to the drag club.

Apparently, the chocolate was to soothe more than one blow.

"Also, Katherine, don't forget about the benefit tonight."

Chapter 4

I pulled into the parking lot behind a nondescript building not far from our apartment. The sign on the pole had a simple purple crown on it and hot-pink lights that flashed the name "Queen Mothers" so brightly they could be seen during the day. Underneath the flashing lights hung another sign thanking patrons for voting them Best Drag Club of 2017.

The issue wasn't Grand's medicine but rather how to pay for it. Since Dad's arrest, I'd learned that health care in this country could be likened to legalized gambling—roll the dice and hope you don't get something that isn't covered by an insurance bean counter's exclusion list. Grand was on Medicare, but since my dad's ordeal, we couldn't afford her supplemental policy, which meant we didn't have the prescription coverage she needed to get her meds. Medicare didn't believe someone with our assets needed assistance. Never mind that the feds currently controlled all those assets.

I had called ahead and let Sheila know I was coming. She sat waiting for me as requested, sitting on a bunch of produce boxes that sagged under her weight, smoking a cigarette and wearing what I guessed was a Tina Turner getup, complete with short sequined dress and spike-haired wig.

She slid off the produce box to meet me, adjusting her skirt in the slide. "Hey, hon. I was so glad to get your call. I was practicing and just got off stage. I heard you had some trouble of the body-snatching variety."

"How'd you hear about my trouble?"

"My girlfriend is a dancer, of the exotic type. She has friends in the same business as the missing girl. It's all over the hooker grapevine that someone body-snatched a dead working girl. She was new, though, so no one knows much about her."

"There's a hooker grapevine?"

"Oh yeah, there's nothing that working girls like more than juicy gossip, especially when it's about one of their own."

"Did your girlfriend know who might have stolen the body?"

"By the time the news got to her, she said they all thought you might be a voodoo priestess, trying to exorcise the girl's bad spirits."

"I'm a lot of things, but a voodoo priestess isn't one of them. I am trying to find the missing girl's body, though. If your girlfriend hears any more, give me a call."

"Okay. I'll keep my ears open. So, what goodies have you brought Big Sheila today?"

I was a woman of few vices. I didn't drink or smoke, and my sex life, when I had one, was boring and normal, devoid of fetishes. But I would literally provide offerings of small children to the gods for my shoe collection. To pay for Grand's medicine, I'd been slowly and painfully selling my shoes off to Sheila and her friends. In times like these, I felt blessed to have particularly large feet for a girl. I was a size eleven, which made me popular with some in the drag crowd. Usually I had no problem moving a couple of pairs a week. If Sheila couldn't use what I had, she always found someone who could. I pulled out the lime-green Manolo Blahnik sandal pumps.

"Oh, hon," Sheila said, the cigarette falling out of her mouth at the sight of them.

I loved the idea of those shoes. The color was inspired, and they were super comfortable but not very practical. I didn't have a lot of things that went well with lime. Plus, they had long leather ties that wrapped around the ankles, and sparkly bobbles on the toe straps. I'd been saving them for an emergency. Given my potential impending unemployment, I thought this qualified.

"You've outdone yourself this time. No one's going to get near these but me. How much?"

"Two seventy-five firm."

"Will you take two fifty?"

"Do I look like Wayne Brady from *Let's Make a Deal*? 'Firm' means no haggling, and if you don't want them, I'm sure I can find another buyer."

"You don't have to get snarky, sugar. You can't blame me for trying to get a bargain."

The transaction complete, I hit the pharmacy for Grand's meds then headed to DC's.

DC lived near the university, on the third floor of an old brownstone with great bones and good upkeep. The building was probably a stunner in its day, a residence for some wealthy businessman and his family that hosted extravagant parties. Now it was gutted and stuffed but still loved.

The apartment had been expanded and carved up into small units to serve as home to PhD candidates, more-studious-than-partygoing undergrads, and a host of young couples like DC and his partner, Kimi.

I bounded up two flights of stairs and, standing in the hallway, heard the music blaring from their unit. I didn't knock because no one would have heard it over the racket, anyway, but went right in instead, using the spare key DC had given me.

"DC!" I yelled, looking around and moving through his apartment. The place was an eclectic mix of interests—part exotic plant- and bookshop, part As Seen on TV store, and part pharmacy. DC enabled Kimi's perpetual hypochondria by always buying her something to save her life. Breathing machines, bandages, medical books, and pill bottles covered the floor and table. I wasn't sure which of them had the infomercial obsession. Devices to tighten their abs, plump their lips, tone their skin, ShamWow the car, and slice and dice the perfect vegetable littered every surface.

Peppered among the clutter were DC's babies—his lush plants, vibrant green even though spring was barely a week old, and his books. That was how DC and I had originally connected. We were both voracious readers, and DC was one of the most knowledgeable people I had ever met. Kimi wasn't allowed near his plants and constantly complained about the number of books lying around.

DC stood in front of an enormous TV, wearing a St. Louis Rams jersey that was so big for his slight body, I couldn't tell if he had anything on under it, and a white headband that stretched around his brown head in sharp contrast to his darker skin. Beyonce's "Single Ladies" music video blared from the big screen. Next to DC, a gray-and-white Persian cat stood strapped into the harness of a vertical slingshot, bouncing to the beat.

"DC!" I yelled again.

A high-pitched scream exploded as he turned around, clearly startled. Once he realized I wasn't a serial killer, a wide smile slid across his face. "Lock up your corpses. Kat is in the house!" he said, pausing the TV.

"Not funny," I said but smiled anyway. I could always count on DC to lighten any situation.

He opened his long, skinny arms. "Come get a hug and tell me all about it."

DC wasn't tall or robust but possessed a commanding presence nonetheless. He was petite for a male, no bigger than five six, animated and energetic in everything he did. He used relaxer on his longish hair, making it silky smooth. He had a sleek figure that never seemed to gain an ounce, even when he tried. Cheekbones any high-society girl would have died for accentuated the smoothest, most beautiful skin I'd ever seen.

I found the hug to be unexpectedly nice. I wasn't overly emotional like DC, but it felt good to be surrounded by a bit of sympathy.

"Now, how did you manage to lose a body?" he asked, taking my hand and leading me to the couch.

"It's your fault."

"My fault?"

"Burns McPhee."

"Oh, honey, if you ran into Mr. Tall, Dark, and Broody, that's hardly cause for casting blame."

Under different circumstances, and if I hadn't been on a man hiatus, nursing my mending heart, I might have been inclined to agree with DC.

"So Burns McPhee stole your body?"

"No, not exactly. He was trying to help me keep it from getting stolen. I think."

I relayed the whole story—how the body had been sneaked away in the sexavator, Burns and Flynn chasing after it with their guns, the white van, and the anonymous tip to the police about my being on the take.

"It's like an episode of *NCIS*. So who was the woman, and why do people want to steal her smelly remains? And who among our morgue brothers and sisters sold you out?"

"You think it was someone at the morgue too?" I asked.

"It's the only thing that makes sense. You said someone tipped the cops that you were on the take and called it in to Dr. Hawthorne before he even got to the morgue, so it was before anyone had even seen you there. Meaning that it was someone who knew you would be working, and since you and I switched shifts last minute, that only leaves people with access to our posted schedule. We have a traitor in our midst."

That was why I loved DC. People always judged him by his appearance, but he was quick and smart.

"We have to find out who the traitor is so that I can get unsuspended and we can have a safe and trusting work environment. Feeling unsafe in the workplace can cause unnecessary weight retention, you know."

"If by 'we' you mean 'you,' I think it's a terrific idea."

"You're the one who gave McPhee the bright idea that he could stroll into the morgue anytime he wanted and peek at bodies. A part of the story I conveniently left out when I talked with the cops, by the way. And now I'm on probation."

"Well, true."

"You know how badly I need this job. I'm making a list." I pulled my notebook out of my purse. My chronic indecisiveness had several side effects, one of which was my list making. Anything that needed sorting or deciding required me to make a list, sometimes culminating in a decision tree, often leading to a task plan. If I was ever worried or anxious about something, which was pretty much all the time, I wrote it down. My current worry list consisted of:

- A prostitute who doesn't look like a prostitute, who gets her dead body stolen
- Creepy body snatcher
- Backstabbing-rat morgue worker
- McPhee and his merry band of misfits

"So, how do you know him, and why did he come looking for you last night?" I closed the cover of my fuzzy pink notebook.

"Burns McPhee is my guardian angel. I'd be dead, a mere footnote in history, if it wasn't for him. A few years ago, before I met Kimi, I ran into some trouble walking to the bus alone from one of my meetings."

By "meetings," DC didn't mean AA or Kiwanis. DC was a registered officer of the Greater St. Louis NORML chapter, the National Organization for the Reform of Marijuana Laws. He ended up working at the morgue through a medical contact in his pot business. The morgue work was temporary until he could get enough money to open his own plant emporium. In addition to the many legal herbs that DC currently sold on the side, he also had a line of medical marijuana. Once Missouri legalized medicinal marijuana, he believed he would be able to patent his more potent line and become more famous than the Jackie O rose.

"It's a long story, but let's just say McPhee and his crew rescued me with their ninja moves from a group of Southern Confederates carrying very large firearms."

"So you ran into some ugly skinheads and McPhee saved you?"

"Now you know how I hate stereotypes, Kat. It's bad for your karma, but more or less, yes. He, Flynn, and Neutron saved me."

"Neutron?" I asked.

"Bug-eyed boy genius. Another one of McPhee's strays. He collects them."

"So who's Flynn, besides someone in obvious need of roid rage therapy?"

"As I understand it, Flynn's been with Burns since they were kids. They were in the Army together. Served in Afghanistan. Flynn is Burns's muscle. He scares me on account of..."

"On account of what?"

"On account of he doesn't like me. He says I talk too much."

I smiled. DC did talk too much. It was part of his charm. The fact that it irritated that obnoxious Flynn was a bonus.

Before DC could continue, the cat let out a shriek. DC made a beeline for the cat contraption.

"What is that?"

"This is a state-of-the-art cat-a-ciser. I told you Dr. Telner, our pet therapist, had recommended one for Morpheus and Niobe. Dr. Telner believes if Niobe has a forum where she can feel strong and powerful, she'll stop trying to chew Kimi's face off in the middle of the night."

Even after all these months, I didn't quite understand DC and Kimi's relationship. They didn't seem like a fit, but they had been together for a while. I knew Dr. Telner had also suggested couples counseling for them, but Kimi wouldn't go, leaving them at an impasse. Kimi had given him an ultimatum, saying either the cats had to go or she would. He looked distraught as he cuddled Niobe in his arms.

"I've had Morpheus and Niobe since they were babies, and they've always been so sweet. But since Kimi moved in, it's been one thing after another. Last night they peed in her ostrich-leather purse. So the cat-a-ciser has to work. Dr. Telner said he doesn't normally sell it to patients but that we're a special case. It's a bargain at two ninety-nine."

"Three hundred dollars on a cat treadmill!"

"Yeah, but they're my babies. What can I do? I have to take them to Momma's. Kimi says they can't stay here anymore. Let me change, and I can fill you in on the rest on our way."

A few minutes later, DC came out looking like a completely different man, wearing a butterscotch-colored suit, his hair slicked back into a short ponytail.

"We are not driving that junk heap of yours. We can take the cruiser."

DC's car was the biggest Lincoln Town Car ever manufactured. The seats were plush maroon velvet, and there was enough room to have a small party in the back. I'd met DC's mom, aka Momma Claiborne, a couple of times before. She was a remarkable woman, strong and sophisticated and approachable and warm. She raised DC and his brothers herself, their dad long gone, while successfully running her own cosmetics business. Her family was originally from the South, but they moved up here after a particularly nasty round of hurricanes in the early 1970s. Her house was a large, fully restored Victorian. It was pink with red trim, but it wasn't that obnoxious Pepto-Bismol pink, more of a mauve. No house in the neighborhood looked like any other, and giant oaks kept watch over them all. Momma's house stood at the end of a long street, looking grand, much like Momma Claiborne herself.

As we pulled up to the house, Momma Claiborne was sitting on the front porch, hatted in a bright-white spring bonnet, sipping on a drink. The hat matched her flower-print dress in bold spring colors. As a large woman, she could get away with wearing bold, flowery dresses. She waved as we got out of the car.

"Hello, Miss Kat," she said as I walked up the steps to the front porch. "How are you doing, hon?"

Everyone was "hon" to Momma Claiborne, males and females alike. Even though she'd lived in the Midwest, or what she called The North, for forty-plus years, her accent was still thick.

"I'm fine, Momma Claiborne," I said and ran up to give her a hug before I went to help DC with the cat carriers.

"Except for the body snatchers," DC added.

"Well, it is body-snatching weather. Hello, son, have you brought me your fur kids?"

"Yes, Momma."

"You know I'd much rather have real grandkids."

When Kimi had moved in with DC, Momma Claiborne had started leaving bridal magazines everywhere and asking when he was going to give her grandbabies. Instead, he brought her cats.

We headed to the back of the house to a sun porch full of plants and flowers starting their spring bloom and let out the cats. This was where DC was most comfortable, with his plants. From the road, it wasn't easy to tell, but the house sat on over an acre of land, one of the pluses of living in the Midwest; houses were sprawling. In the back of Momma Claiborne's house sat several greenhouses that DC used to grow his plants and herbs.

We had a seat on the settee.

"So how does McPhee rescuing you lead to him being in the morgue and trying to steal my body last night?" I asked.

"That's a whole other tragic tale. All I know is that since the prostitute killings started last spring, he's been in the body business. I think it has something to do with Gillian Mathers."

"Gillian Mathers?" I searched my memory bank for the name. "Isn't she the dead reporter from the *Post*?" The occasional conspiracy theory about her death had been the only thing to push my dad off the front page every now and then. "What does he have to do with her?"

"Rumor has it Burns and her were an item in high school and maybe longer."

"Okay, but I thought the reporter's death was a robbery gone wrong?"

"Apparently, about six months ago, she called him with a story about some psycho serial killer murdering prostitutes. She asked for his help. Less than a week later, she turned up dead. I'd say he doesn't think it's a coincidence and maybe also that he's nursing a bucket of guilt."

"So you've been letting him play peek-a-boo with any dead prostitutes that come into the morgue?"

"I owe him, and I always pay my debts. Plus, just look at him. He's like a walking tragedy. He took Gillian's death really hard. The police have swept it all under the rug and are getting nowhere on the prostitute murders. He's one of the good guys trying to make something right. I didn't have any moral objections to that."

I thought back to the way McPhee looked when he told me about the death of his best friend potentially being connected to the missing girl. That look in his eyes. He looked like a strong man trying to hold it all together. For a moment, I felt sorry for him. Still...

"So if he's one of the good guys, why wouldn't he corroborate my story to the police, then?" I asked.

"After Gillian was murdered, Burns and the local police exchanged some troubling communications. My guess is he's pissed off the cops enough and doesn't want to get himself in any more trouble. That, or he knows something he doesn't want them finding out."

"That Detective Driscol sure didn't like me mentioning McPhee at all. His forehead went all wrinkly, and he started rubbing the bridge of his nose, like he was stressed out. And I can't believe they think I was in on it."

"Well, you might have ties to the Italian mob." He smiled big.

"Oh, please. About the only things Italian in my family are my dad's suits and my love for gelato. But you're right. Someone at the morgue is trying to make it look that way. Who would do such a thing? I've been so nice to everyone."

"It's not your fault, really. People here just don't appreciate free fashion tips." DC got up and started fussing with his plants.

I hugged the accent pillow to my body and contemplated the situation with my coworkers. DC and I had hit it off instantly. We were reading the same book the day I started. He had noticed me drooling over his scientific journal collection, and I helped him pick out the perfect accessories to go with his suits.

With everyone else at the morgue, things had not gone so smoothly. No matter what I said, it always seemed to be the wrong thing. "Some days, I feel like I'm in a foreign country. We don't seem to have anything in common. I wear bright, inviting colors, but no one will talk to me."

"Look, sweetie, no one can blame you for being slow to adjust to your new circumstances, and not everyone can be as open to newcomers as I am."

"Maybe. But if we're going to smoke out the weasel in our midst, I'm going to have to change that. We need a plan." I crossed my legs underneath me and took out my notebook to review everything again.

"Well, whoever wiped the video had to have computer expertise to do that, and with that level of skill, they could have hacked in and looked at the morgue's schedule. That's how they'd know you were the one working," he said, pulling some dead leaves off one of his plants.

"Okay, so our first priority will be to figure out if any of the other morgue attendants have good computer skills. If they won't talk to me, maybe one of them will talk to you?" I looked up at him, hopeful, knowing it was a stretch of a favor.

"I don't exactly mix with the morgue crowd. If we really want information, there's only one good source..."

"Don't say it." I closed my eyes and took in a deep breath.

"Marshall," he said in a firm tone.

"I asked you not to say it," I said, exhaling the breath I was holding. "I'm not sure I can stomach Marshall this early."

"We need info, and Marshall's a man in the business."

I needed the information. And not just for me. "It's all so awful. This girl, the Jane Doe they took, was beautiful and young, younger than me. And someone beat her to death. Now someone's taken her. She deserves for people to know how and why she died. And she deserves respectful closure."

"I've got to be going, Daryl." Momma Claiborne strolled to DC. Despite her size, she gave the impression she could float. "It's my beauty day. Make sure Kat gets some of my leftover fried chicken. I swear that girl's gonna wither on the vine. And if you go anywhere, make sure you lock up the house." With a kiss to DC's cheek and a wave to me, she was gone.

We grabbed the chicken as instructed, and with food in tow, we headed out to the greenhouses for lunch in the garden. As we rounded the bend, heading for the table and chairs by the first greenhouse, DC became noticeably tense.

"Oh, damn! There's someone in there."

"Where?"

"In the greenhouse, on the left. See? Watch, there's light flashes moving around."

I peered at the window of the greenhouse in the distance, trying to look casual in case we were being watched, and there it was, a gleam of bright light, as if the sun's rays were hitting a diamond and reflecting back. "Maybe Momma let someone back here?"

"Not without telling us, and she's headed for her beauty day."

"Maybe it's an animal," I said, trying to keep DC from freaking out and running screaming from the house. "Let's go check."

We quickly clambered out the back door and into the garden between the main house and the greenhouse. Crouching down, we crept near the greenhouse to get a better look.

"You go first," DC whispered.

"Why me?"

"Your family has more experience with criminal activity, and besides, I just did my nails," he said, sticking out his pristinely manicured hand to show it off.

"My dad's in prison for money laundering. That hardly qualifies me to take on an armed intruder," I whispered as we moved past the door of the first greenhouse, toward the door of the second. The greenhouses were both long and narrow, with little narrow paths running between the rows of tables holding the plants and cuttings.

"Armed? You think they have guns?" DC asked in a high-pitched whisper.

"The Department of Justice estimates that a home invasion occurs every ten seconds or about eight thousand times a day," I whispered back, reaching for a rake and a hoe leaning against the greenhouse. "But an article in the *Journal of the American Medical Association* showed that the intruder was armed in only about twenty percent of home invasions, so maybe not," I continued, handing him the rake and mumbling as much to myself as DC, although he always seemed to appreciate my journal references. "But it's good to be prepared."

We slinked around the side. "Also of note, thirty percent of the time, the intruder was someone the victim knew."

"I'm getting out of here, anyway," he said and turned back to the house.

"Don't you want to know who's in there?" I asked, tugging his shirt and pulling him back.

He smacked at my hand. "All right, now. There's no reason to get physical."

"Then man up. I'll go first, but you better have my back," I said, and raising my hoe, I slowly opened the door.

We looked utterly ridiculous, and if the intruder was anything more than a raccoon, we were in trouble. Even then, I wasn't sure we could handle it.

"Bloody hell, you idiot. What'd you go and do that for?" said a gruff, obviously agitated voice from the rear of the greenhouse.

"It looked sharp. I wanted to see if it would hurt," a softer, more juvenile voice replied.

"You know, for a genius, you're a real dumbass. I can't take you anywhere without you getting into trouble," the first voice said.

Whoever they were, they were too swept up in their own internal conflict to notice that we had come into the greenhouse.

"Let's split up," I whispered. "We'll surround them."

"Okay, let's go that way," DC said, almost clinging to me as we moved.

"That's not really splitting up."

"What if they attack me?"

"Use your rake and rake their eyeballs out."

"Okay, good idea. It sounds like Izzy got one of them, anyway."

Izzy was DC's giant fishhook barrel cactus. He had several, and Izzy was the biggest. It stood almost as tall as me, with sharp protruding spines that would nip someone's skin at the smallest brush.

I circled to the left, wielding my hoe like a fierce weapon, and DC headed to the right. As soon as I got to the back of the greenhouse, I recognized one of the men as none other than Flynn and stood up tall from my left flank position.

"What are you doing here?" I asked, standing up.

The men appeared startled, and the scrawny one screamed, pulling his gun and firing into the ceiling. One of the Plexiglas ceiling tiles instantly shattered, sending the plastic glass raining down on top of us and causing DC to let out a wail. I ducked for cover to avoid the falling glass and any further potential stray bullets.

"You idiot," Flynn yelled, taking the gun from the scrawny kid before he could do more damage.

Once the glass stopped falling and it appeared Flynn had the renegade shooter under control, I came out of hiding. DC already stood in the middle of the greenhouse, chastising the kid.

"Neutron, I'm gonna sue your scrawny little ass for ravaging my abode."

"Technically, this is your mother's place," the kid replied, clearly not realizing that he was winding DC up even more. The kid was short and wore glasses—which made his bug eyes look twice as buggy—jeans, and a T-shirt that paid homage to Slayer.

"You do know who you're talking to, right?" DC asked, pushing his way toward the kid, Flynn in between them. "I'm an officer of a premier horticulture organization. I have money and power behind me. Don't think you can just march in here and deface my sanctuary."

"I hardly think the local pot growers' association qualifies as a premier horticulture society," the kid quipped.

"We're a substantial force in the economy, and I'll show you how much power we have, you property-wrecking dumbass!"

"Oh, shut it," Flynn said. "And calm down. I'm sure Burns will pay for any damages."

"What are you two doing here, anyway?" I asked, stepping in before DC could further escalate things.

"Burns sent us," the scrawny kid said.

"McPhee has you following me now?" I asked.

"I'm Neutron," he said, offering his hand. When I didn't take it, he gave a slight bow.

"I thought you said he was a genius," I said, looking at DC.

"Really?" Neutron looked up from dusting himself off and smiled at DC.

"A genius with no damn common sense. What made you think that firing a gun in a glass building was a brilliant idea?" DC asked.

"It was an accident. I'm injured," he said, showing his bleeding finger, "and I was startled."

"Because you stuck your damn hand on a giant prickly plant," Flynn said, and the three of them started arguing again.

"All right!" I yelled over their commotion. "Only one of you gets to talk, or I swear to God, I'm going to beat each of you over the head with my hoe."

"She can do it too," DC said in my defense. "She's a black belt, and her dad works for the mob."

"DC! You, Neutron. Why did Burns send you to watch us?"

"You're being followed."

"Followed? By whom?"

"We don't know, but we tracked them here. They have a car outside Momma's house, so we circled through the back."

Before I could ask any more questions, gunshots fired into the greenhouse from every direction. We all hit the floor.

Chapter 5

When the shots started spraying, the glass of the greenhouse shattered. We ducked the falling shards and made our way out the back of the greenhouse, through the grassy alley, racing to the SUV.

And we ran smack into the body-snatching man from the morgue. I stood inches from him, frozen. He stood in the middle of the road near the SUV, still, his machine gun casually tossed over his shoulder like dry cleaning. He smiled at me.

"Kat!" DC's voice broke my freeze.

I ran to the truck. The door popped open in front of me, and I dove in as the engine revved. I sat upright and straightened my outfit while Neutron floored it. We drove right past the man, who was still standing in the road. His stare followed us as we passed him. He barely moved except to give me an evil grimace.

"Am I shot? Someone check me. I feel holes in my suit. I think a bullet grazed my midsection. Someone check me." Once we had all made it into Flynn's SUV, DC frantically patted his body, looking for wounds.

"You bloody idiot, you're not shot!" retorted Flynn.

"Bloody? Where's the blood?" DC asked.

"It's an expression," Flynn replied.

"I've seen my maker today, and it's all y'all's fault. I feel ill," DC said and put his head between his knees.

"Do not hurl in my truck!" Flynn yelled.

"Stop yelling at him," I said. "You're only making him more hysterical."

"We're gonna need protection now. Someone's gonna have to get me a new identity," DC went on.

"Did you know that the Federal Witness Protection Program spends over forty million dollars annually providing new identities?" I was tired, my patience was wearing thin, and I wanted him to change the subject.

"Really, forty million?" The question was muffled. DC lifted his head. "I would have thought it was higher than that. We need to figure out how we're going to get our slice of that forty million." DC became calmer as he contemplated how we would do that.

"How did you know we were being followed, anyway?" I asked them.

"We were following you and figured out that we weren't the only ones," Neutron said, his bug eyes shifting from the road to the rearview mirror to the side mirrors and back, nonstop.

"Why were you following us?"

"To see if you knew where the stolen body was."

"I'm on probation for that and almost burst a lung chasing that same maniac corpse kidnapper through the hospital as I was trying to help you. Do you honestly think I have anything to do with it?"

"Dunno. Rumor has it your family may have mob ties. There could be a connection," Neutron said.

"That's true," DC chimed in. "You could be dangerous and just not know it."

McPhee's office was in Clayton, an inner-ring suburb of St. Louis, and the county seat. It was a bustling business and cultural district and home of the annual St. Louis Art Fair. We pulled down a narrow alley and key carded into a garage under a towering building. We got on the elevator, and Neutron key carded again, pushing two buttons.

The elevator whirled to life and stopped after a short hop, the doors opening to reveal a sleek steel door with McPhee Security etched into it. Key-carded doors flanked both sides of the elevator hallway. No other signs appeared. The lighting was low, and there were no people.

Flynn got out first. "I'd say it's been a pleasure seeing you again, but we'd both know I was lying. Have fun."

Neutron pushed another button then followed Flynn out the doors. The doors started to close.

"Burns, what kind of idiots do you have runnin' this place?" DC asked. "Do you know what that bug-eyed moron did to my greenhouse? Do you have any idea how much damage has been caused? And I don't even want to know if those lunatics with the guns shot up Momma's house, because if they did that, I'm sendin' Momma for you and that bug-eyed moron."

"DC, my friend," Burns said, moving to meet DC, an almost smile curving the corners of his mouth, his eyes brighter, warm with affection. He draped his arm around DC and squeezed lightly. "I hear you were very brave today." This flattery stopped DC's hysterics cold.

"Yes, I guess I was, wasn't I, Kat?" he calmly asked, smiling at me.

"Yes, you were," I agreed, happy to see DC's smile.

"I hear you handled yourself quite well too. Is it Katherine or Kat?" Burns locked his eyes on me again. He moved close enough I could smell him. McPhee smelled exactly like I would have imagined if I had thought about it—yummy and musky.

"In 1989, Katherine was the twenty-sixth most popular girl's name of the year. My parents were traditionalists."

Burns didn't even try to hide his amusement at my social tic, which caused me to instantly blush and turn away, looking about the room. "DC calls me Kat, but I like him," I said, glancing at him. At that, McPhee looked... hurt, maybe?

"Burns is an interesting name. Family origin?" I asked, hoping a change of subject would help.

"Yes, sort of. My mother's way of paying homage to our deep-rooted Scottish origins and her love of poetry."

I searched my memory. "Oh, Robert Burns, then!" I turned toward him. "'But little mouse, you are not alone in proving that foresight may be vain: The best laid plans of mice and men...'"

"Go often awry and leave us nothing but grief and pain for promised joy," he completed, stepping closer, his eyes locked to mine.

"Yeah, well, I'm not so sure where the joy is, but my day has been nothing but pain and grief," DC said as he examined one of the holes in his suit.

"Ah, but you are the fierce Braveheart," he said with a chuckle, a thick brogue coloring the words.

"To be honest, I'm not sure we fared all that well," I added. I was feeling overwhelmed. I hadn't expected my day to include a shootout, and now I was in a strange office, talking to a man I originally thought was one person but who now seemed to be someone else. Steadying myself, I began looking at the pictures of Ingenisys's projects around his office. "What is Ingenisys, anyway, Mr. McPhee?"

"Burns, please. We match business investors here with worthwhile projects in the Middle East."

"Isn't the Middle East dangerous?" I eyed a photo of Burns surrounded by village children playing soccer. He looked... happy. For whatever reason, since I'd met him, he looked more haunted than anything. I wondered if that look had to do with my missing body and the death of Gillian Mathers.

"It can be, but that makes the projects more important. It will never get better there if the economy doesn't change. That's something I would think you would understand with your economics background."

I raised an eyebrow. Not many people knew I had a minor in Econ, an appeasement to my father. Burns's gaze became intense again, even as he casually leaned against the side of his desk.

"There's some great new research on positive outcomes from pooled microlending that could help your cause," I said.

He held up a *Journal of Internet Banking and Commerce* from his desk. "It's a little thick to get through. I'd be interested in your perspective sometime."

"You run the business?" I asked.

"This branch. It's headquartered out of New York. An Army brother of mine is the founder."

"And you run the security business we saw on the floor under this?"

"Yes, it helps pay the bills, and clients rich enough to afford security tend to make good prospects for investing."

"Burns is a security genius," DC said. "He's a badass Special Ops guy who can take you out with a single finger. I've seen it before. You don't want to get him mad. He's gonna teach me." DC made karate animations. "Especially now that I have to change my identity."

DC was interrupted by Neutron's reappearance. He had changed from his camos into Dockers and a button-down.

"Neutron, why don't you take our hero here to see Bradley for a change of clothes?" Burns asked as Neutron approached with a scrunched-up face.

"I think my life's been in jeopardy enough today. Bradley will shoot on sight."

"Who's Bradley, and what did you do to him?" I asked, turning to DC.

"Bradley's our office manager, and DC set his desk on fire," Neutron said.

"Now, come on, you know it wasn't quite that simple. Okay, maybe it was. But I had a hankering for s'mores. That's not a craving you can dismiss lightly, all that melted marshmallow and chocolaty goodness." DC smiled. Chocolate was one of his favorite things. "The cigarette lighter got hot. I ended up with a blister. We're lucky my whole finger didn't burn off." He held up his index finger for inspection.

"Fire is very bad for your skin," I said, holding in a laugh.

"When Bradley's done, you can bring him to the ops center and walk him through the background reports on the other morgue employees. Maybe try to get a sketch of the man who took the body," Burns said.

I could have sworn I heard a groan from Neutron.

"Background reports? Burns, we seriously have to talk about gettin' me a new ID if I'm gonna be identifying corpse-napping murderers." As Neutron tried to push him toward the door, DC grabbed Burns's arm to show him how seriously he'd taken the morning's events.

"Go with Neutron, DC. I promise we'll talk later."

Neutron lured DC out of the office by asking him about what he wanted to change into. He must have known DC had a fashionista streak. As the door shut, DC's voice could still be heard, harassing Neutron about available attire.

Finally, we were alone. With DC gone, Burns's full attention fell on me. His dark eyes locked onto me like missile-tracking devices. I reminded myself that I was here because he'd lied. Feeling my anger rise, I met his stare with what I hoped was my own glare. "You got me put on probation. I'm going to lose my job."

"I'm sorry, but there weren't a lot of good alternatives."

"How about telling the truth?"

"I could have told them I was there because DC and I have an arrangement where he lets me see bodies of dead prostitutes, but I'm betting you wouldn't want DC to be the one on probation."

He was right. I wouldn't. Still, I said, "You don't know anything about me."

"I know you've left a fairly prestigious life to come back here and take care of your mom and sick grandmother, under some less than optimal circumstances. I admire that kind of loyalty."

I must have looked surprised.

"I own a security firm, remember? Look, Kat," he said, stepping around the table toward me, his voice softening as he got closer, "I'm just saying that given how protective you seem of the people you care about"—his body moved within inches of mine—"how protective we both are"—he reached his hand toward my hair—"I assume we agree that getting DC in trouble is not on the option list." He pulled some Plexiglas out of my hair, brushing his fingers lightly across my cheek with the softness of fluttering butterfly wings.

We stayed like that for a moment, me taking in the contradiction between his authoritative manner and his soft actions. Finally, I nodded.

"Good," he said, putting his hand down. "I'm glad I have your support. Now if you'll excuse me," he said as if turning to go, looking casual again, almost dismissive.

"What?" I was taken aback. A minute ago I was almost yelling at him. I would not be manipulated. I would get control of the conversation and squish him like a bug.

"I have some meetings to attend to. I'll call Bradley to—"

"Oh no," I said, my voice rising. "We are not done here. I've been suspended and shot at, and I'm sleep deprived. Just when I thought my life was on an upswing, you show up, that beautiful girl is stolen from me, and my life is back to ground zero. Here I am, soon to be jobless and worrying sick about how my family will cope. You are not going to dismiss me like I'm one of your blond, Bumpit-wearing, Stepford secretaries who does whatever you say." I was exasperated and flailing my hands.

Burns paused. Phone in hand, he stood there as if waiting for me to finish.

"You're right. I wouldn't want DC to get in trouble. He's been a great friend since I moved here. But I only have to look around to know you're a smart guy. You could have made up a reason for being there that would have kept everyone out of trouble."

"Like what?"

"You could have told them you were in the hospital visiting a sick friend."

"And what would I have said when they asked me who that was?"

"You could have told them you were there for the ice cream. All right, that's ridiculous," I said, calming down to a more reflective tone. I knew I was reaching, but I also knew I wasn't wrong, despite how Burns was making me feel. That was the thing, though—I shouldn't have been feeling bad. None of us should have. DC didn't want to look at the body. Burns did.

"Why did you have to tell them anything at all? You didn't have to mention DC to tell them that you were there trying to get a look at the body. Maybe you're a body groupie." I had him finally. We both knew it. He put down the phone. "But you didn't want to tell them that, did you. Because then you would be the one in trouble instead of me."

"No, I didn't," he answered honestly, shocking me.

"Okay, then."

"Telling the police why I was really at the morgue would have created a complicated situation that I'm not prepared to handle right now." He said it softly, that haunting look coming back to his face.

"Because you want to know who killed Gillian Mathers?"

He looked surprised at my question.

"I have my sources too."

"Your source has a flair for drama, and he talks too much," he replied, smiling.

"Yes, but he's very charming." I smiled back at him.

"Kat," he said, his tone more serious, "six women are dead. I don't think for a minute that this guy is done. Potentially more women's lives are at stake. At the very least, a murderer is wandering around free because the police have been unable to find who killed these women and my friend. If they aren't going to do their jobs, I need them out of my hair so that I can do it for them."

He was trying to appeal to my compassionate side now, and it was working. I couldn't decide what to do about this mess we both seemed to be in. Instead, I pulled my list from my purse, sat down at the little conference table, and began writing.

"What are you doing?"

"Updating my list." I said it as though it was a normal occurrence and he was the weird one for questioning it.

"Your list?"

"Yes. Rule number eight. If there's something to be figured out, it requires a list for fact gathering and puzzling. Although, I don't think that's really a rule. I think my mom made it up to help me cope with my anxiety."

"Okay. And has your list helped you figure out who was follow-ing you?" he asked and sat down next to me.

"No, I don't know who's been following me, besides your men, that is." I wrote that down, that Burns's men were following me.

"I wasn't sure that you weren't involved yet. I wanted to keep tabs on you until I figured out you weren't in on taking the body. Your dad's in prison for working with the mob. For all I know, you could have been connected."

"Why does everyone think I'm some kind of mob princess?"

"Princess, maybe." He grinned. "Between that sexy brain and killer smile, you don't give much of a mob vibe, though."

I looked up at him. "Thank you."

"But the newspaper articles about your family aren't helping," he added.

"No. They aren't, but you say 'racketeering' and everyone jumps to 'mob.' It gets a bad rap. Racketeering is one of the smallest federal crime categories, representing less than one percent of all arrests and increasingly involving white-collar crimes. It's like winning the crime lotto."

"Of course you'd know that." He smirked and leaned against his desk, his look turning contemplative. "Do you know what's going on with your dad?"

"Not really. He keeps saying it's all some big misunderstanding. If you think *I'm* low on mob vibe, you should meet my dad. Everything happened so fast, before I could get back here. By the time I arrived, the house was empty, Dad was in prison, and no one would talk to us."

"Appearances aren't always what they seem. Especially when people are close to us, we can have a hard time seeing what's going on." I felt like we weren't talking about me anymore. Burns became distant, and I was getting uncomfortable.

"So do you know who was following me?" I asked.

"Not yet. But if you weren't in on the body snatching, I thought you might need some protection. Then you showed up at DC's, and I had a double incentive. I'm very fond of him and would hate to see anything happen to him."

"Funny, I was thinking something similar. DC's the only reason I have to trust you at all."

"At least we can both agree that we have excellent taste in friends. Hey, it may not seem like it, but I am genuinely sorry for the trouble you're in. It's a tough situation all around. Can you think of any reason someone would tell the police you were involved?"

"Honestly, at first, I thought it might be you. But there are only so many people who had the access to know I was working instead of DC. My whole life is upside down now." I turned back to my list.

Burns looked at me with sympathy and was quiet for a moment. We sat there in a surprisingly comfortable silence, me looking through my list, Burns apparently lost in his own thoughts.

Finally, he said, "Will you come with me? I want to show you something."

I looked at him warily.

"Please? In the interest of us getting off on a better foot," he added.

I nodded. He led me out of his office, past the auto-bot workers, and into a stairwell. He key carded us into another door and into another hallway, where he put his hand into a fingerprint reader. The door made a humming noise then clicked open.

Chapter 6

In front of us was a large room. Giant televisions flanked one of the walls, displaying security camera footage. Pictures of my morgue colleagues were pinned on the adjacent wall, and underneath was scribbling I couldn't make out. My morgue ID picture was in the center of the photos. That was not a good hair day for me.

Two rows of long, curving desks covered in computer equipment sat in the middle of the room, facing the televisions. On the far wall were pictures of girls, one of whom I recognized as reporter Gillian Mathers. In the same grouping, strings with pushpins connected various people I couldn't make out. It looked like something out of the CIA or police central.

"Welcome to the war room," Neutron said, looking up from one of the computer stations. DC sat next to him.

"Hey, Kat. It's like the Batcave, isn't it?" DC asked as Burns and I moved into the space.

"It had to be one of them." I crossed over to the wall with the pictures of my coworkers. "There were only a handful of people who knew I would be at the morgue last night instead of DC. Someone with Dr. Hawthorne's direct number." I stared at the collection of misfits. "Why are there only a handful of people's pictures on the wall? There are at least twenty people on the morgue staff."

"These are the people whose alibis we weren't able to corroborate. You weren't on there until last night."

I squared my hips and looked at Burns, wondering whether he was serious. "I have an excellent alibi for last night. You should ask the owner of this security firm what I was doing when the Russian stole the body."

His eyes brightened, and a smirk came to the corner of his mouth, but he didn't respond.

"Why is Dr. Hawthorne up there? Surely you can't think he's involved in any of this. He's a nice old grandpa."

"No, I don't think he's involved. He's squeaky clean. Boring life. Goes to the same barber twice a month. Belongs to the Elks. Nothing unusual in his finances other than he pays too much for haircuts." He walked across the room toward me, staring at the board as he did. "What do you know about the rest of them?" Burns stopped next to me and stuffed his hands into his pockets.

I moved toward the board and cleared my throat, pointing at one of the pictures of a baby-faced guy, more boy than man, with feathery brown hair and a sky-blue shirt. "Henry is an Autumn. He really shouldn't wear blue. It washes him out."

"I'll pass that along the next time I see him."

"Well, it's not like we're all besties. These people work at a morgue. They aren't exactly known for their outgoing social skills."

He cocked his head and looked at me sideways. "You work at a morgue."

"Not on purpose."

"DC works at a morgue."

"Exactly. He's not quite what you would term mainstream." I turned toward him and folded my arms across my chest. "Why do you care about any of them, anyway? What is all of this?" I searched for an answer in his eyes, taken in by their intensity.

He ran his hand through his hair and sighed. "This isn't the first problem we've had with the morgue staff."

"What do you mean?"

"After Gillian's murder, some of the key forensic information in her case went missing."

"Missing?" I looked at the board and tried to decide if one of them could have been involved in all of this. They all looked like such misfits. For one of them to be so calculating seemed improbable.

"Yes. Dr. Hawthorne claimed it was a clerical error. He believes the evidence is still at the warehouse, just misfiled."

"But you think that's too convenient?"

"Kind of like the daughter of an accused mobster being implicated in a body snatching of our only lead in months."

"Thanks for that, I guess." I reached up and took one of the pictures off the board. "This is Meg." The picture was of a cheery-looking brunette in a bright-green blouse. Although I could see the resemblance, the person in the picture didn't much resemble the woman I worked with. In real life, Meg had a pierced eyebrow, wore heavy black eye makeup, and wouldn't be caught dead in bright green. I moved her picture next to Henry's. "She has the hots for Henry, but I'm not sure either of them realize it."

"Really?" Burns brought his hand to his chin and rubbed it.

"Totally. I have a nose for this. I have to say, though, they both seem as harmless as hamsters."

He pointed at the picture of Meg. "She has a bit of a checkered past. Juvie stay. And he has interesting sums of money moving in and out of his bank account. Sums a morgue worker shouldn't have."

"If you want motive, Marshall here has it in spades." I pointed at the picture of Marshall Traupe, a round man with greasy, curly hair.

"What do you mean? We didn't find any reason to think Marshall is involved. Like a lot of the others, he just couldn't be ruled out."

"If there's something illegal going on at the morgue, I guarantee Marshall both knows about it and has found a way to profit from it. If I were looking for information on people in the morgue, Marshall there would be my first stop. But bring cash."

"Interesting." Burns rubbed his chin.

"Why is Dr. Jaffe on the board?" I moved to look at Dr. Jaffe's hospital employee mug shot. He had large bags under his eyes and needed a haircut. "He doesn't work at the morgue."

"No, but he was the attending physician the night Gillian's forensics went missing, and he's massively in debt."

"Money troubles would fit. He's very grumpy. He could use a couple of sessions with my yogi master, Tahkaswami. Plus, he really doesn't like me."

"How come?"

"I have no idea. I always try to bring cheer to the autopsy room whenever we work together. He's very unappreciative."

"I think you're cheery." Burns grinned. He pointed at the picture of a man with a biker jacket and a blue cross tattoo that stood out against the tan skin of his neck. "What about him?"

"Sam? He looks dangerous from afar, but his fondue is way too good for him to be a crook."

He took the picture of Sam off the board and studied it. "Sam Allen Winston, despite his fondue, has a rap sheet a mile long. You said a minute ago, 'when the Russian stole the body.' How'd you know he was Russian?" He looked up at me.

"Like I told the detectives, he had Russian mobster shoes."

"I didn't realize there were specific shoes for Russian mobsters."

"That's why it's important to have someone around you who knows fashion. But why does that matter?"

"Sam here, with the killer fondue"—he turned Sam's picture toward me—"did time in his youth for boosting cars for a Russian chop shop."

"We have to tell the detectives all of this. It could help clear me." I reached for my cell phone.

"I wouldn't advise that, given the situation." He took the phone out of my hand. "The last prostitute who went to the police ended up dead." He slid the phone into my bag. "Your best bet at this point is to lay low."

"Lay low?"

"No offense, but look at you." He stopped and looked me up and down and slid his hands into his suit pockets.

After my internal morning debate, I had dressed in a short, fluttery black skirt over black leggings, with a turquoise sweater capped by a lovely jewel-toned scarf. I'd gone with matching turquoise wedges.

"What's wrong with me?" I said, looking myself up and down. Besides being a bit mussed from the shooting and running, I thought I was well within body-chasing fashion etiquette.

"Nothing's wrong with you. Far from it. You're gorgeous and smarter than the average bear, but I'm pretty certain you have about as much experience with hardened criminals as a Brownie troop. Heck, I'm surprised you didn't break your neck running in those heels."

"They're wedges, not heels. I ran perfectly fine in them, thank you. I must have missed the fashion chapter in the handbook for body chasers."

"Have you ever shot a gun?"

"Besides in a video game?"

"Kat, I don't know what's going on here, why someone has chosen to involve you in this, but after today's shooting, you should realize that it's dangerous. Let more-serious people handle it."

"So, I'm not serious now?"

"I didn't mean it like that. I like you. I want you safe."

I rubbed my temples. I wasn't able to get out a further response before I saw alarm fill his eyes. He was at my side in an instant and took my hand in his, bringing my arm up where he could look at it. Heat rushed to my cheeks. My pulse quickened.

"Around seventy-five thousand people a year survive gun injuries," I managed to get out, looking at him.

"You're bleeding." He held up my arm and turned it where I could see it. Blood soaked through my sweater. He pushed my sleeve down, took some tissues from the table, and blotted my arm gently in an effort to clean it up.

"Ow! That hurts." I'd barely felt the small cut, but it hurt so much when touched.

He maneuvered me to a small kitchen area on the side of the war room, washed off my arm, and smoothed a Band-Aid over it.

"It's just a scratch," I said, pulling my arm back with a little more force than I had wanted.

"Do I make you nervous, Kat?" he asked, his finger lightly running down my arm.

My anti-man radar blared loudly. "Let's review. Since I've met you, I've lost a corpse, lost my job, been followed by thugs, my friend's place has been demolished, I've been shot at repeatedly, and now, through zero fault of my own, I've apparently pissed off some very bad men. Yes, I'd say you make me nervous."

"Do I need to seal it with a kiss?" He looked up at me.

"That won't be necessary. I didn't even notice I was cut until you pushed on it." I shoved him out of the way to give us some space, hoping he hadn't noticed that I was flushed. I was glad that he trusted me enough to let me see his war room, and he might have been nicer than I thought before I came there, but we were still at an impasse. Without him, I had no way to prove that I wasn't involved in the body theft. If he didn't change his story, I would end up homeless, my complete collection of Jimmy Choos pilfered for a pittance. "So you still won't corroborate my story?"

"Nope," he said and leaned against the counter. He apparently hadn't even thought twice about it. Smug jerk. I would forget what I'd said about him being nice. "I can't afford police involvement right now, and I'm quite happy with you being sidelined." He grabbed a bottle of water from the refreshments on the table, handed one to me, and opened the other.

"Is that right?" I asked, opening mine while considering his words. I wasn't any happier than Burns was about some madman following me and involving me in body snatching, but this was still making my life more of a mess than it already was. That wouldn't do. "Then, I guess I'm left without many choices," I said, digging through my purse for my phone. "Do you know if Detective Driscol works today? He seemed to know quite a bit about you, so I assume you're old friends." I pretended to ponder the question while searching. "Never mind. I'm sure the main police operator will know." I pulled out the phone.

"I already told you, involving the police is a dangerous move for you."

"Oh, I already have people shooting at me. Even if the cops don't believe me about your involvement, I'm sure they'd be very interested in your little war room here. Based on how Detective Driscol reacted to your name when I gave you as my alibi, I think they would at least feel obligated to jam you up some. I doubt he's on Snapchat, but I'm sure even his phone can receive pictures of this war room of yours. Then, while they're busy dealing with you, I'll start looking for my missing body and clear this mess up. How safe do you think I'm going to be if I end up living on the streets?"

He scowled. I pretended to push a number and held the phone to my ear.

He set the water down on the counter without saying anything, staring. Probably calculating.

I took a picture of Burns. "Yes," I said to the pretend police officer, "can you please tell me how to get some evidence to Detective Driscol? I'll wait." I held my phone and pretended to wait, trying to look like I wasn't really a nervous wreck, and asked him, "Do you think the men shooting at me would be interested in your murder board too?"

Burns stood up and ran his hands through his hair. "Fine. Stop."

I hung up the phone, doing a happy dance on the inside. "Then you'll corroborate my story?"

He took a moment and appeared to be thinking. "No. But I have a proposition for you."

"A proposition?" After putting my phone away and picking up the water, I took another drink, eyeing him over the top of the bottle.

"Relax, it's not that kind of proposition." He smirked.

As if I would think that.

"Someone in that morgue is connected to this mess. I'm sure of it," Burns said.

"To the murders?" I asked.

"Maybe. Maybe they're only involved in the cover-up, but they can lead me to who's responsible. But I can't get to those people the same way you can, and as much as I appreciate him, I don't think I can trust DC to do it on his own. You get me information on your peers plus whatever information there is on the missing body from the morgue, everything from the crime scene to initial forensics and anything else they had on Joy. In return, I'll find a way to take care of the hearing next week. And no cops."

"So Joy was her name?"

"Maybe. A girl named Joy was working with Gillian on the killings before Gillian's attack, and now Joy's missing. As far as we can tell, there's only been one Joy working the corners in the city, and the body of the dead girl that came in doesn't meet her description. That means my girl is still out there," Burns said.

"Do you think maybe Joy is just a name she gave your reporter friend?"

"Could be. She didn't really have a reason to, though. Gillian was helping her. None of the other prostitutes were high-profile. The police didn't spend much time looking into the deaths, and the trail on Gillian was cold almost the minute she was killed. There's not a lot to go on. When the body came in, I thought we might finally get a lead. Now I'm worried that this means he's starting his killing spree again."

"Do you think that's why he took her, to cover up another serial killing?" I asked.

"I don't know. It doesn't make sense."

"He gives me the willies," I said.

"Who?"

"The man who took the body. He showed up at DC's today too."

"He gives you the willies?"

"Yeah, the willies," I said. "You know, the heebie-jeebies. He has this psycho look, not that I've been around a lot of psychos, but if I had, I imagine that's what they'd look like. Why would they dump her to start with if they didn't want her found?"

"That's why I need access to the forensics your boss did at the scene, to figure out what they're hiding. Right now, we have nothing else to go on," Burns said.

"There are people shooting at me."

"You're in luck, then, that you happen to know a highly trained group of security operatives. I can assure you that you and your family will be safer with me than the cops. Plus, we might just figure out who falsely accused you of stealing the body."

"Okay, it's a deal." I screwed the lid back on my water bottle and stretched out my hand. "I go all secret double agent on my morgue colleagues in exchange for you fixing my hearing so I'm not suspended." For the first time in twenty-four hours, I felt like something had finally gone my way.

"Good." He took my hand and shook once but didn't let it go. "But otherwise, will you please stay out of things?"

"Because of my shoes?"

He smiled and let my hand go. "In the Army, everybody has a skill, and everybody follows orders. You seem good at collecting information. So collect and let me run the mission and chase the bad guys."

"So I follow orders?"

"You're quick. Must be that Harvard education." He tugged my scarf and smiled playfully. "Do you have a plan for how you're going to get the information?"

"There's only one good way to get that many people to open up." I held the closed bottle to my lips and began making a mental list of everything that would be needed.

"Therapy?"

"No, silly. We're throwing a party!"

A commotion in the war room drew us back. DC, Neutron, and Flynn were arguing.

"Tom Cruise did not put a hit out on you and the Skirt," Flynn said as Burns and I reentered the conference room. Neutron pressed some buttons on a tablet computer, and a giant image of Tom Cruise flashed on the large television screen in front of the room.

"Well, that's who he looked like. I can't help it if your program can't accurately capture the nuances of various white people. Burns, tell him it's not my fault his program is dumb." DC crossed his arms. I could have sworn I saw him push his bottom lip out in a pout.

"Maybe Kat will have better luck later." Burns placed his hand in the small of my back and led me toward Neutron then tilted his head close to mine. "You've already met everyone, I believe. Neutron runs comms and electronics." He gestured with his free hand. "And you met Flynn last night. He runs ops."

Flynn grunted hello.

"Is Flynn his first name or his last?" I asked.

"It's just Flynn, like Madonna but not as hot," Burns said, causing Neutron to laugh and Flynn to look annoyed.

DC got up from the chair and walked over to us. He looked from me to Burns then back to me. "Well, don't you two seem chummy."

Burns's hands went into his pockets. The cold spot he left in the small of my back made me shiver.

"We are not chummy," I insisted.

"You look pretty damn chummy to me. Wouldn't you agree, Neutron?" Flynn asked.

"I think he's got you there." Neutron adjusted his glasses as if trying to get a better look at us.

"What happened to you wanting to claw his eyeballs out?" DC searched my eyes for some clue of my Zen transformation.

"And I thought we agreed we couldn't trust the mob princess." Flynn kept his eyes on Burns.

"For the record"—Neutron raised his hand from his seat at the computer—"I didn't think that."

"Put your damn hand down. We're not in grade school," Flynn said.

"We've made an arrangement of sorts," Burns said as he leaned against the long table across from us.

"You made a deal with the pageant princess?" His mouth agape, Flynn looked at Burns.

"Why do I have the feeling I'm not going to like what we've agreed to?" DC looked at me out of his left eye, something he did frequently when he was suspicious.

"It's a great deal. You get to do what you do best—be your lovely social self." I smiled.

"Uh-huh." DC waited as if expecting me to finish.

"Look, all we have to do is get Burns information about the people who work in the morgue. No big deal." I shrugged and turned to go look at the morgue attendee board.

"We're going to supply information? You and me?" DC uncrossed his arms and pointed at us.

"Yes, in exchange for getting me out of my hearing. I think it's a wonderful trade."

"If by 'wonderful' you mean 'it won't work because they all see me as out of their league and no one likes you,' then yes, I think it's an excellent trade." DC joined me by the picture board.

"Now, don't be a Debbie Downer. I have it all figured out." I looped my arm through his. "We're going to throw a party." I turned us around to face them. "Ingenisys and McPhee Security are going to sponsor a morgue makeover. You know, giving back to the community right here instead of overseas, especially in light of the recent security trouble."

DC laughed while Flynn groaned. "And just how do you think you're going to get permission for that, Ms. FBI's Most Wanted?" DC asked.

"Let me worry about that," I said, mentally running through a list of connections I still might be able to call on to make that happen.

"Burns, we are not." Flynn held out his arms as if he were pleading for his life.

Neutron stood up. "I love decorating."

"She means real wallpaper, not the virtual kind," Flynn said. "Not that it matters, because there's no way we're doing this."

"The morgue could use a face-lift." DC gazed toward the ceiling. I could tell the idea was growing on him. "Especially with all that crime scene tape."

"Exactly. We'll paint and accessorize and make a new employee break room area. I'd kill for a coffee bar." I could see it all in my head. It would look beautiful when we were done. And then maybe people would like me more.

"I think it's a great idea, but how exactly are you going to get old man Hawthorne to go along with it?" Neutron asked.

"Leave Dr. Hawthorne to me. I'll tell him I'm donating it to make up for all the trouble. Besides"—I put on my best coy expression—"I'm brilliant at convincing old men to see things my way."

"I don't think that's really in question." Flynn crossed his arms in a huff. "But I don't see how any of this helps us at all."

"Kat and DC have a connection on the inside. The party will be a good excuse to get closer to each of the employees we aren't sure about." Burns pointed at the pictures on the board. "She's also going to get us access to the forensics that Dr. Hawthorne took from the murder scene so that we can try to figure out where the girl was killed." He took the lid off the water he'd brought back with him and started to drink.

"And with Burns as your boyfriend, the McPhee Security team will be with us every step of the way." DC opened his arms wide as he said it, as if announcing a new product for a commercial.

Burns spit out his water.

"Priss and Burns are not involved!" Flynn said. He might have turned a bit green.

"I'm off men," I added.

"Did you fools see my clothes? We have people shooting up my momma's house, some psycho Russian stole a body of a dead girl, and one of those misfits over there"—DC marched to the wall and pointed at the pictures on the board—"got us involved in this, blaming our poor Kat." He turned to me and gestured sympathetically. "You think I'm going back in there alone, you've got another think coming."

"It does make sense," I said.

Burns wiped the water from his chin with the back of his hand.

"Nothing about any of this makes sense," Flynn huffed.

I didn't think it was possible for Flynn to pout even more, but somehow he managed it.

"I think it sounds like great fun," Neutron said.

Everyone looked at Burns, clearly waiting for a response, but he didn't say anything. Instead he drank more water, this time swallowing. Finally, he screwed the cap back on the empty bottle. "Then I guess it's settled." He set the bottle on the table and stood up. "I have to go. I have a meeting. I'll be in touch. I'm glad we could come to an agreement," he said as he turned to leave, taking my hand to shake it. Not a real handshake, but a male-female handshake, where he sandwiched my hand between his two.

I was sure the only point of the exercise was to make me uncomfortable, which it did. Burns McPhee was dangerous on a lot of fronts.

Chapter 7

Anytime a group of people banded together, they invariably mimicked ecosystems in nature. Although different systems met people's needs in different ways, they all required certain systemic elements. For example, every environment tended to have predators that kept the smaller, more rapidly reproducing populations in check, such as lions on the savanna and sharks in the oceans. Likewise, groups such as sororities, old age homes, and morgues all had people who took on systemic roles. There was the leader, the cheerleader, the martyr, and of course, the historian, someone who brokered in information, knew all of the group's secrets, and often knew plenty about the competition.

In the case of the morgue, the historian was smarmy and a bit on the pudgy side.

With Burns convinced and the party plan established, my next move was to put the plan into motion. That meant making contact with someone who could get the information wheels turning, even if that someone was slimy and irritating. DC called the morgue and got the schedule for the day. Marshall wasn't working. That left one option for meeting with him, Marshall's makeshift office—Marley's Pub. At that point, DC had claimed he had to go check on his cats. In reality, I had about as much chance of getting DC to go with me to Marley's as he had of getting my grand to one of his "meetings." We agreed we'd catch up later.

I parked in the lot at Marley's and considered my approach. Undoubtedly, Marshall would want something. I steeled my nerves, trying to convince myself that whatever he wanted, within reason, would be worth getting Burns to corroborate my story.

My thoughts were interrupted by the ringing of my cell phone. "Hello."

"Good morning, Katherine."

The accent on the other end of the phone sounded thick and Russian, like something out of a bad James Bond movie. The more he talked, the more my neck hair stood on end. "Hello. Who is this?" I knew who it was. The edge in his voice matched his evil stare, but I needed to stall to gather my thoughts.

"I think you know who this is, Katherine. You've made things complicated for me."

"I'm sorry? I don't quite understand."

"What should have been a very simple recovery operation has now turned into a large police investigation, impeding my effort. It's made things worse for me with my employer, and this is your fault."

"You stole my body."

"*Your* body?" he yelled, clearly agitated. Heavy breathing blew through the phone for several seconds before his voice returned to a monotone. "This is your fault, you and the women like you. But it's okay. I think we have a special connection, Katherine. I'm sure we can come to a mutual arrangement to make up for your rather bad behavior."

"What kind of arrangement?"

"I'll be in touch soon, dear. And stay away from the police. I would hate for anything bad to happen to that beautiful—"

I hung up before he could finish. My hands shook. I forced myself to get up, despite wanting to hide under the covers. The man with the eerie grin was crazy. And he knew my phone number. I needed to get moving to take my mind off of it. I had a plan to execute.

LAST YEAR, THE COUNTY passed a no-smoking ordinance. Now, all the nicotine junkies could be found across the street at Marley's. In addition to dying of lung cancer and smelling like humidor refugees, hospital employees who smoked would now also come to work half sauced.

I took a deep breath before entering. Marley's was not a place people went for the atmosphere. Grime caked the bar top. An aroma of puke and whisky wafted through the place. The food was lousy and the drinks watered down. But at noon on a Tuesday, the place puffed like a chimney. I tried to make my way through the puff cloud to find Marshall Traupe.

Marshall was an unctuous rat. He had no redeeming characteristics whatsoever. He used people at every opportunity and would take great delight in my owing him a favor. As the hospital gossip, though, he was also the person most likely to know who the morgue rat would be. And he would tell me—for a price.

"Sugar lips," he said in a muddle as he watched me approach and tried sucking on his straw. "I hear you had quite the busy evening."

"Stuff it, Marshall."

"Now, babe, is that any way to talk to Uncle Marshall?"

Marshall was an overweight thirtysomething know-it-all. In school, he wouldn't have been the kid anyone felt sorry for because he got picked on all the time but the kid everyone hoped would get beaten up the next time he opened his yap. He had greasy slicked-back hair, and he always smelled like french fries.

"I need some information." I looked down at him in the booth, contemplating whether my health could handle my sitting down in the filth.

"Babe, you're talking to me that way and you need something from Uncle Marshall? Well, now, you might want to reconsider your approach here." He stuffed a french fry in his mouth.

When speaking to women, he referred to himself in the third person, as "Uncle Marshall," not realizing that women instantly classified him as the creepy uncle. Marshall was the only person I'd ever met who could make the word "babe" sound completely and totally disgusting. But he had a point. I needed his help.

Putting on my happy face, I tried again. "Okay, Marshall, would you mind terribly giving me some information?" I slid into the booth.

"See how much better that is when you're pleasant," he said and moved to put his arm around me.

"I am trying to be pleasant, but I swear to God, if you lay one finger on me, I will flatten you. I have three years of self-defense training, and I'm not afraid to use it." I flashed my best smile, stopping him in his tracks.

"Since you put it that way, I might be able to help you out. What kind of information are you looking for?"

"You're aware of my troubles last night?"

"Babe, you'd be hard-pressed to find someone here not aware."

"Someone at the morgue set me up." I picked at the basket of french fries. They would be murder on my complexion, but I hadn't eaten since before the incident.

Marshall smiled. "Gee, I can't imagine who would want to do that." Grease squirted down his chin as he stuffed more fries in his face while talking.

"Never mind." I stood up. "I knew this was a mistake."

As I turned to go, Marshall grabbed my arm. I glared, and he dropped it.

"Babe. I was just having some fun. There's no reason to get all testy." He motioned me back into the booth. "Why do you think someone from the morgue was involved?"

"Someone called in a tip to Dr. Hawthorne's private number, implicating me in the body heist. So it had to be someone who, one, knew Dr. Hawthorne's private number, and two, who knew I'd be covering for DC last night. Only someone from the morgue would know those things. Plus, as you have so astutely pointed out, I am not exactly well-liked by my coworkers." I picked up a cold fry and stuffed it in my mouth, letting the salty goodness soothe my ego.

"I can think of nothing I'd rather do than help out such a lovely lady as yourself." Marshall took a napkin from a pile in front of him and wiped his chin.

"Really?" I cocked my head cautiously.

"For a trade, of course." He put the napkin over the fries, putting me out of my grease- craving misery.

"What do you want?"

"A bowling partner."

"What?"

"This guy I went to high school with bet me that I couldn't get a chick to be my partner for our mixed doubles league. I need a babe to escort me on Thursday nights," Marshall said.

In St. Louis, you knew you were talking to a local if they asked you where you went to high school within the first five minutes of the conversation. "Bowling?"

"Yeah, the little red-and-blue shoes and the ball that knocks down the pins. A small price to pay for my wealth of information."

"For how long?"

"Six weeks."

"Six weeks? Are you nuts? I'll find the rat myself," I said and started to get up.

"All right, all right. You only have to show up for the first two nights so that I win the bet. After that, I'll find someone else who wants some of this," he said, lifting his shirt and making me want to vomit.

"Fine, now how much do you know about our coworkers?"

The half-drunk man next to me had decided I needed to breathe in as much smoke from his cigar as he did, making my stomach churn.

"I need to put some feelers out to make sure I'm giving you the best info. But for starters, you should take a look at Dr. Smarty-Pants Jaffe."

"You're just saying that because he always busts your chops."

"Babe, I have more integrity than that." He sucked up the last sip from his glass with a loud, obnoxious slurping sound.

I stared at him.

"Well, okay, I don't really. But I'm telling you, word on the street is that the cranky doctor has a gambling problem. And it's no secret that the one person in the morgue he likes less than me is..." Folding his hands into guns, he pretend-fired them at me.

"That's true, I suppose. What about anyone else?"

"I'll have to tap into the power of my extensive network," he said. "Aren't you glad you had someone like Uncle Marshall you could come to, babe?" He flexed his fingers then tried to put his arm around me.

"You won't be able to bowl with a broken arm," I said.

He stopped midflight. I pushed the drunken man off me and turned to go. At least I was leaving with a lead. I knew there was something more going on with Dr. Cranky than just a lack of sleep.

"So, Thursday at six. I'll pick you up," Marshall shouted as I pushed the door open and let my lungs re-expand. "And wear something sexy!"

I emerged from the smoking chimney a little green and gasping for air. The blooming trees presented a sharp contrast to the death-inducing cancer palace behind me.

Sitting on a bench, I mulled over Dr. Jaffe's gambling problem. At first I thought he didn't like me just because he was an over-worked, sleep-deprived intern. Strange things happen to the human body when it is deprived of sleep. But he was always questioning me about things. "What's the name of this artery? How does this piece of anatomy connect to that?" He didn't do it with the other attendants, only me. I felt like he was on a mission to perpetually make me feel out of place and incompetent and get me fired.

I had no idea how I would get him to talk about his gambling problem, or whether he was the one who ratted me out. I needed a plan to prove Dr. Jaffe was the one who'd set me up.

Lost in thought but feeling like I could breathe again, I headed for the parking lot between Marley's and the hospital. That was where I saw Henry. Arguing with a woman.

I ducked down between the cars to see if I could get closer. The parking lot was a maze from that angle. I peered at their feet. The woman wore a pair of ugly brown Mary Janes, which instantly set off warning bells. I'd never known anyone pleasant in brown Mary Janes. Henry nervously drew shapes into the gravel parking lot with his sensible brown loafers.

After maneuvering through the various vehicles, I perched behind a rusted El Camino. Part car, part truck, it was the equivalent of a car mullet, but luckily it was long bodied while not very high in the air, giving me a good view of the two arguing.

The woman wore a tight button-down peach cardigan over a tight black pencil skirt. Even though she had a slender physique, she looked as though she might burst out of her outfit in any number of places. She had full, flyaway golden hair, and her accessories included wire-framed librarian glasses and an ugly scarf.

The woman ripped the scarf from around her neck and draped it over Henry's arms, trapping him. "We've been all through this, Henry. It's really the only way." She pulled him into her with the scarf. For a minute, I thought they were going to kiss.

What? If Henry had a girlfriend, Meg would be crushed.

"I handled her this time, but I can't do any more." Henry ducked under the scarf.

Handled who? I wondered, and did "this time" refer to me? Remembering the suggestion from the *PI for Dummies* book, I pulled out my phone and started recording to ensure I caught everything said and to make it easier to go over later.

"That's not good enough. Either you take care of business, or I will. You aren't off the hook here until she's completely taken care of."

"What did she ever do to you?"

"As I told you before, it's best for the family."

"Family" could have meant the mob.

Henry stared at the ground and let out a big breath. "I think she's on to me. She's starting to ask a lot of questions and has surrounded herself with people."

"You're going to have to find a way to turn the screws, Henry. She has to be stopped. My plan can't go forward until you've taken her out of the picture. Now, do you have my money?"

"Yes, but this is all I'm going to be able to get for a while. Since yesterday, the morgue has turned into a zoo. Everything is being watched." He pulled a large stash of cash from his pocket and counted it.

The woman grabbed the bills, turned on her nasty brown Mary Jane heels, and marched away. She slid into the driver's seat of a gray sedan.

Henry stood alone in the parking lot, looking as if he'd lost his best friend. "I made the call. That's all I'm going to do!" he said to himself, just loud enough for me to hear. He stuffed the remaining bills into his pants and headed across the street to the hospital.

On the case for only a few hours, I already had more suspects than I knew what to do with. Figuring out which of them was a traitor could prove to be harder than I had anticipated.

I pulled out the *PI for Dummies* book and started reading. I needed more skills if I was going to figure this out.

Chapter 8

I looked down at the instant swill in the small Styrofoam cup and had a pang of desire for something from a good coffee shop. Usually caffeine helped calm my nerves. Today, I wasn't sure what to expect on my first day back since the incident, especially now that I was on probation until my hearing. But I couldn't bring myself to ingest what looked more like murky brown dishwater than coffee. I went to toss it into a trash can on the sidewalk in front of the morgue doors but came to an abrupt stop at the sight of Detective Driscol leaning against the can.

His unremarkable appearance hadn't changed since our last encounter, except that he looked a little more disheveled than usual with a partially untucked shirt and wrinkled slacks that looked as though he had slept in them.

"Nice to see you without your attack pig." He forced a smile as if to indicate his comment wasn't serious.

"A work environment isn't a good place for her. She has a delicate constitution. Is Detective Lambert with you?"

"She lets me out on my own on occasion."

I blinked at him.

He rubbed the back of his neck with his hand and sighed. "I had a follow-up meeting with the hospital administration. They mentioned you would be returning to work today. I thought I'd say hello." He tried another fake smile.

We both knew his explanation was a bunch of hooey, but he seemed obligated to go through the motions. I, however, had a different agenda for my day and needed him to move along to the real reason he wanted to see me.

"For a moment, I thought you might be here to accuse me or my family of a new crime we didn't commit. Thank you. Now if you'll excuse me, I'm a bit late already." I passed by him at a brisk pace and headed for the morgue doors. The click-clack of my heels hitting the concrete echoed under the overhang that ran from the trash can to the morgue door.

"I heard you went to see McPhee."

From the volume of his voice, I could tell he had turned around but hadn't followed me to the door. I turned to face him but stood my ground. "I don't suppose I should be surprised that you're following me."

"I make it my business to be informed." He stood up a little straighter. Better posture didn't make him look more threatening, but it did relax some of the wrinkles in his trousers.

"Given that two days ago, you were clinging to the belief that McPhee and I had never even met and that I was, I don't know, hallucinating his appearance in the morgue, I'm not really inclined to discuss that subject." I reached for the doorknob.

"All right. I'm sorry." He hurried over to me. "Look, Kat, I think we may have gotten off on the wrong foot here."

"You accused me of being a liar, a thief, and a Billy Idol fan. And you insulted my Maybell. I'm not sure what footing you thought we would be on after that."

He looked at the ground before responding, as if searching for what he would say next. Before I could figure out why he would confront me without a better plan for how the conversation would go, he looked up. "I checked in with our organized crime division. They confirmed that there's been some strange goings-on in the Russian syndicate."

I blinked some more. While I felt vindicated that he had at least checked out my hunch, for all I knew, his next move would be to tie my dad and me to the Russians.

"Did McPhee give you any information about the case?" Driscol asked.

"So that's what this is about? You want to know what McPhee knows and, for some strange reason, think I'm the person who will give it to you?"

"I hoped we could come to an understanding. McPhee might be a pain in the ass, but I don't believe he's the loon some on the force have painted him to be," Driscol said.

"So you believe him about his best friend's murder?"

"I don't know what I believe right now other than there's more going on here than the facts suggest. You may be mixed up in more than you realize. You need to be careful with McPhee."

"Funny, he said the same thing about you."

"I understand that cops probably aren't high on your list of friends right now. But McPhee is a singularly focused man, and the one thing I'm certain of is that you will be expendable the moment he thinks you may be an impediment to his goal of avenging the reporter's death. If you ever need anything"—he took a business card from his pocket—"give me a call at that number."

I took the card, and without saying anything else, he turned and walked away. I felt much better knowing he had checked into my claims about the Russians. Maybe we could find a way to help each other. I made a mental note to send him a thank-you card.

After I put the business card in my bag, I turned my attention to the morgue. I had a big agenda for the day and couldn't get distracted.

Standing in front of the morgue doors, I rubbed my sweaty palms together. As part of my probation, my badge had been confiscated. I was allowed on the premises only if I had a babysitter. I knocked on the door.

Through the long, narrow sliver of glass, I recognized Marshall's pudgy cheek. He blinked at me several times. I smiled.

"I'm sorry, but we can't allow hardened criminals in such a highly sensitive area," he said loudly through the door. "But if you're willing to provide certain services..."

I banged on the door, causing Marshall's cheek to bump from the reverberation. "Can it, Marshall, and open the door."

"Ouch!" The door opened. "You aren't going to make friends that way, you know."

As soon as I entered, the buzz in the morgue hushed. Everyone turned to look at me, making me flush three shades of scarlet.

As I looked around the room, I couldn't help wondering which of them had sold me out.

"All hail the return of our own criminal-chasing heroine," DC announced with a golf clap.

"Hello, everyone." I waved slowly. DC and I had prepared for this the night before, but now that the time had come, my stomach seemed less settled on the idea. Which was strange, because I never got nervous talking in front of people.

Then again, I thought everyone had always liked me. Since everything had happened with my dad, I'd come to realize that most people liked me only because of my dad's money. It was a betrayal of the worst kind, like finding out my favorite makeup was viciously tested on poor defenseless animals despite the company's proclamation of being cruelty-free.

No one here cared about any of that, though. One of them wanted to hurt me.

"First, I want to apologize for all of the trouble."

"Did you really help steal the body?" asked a meek voice far across the room. I had to search to find the owner. In the back of the room and leaning against the computer table facing the brown wall was a small woman wearing Professional Goth. Her formfitting black silk ruffled shirt had buttons that peeked out from beneath a velvet blazer. Her skirt was a long black-on-black damask. The color blended with her hair, the only other color in the whole outfit being a newly acquired red hair stripe that ran in a ring from one ear to the other. I wondered whether the color was permanent. She carried a vintage black-and-white drawstring bag.

"No, Meg, I didn't help steal the body."

"Don't be so modest, babe." The pudgy-faced Marshall stood near a cubicle, a doughnut in each hand. "I tried to tell Dr. Hawthorne you were trouble," he teased in a grinning doughnut muffle. Marshall wore his usual light-colored polo shirt—too small for his torso, so his stomach always stuck out—and khaki pants. All of which he covered with a long white lab coat, hoping to confuse people into believing that he was more important in the hospital than he really was. One time he was suspended for pretending to be a doctor. Thankfully, a nurse figured him out before some poor old guy went to surgery for removal of a tumor he didn't have.

"The suspension is just a precaution." DC moved closer to me. Strength in numbers. He always looked strange to me here at the morgue and wearing scrubs. They never seemed to fit his slender figure quite right, making him look like a schoolkid who had stolen his parent's work uniform for show-and-tell. "You know, kind of like how women treat you. Cautiously and in need of supervision, pending legal action."

"What DC meant to say," I said, glaring as I turned past him, "is that while I wasn't involved in the body heist, except to try to stop it, I'm very sorry that it's affecting everyone here so much. And it's made me realize that we haven't really had the opportunity to get to know each other as much as I'd like."

A loud clanging came from the side where the coffeepot was. Sam Winston had a wrench in his hand. He beat the defective coffeepot, reciting several expletives as he did. The thing was always on the fritz. The blue-gray cross tattoo peeking out at his neckline matched his blue-gray scrubs today. "That's okay, kid. We aren't exactly a social club here." He turned around, coffee cup in hand, eyeing me over the top of it.

I eyed him back, wondering why Burns had used his full name as if he were a serial killer—Sam Allen Winston. He hadn't used the middle name of any of the other workers. His bald head reflected the bad lighting coming from the institutional fixture above him. Coffee clung to his goatee before he reached up with a scar-covered hand and wiped his chin. Looking at him closer, I could imagine him digging a shallow grave for Joy's body. I tried to shake off the shudder.

"True, but I can't help but think I haven't gotten off on the right foot here. I want to make it up to everyone. Plus, look at this place." I watched as heads surveyed the room. "We deserve a better working environment than this. We're lucky OSHA hasn't shown up."

"Yeah, right. What were we thinking, squandering our interior decorating allowance," Marshall said, holding up a broken coffee cup.

"A 2010 study confirmed that pleasantness of working environment has a direct impact on employee morale, productivity, and satisfaction," I said.

"Are you saying we aren't worth a nice space?" Sam eyed Marshall and flipped the wrench still in his hand into the air.

"Yeah, what does that mean?" Meg moved forward.

For a minute, I thought she might bop Marshall with her bag. I was starting to like her.

"Don't blame the messenger." Jelly dripped down Marshall's chin. "All I'm saying is that with the bad publicity we've received thanks to Miss Slippery Fingers here"—he pointed at me—"I don't think there's going to be budget for undergoing a makeover anytime soon."

"That's where you're wrong," DC said. "Kat's got it all figured out. Tell 'em, Kat."

"What would you think if I hosted a morgue makeover party and open house?" I spoke slowly, accentuating the important words and trying to sound cheerful. I smiled big.

"I thought you didn't have any money?" a soft voice I recognized as Henry said. He popped out from behind another cubicle wall. The supple roundness of his face coupled with his floppy feathery hair always made me want to squeeze him like a teddy bear.

"Well, I don't. But my family's been fundraising for worthy causes for years. And I can't think of a more worthy cause than you all."

"Plus, her new boyfriend has money connections, and he's into security. After what happened, no one can doubt that this place needs some new security," DC added.

I didn't think the reference to my new fake boyfriend was necessary, but mentioning that he worked in security seemed to have some impact.

"You do such unsung work, I think you should be celebrated." I put my hands on my hips in a cheerleader stance—eyes forward, shoulders back. A study of body language had confirmed that for some weird reason, that stance always seemed to make people peppy. This situation called for pep.

"Will there be cake?" Meg asked.

"Oh yes, definitely cake," DC said. "But y'all have to help."

"Help? I'm not a very good baker. Meg's the creative one." Henry blushed.

"Not with the cake," DC said.

"With the makeover. You know, the painting and stuff. There's pride in ownership. Don't you think it would be a lot nicer to come to work if the morgue didn't look like such a… morgue? I mean, look at this place! It's depressing," I said.

"I wouldn't mind helping. I've been known to be pretty handy." Sam clanked the wrench down on the table next to the coffee maker.

"Us too. Right, Henry?"

Henry kept eyeing Sam's wrench. "If Meg's in, I'm in."

"Excellent! Then it's settled. I'll talk to Dr. Hawthorne about it, and we'll aim for next Saturday."

"Talk to me about what?" Dr. Hawthorne came out of the morgue room.

Everyone then returned to their work as if things were normal. DC and I followed him to the back of the main entry room, toward the computers. Marshall trotted behind us like a stray puppy afraid he might miss something.

Dr. Hawthorne was in an ugly off-white short-sleeved shirt, buttoned all the way to the collar. I wondered why men didn't realize that short-sleeved dress shirts were not attractive. Several pens protruded from his pocket.

"I'm not sure I can handle any more surprises at the moment," he said.

"Kat has an inspired idea, doesn't she, Marshall?" DC asked.

"How should I know?"

"Pins and shoes, Marshall!" I glared at him.

"Oh yeah. It's definitely inspired, Dr. Hawthorne." Marshall whimpered as DC pushed him into the computer area, leaving me standing at Dr. Hawthorne's desk.

"Now, you have to have an open mind. I found us a sponsor who wants to throw us a makeover party. We'll remodel the morgue and then have an open house so the community can come and learn all about us."

"A remodel of the morgue and a party? I don't think so, Katherine." His tone was unusually sharp. He suddenly looked panicked.

"But Dr. Hawthorne, you have to say yes. It's free for the morgue, the benefactor is willing to buy us some of the new equipment you've been wanting, and I think it would really help everyone's morale."

"Who is this mysterious rich benefactor?" he asked.

"Oh, Kat landed herself a new man. He owns an investment and security firm," DC chimed in.

I smiled and tried to look confident. While I had expected some resistance from the administration, I hadn't quite expected Dr. Hawthorne to say no to free equipment—or to be so suspicious of the plan.

"I thought you were engaged to that Boston fellow," the doctor said.

"Our Kat leads a complicated life. It was true love at first sight," DC said. I elbowed him to get him to stop talking.

"Regardless of my relationship status, this is a good plan. It's free money for state-of-the-art security equipment that Lord knows the county can't afford right now, and the party for the community will help counter the recent bad publicity. We could even auction off some of the stuff from the old evidence-holding room."

Dr. Hawthorne knocked over his drink on his desk. "Oh goodness, someone grab some towels!"

We all worked to help clean up the mess. By the time we were through, Dr. Hawthorne seemed calmer. "Well, Katherine, I'm not opposed to free equipment, but we will have to get permission from the administration, which, given everything that's happened, is no sure bet."

"Oh goody," DC squealed, jumping up and down and clapping.

"Thank you, Dr. Hawthorne. You won't regret it."

"Don't thank me yet. We still have to get approval. Now, back to work. You'll be working with Dr. Jaffe today, Katherine. Marshall will help assist, but we have a family-requested autopsy today, and you're the best closer."

Closers were technicians who put the body back together after all the autopsy work was complete and the body needed to be readied for the mortician. My three years of sculpture class had made me the best closer here.

My heart sputtered. This would be the first time I'd seen Dr. Jaffe since Marshall had told me the doctor might be involved in implicating me in the body theft.

Chapter 9

When DC and I had made our plan the night before, I hadn't expected to run into Jaffe today. I had no idea what I would say to him or how I would get him to admit he'd played a role in setting me up.

On top of it all, I had Marshall to deal with. The two of them together would be a lot to handle.

I sighed and headed to get ready. I bundled my hair into a pony and suited up before putting on the cute hot-pink surgical hair cap DC bought me for my birthday and coordinating with matching pink gloves. Before entering the room, I pulled out my bottle of Clive Christian perfume and spritzed. Granted, it was an interesting way to use three-hundred-dollar-a-bottle perfume. But I wasn't getting out to many fancy clubs these days, and I couldn't bring myself to sell it. That would be like admitting defeat. Plus, the pleasant smell helped me stay in my happy place during an autopsy.

"You're late," Jaffe said, not looking up.

As a med student and resident, Dr. Jaffe operated most of the time on two hours of sleep and too much Red Bull. He was an order-barking jerk and a pig. Not the nice Maybell-type pig or even the creepy Marshall sexist pig but the more pedestrian slob kind of pig. An autopsy room needn't look like something out of a Quentin Tarantino movie. Autopsies could be neat and tidy. Despite his sloppy habits, he was a clean-cut guy with an unusually long, narrow head. No one's head should be that long.

"It's to be expected," Marshall said. He leaned in close to where Dr. Jaffe was cutting. Dr. Jaffe stared at him, and he backed off.

The doctor had completed the initial cut. I tried not to look as I moved to the other side of the table. "I had some business."

"This isn't your sorority," Jaffe said and, after making his last cut, finally looked at me. "What are you wearing?"

"Working in a morgue does not preclude good fashion sense." I proceeded to the body.

The business of death was a giant bureaucracy that was all about the money. After a death was reported, the medical examiner determined the need for an autopsy and gave it a particular designation that indicated who would pay for it. Medical examiner jurisdiction ruled when foul play was suspected, as with Joy. That meant the county paid. An autopsy for a hospital death had to be approved by the hospital pathologist for the county to pay. If the hospital pathologist declined, then the family could request to have an autopsy conducted by a private pathologist for a fee. Doctors were always complaining about these death designations. When a patient died unexpectedly, doctors liked to know why. Due to funding limitations, Dr. Hawthorne often had to decline autopsy requests.

Today's autopsy winner was Dr. Hutchinson. He had a male—white, sixty-three—die after a simple operation. When Dr. Hawthorne wouldn't budge after denying the funding, Hutchinson convinced the family to pay for it. Jaffe, the jerk, was here doing his bidding as usual.

"Who can tell me what pulmonary surfactant is?" he asked.

I blinked at him. This wasn't *Jeopardy*.

"I'm sure I couldn't surpass your level of knowledge greatness, Doctor," Marshall said.

I thought I saw Dr. Jaffe's eyes roll.

Ignoring the question, I instead stared at the face of the man on the table, studying it, trying not to get blood on my pretty gloves.

"What are you doing?" Jaffe stopped what he was doing and stared at me.

"Looking at him."

"Why?"

"Because he has a story to tell, and I like to know who's telling it before I start."

"Blessed with the A-team today," Dr. Jaffe mumbled under his breath. In fine Tarantino fashion, he'd strewn blood everywhere, and I had to walk carefully so as not to slip. "Are you wearing perfume?" Jaffe sniffed as I passed him.

"Smell cells are renewed every twenty-eight days, so every month you ostensibly get a new nose." His questions were irritating and getting on my nerves. "You forgot the string." I pointed at the man.

"What?" Jaffe barked.

"This man will be going to the mortician soon. You need to leave a trail so the mortician knows where to go. Otherwise, the body ends up less family-friendly for the showing. I know you doctors don't care about such cosmetic things, but it's important to the family."

He stared at me for a moment as if he didn't quite know what to say.

"Seriously?" Marshall was such a kiss ass. He looked at me over his mask with his weasel eyes. "It's your fault Dr. Jaffe is behind today, you know, with your body snatching and all." He wrinkled his nose as if he'd snorted feathers and might sneeze.

"As I've already said, I had about as much to do with that poor girl's body being stolen as Dr. Jaffe here." I pointed at the doctor.

"Me?" He stumbled into the instrument tray, catching it before it toppled. "Why would you say that? I didn't have anything to do with it. Why am I always stuck with idiots?" He took off his gloves and threw them on the floor dramatically. "I'm done here." And he stomped off, leaving me with Marshall.

I hadn't had a chance to absorb Dr. Jaffe's freak-out at the suggestion of his involvement before Marshall started in again.

"Do you think he's mad at me? What if he tells Dr. Hawthorne?" He brought his hand up, almost covering his mouth. His bloody, gloved hand. I tried not to hurl.

"Right. He might be in there right now telling Dr. Hawthorne what an incompetent idiot you are," I said. "You better hurry." I tried to look alarmed. Marshall started to look alarmed, too, and followed Dr. Jaffe. I breathed a sigh of relief.

My mind wandered to the missing body. Today was the day we should have been doing the autopsy on Joy. I supposed the good news was that thanks to the body theft, at least someone was paying attention to her death now. I wondered if anyone besides Burns would have even cared about her murder if her body hadn't been stolen. What was one more dead prostitute, after all? But Joy had a story, and it deserved to be told. I decided to clean up then go see what I could find on the other murders.

"Psst."

I heard a sound coming from the hall. I looked up but didn't see anyone.

"Psst."

I heard it again and went toward the hall to locate the noise. Before I got there, DC intercepted.

"How'd you get in here, Wiggins?" DC asked.

Jorge Wiggins, a mortician from one of the local funeral homes, stood dressed in a suit that didn't quite fit him. He had a noticeable lisp and overly moussed hair. "I heard you had a hot one."

"And what, you thought we'd just give him to you if you weaseled your way in here?" I asked, coming into the hallway.

"With the trouble the chickie's been having," Wiggins said to DC, pointing at me and taking a roll of bills out of his pocket, "I thought you all might be persuadable."

Competition thrived in the county's funeral business. I'd heard about other dieners taking kickbacks for sending business to particular funeral homes but didn't think it was true.

"Put that away and get out of here, you moron," DC said, pushing the man back up the hall.

"Wait!" I said, grabbing Wiggins's arm and tucking it under mine. "How are you doing?"

He eyed me warily. "Why? What do you want?"

"Nothing. Nothing. I'm just worried about you. You know, with the police snooping around and all," I said. "We wouldn't want any suspicion to fall on you, would we, DC?"

"Oh no," DC said, quickly catching on to the plan.

"Why would the police think I had anything to do with this?" Wiggins began to sweat as we walked toward the door.

"Well, here you are, aren't you?" DC said. "It would look awfully suspicious to the police, don't you think, if someone told them you were here soliciting bribes when a body had recently gone missing as a result of a bribe?"

"Terribly suspicious," I agreed. Wiggins tried to pull his arm away, but I held firm. "Now, if you had any insight as to who here at the morgue was on the take, we might be able to persuade the police to consider them as a suspect instead of turning their attention on poor you." I batted my eyes at him.

"All right! Stop. I get it." Wiggins yanked his arm out of mine. "I'll tell you. But you have to swear you won't tell him you heard it from me."

"Scout's honor!" DC held up a peace sign.

Wiggins looked at DC then me. I nodded.

"It's Henry Johnson."

"Henry? Sweet, mousy Henry?" DC asked.

"Sweet my ass. That guy's got a serious problem. He's into me for about three Gs a month."

"What does 'into you' mean? And keep it clean. I don't need you scaring my delicate insides with your gross images," DC said.

"Relax, it's nothing kinky. He funnels me bodies, and I give him a kickback. He lets me know they're here before he alerts any other home and then tricks the family into believing sending the body to me was all official procedure. I get 'em to sign off the paperwork when they come in to talk about it."

"Maybe that's where the money came from and not from ratting me out," I said. I explained to DC about the woman, Henry's mention of the call, and the big wad of cash I'd seen him with yesterday. "You gave him up awfully quickly," I said. "Why should we believe you?"

"I'm looking for a replacement. That's why I'm here today. Thought you might be interested, given your... issues. That guy's not quite right. Mark my words, something's going to happen with him, and then I'll be out of a body supply."

"At least you have your priorities in order," DC said.

"Damn straight." Wiggins pulled at his suit collar as if it were suffocating him.

"Has he ever told you what the money's for?" I asked.

"No. We're on a don't ask, don't tell policy. So, are you gonna give me the body in there, chickie? I pay well."

"He's already spoken for." I carefully stepped back onto the edge of the linoleum.

"Bummer. Okay. I gotta go before someone sees me talking to you. But if you want to do some business, give me a call next time." Wiggins pushed through the morgue doors as he ran a handkerchief over the top of his sweating head.

"Damn, you're like a moron crime magnet," DC said.

"This has been a whole weird day. When I asked Jaffe about being involved in Joy's disappearance, he freaked out. And Marshall was falling all over himself to suck up. It wouldn't surprise me if, despite his agreeing to help me, he's really the one who called me in to Dr. Hawthorne. And by the way, have you ever seen Dr. Hawthorne so twitchy?"

"Winston's the one who scares me. Did you see him with that wrench? And now this thing with Henry. It's always the baby-faced ones who turn out to be the mass murderers," he said.

"Poor Meg. Do you think we should warn her?" I asked.

"Maybe she's in on it. You're a girl. You should try to bond."

I let out a sigh. I couldn't remember the last time I'd been able to see my girlfriends. Meg was a little on the strange side, but I thought it might be nice to have some girl gossip time. "Okay. I'll try to set something up with her, tell her I need her help getting ready for the party. At least things are going according to plan. I'm sure between Burns's connections and my family's, we can get the hospital administration to accept the proposal. But I did get a strange visit from Detective Driscol. Any word on Joy's forensics yet?"

"Everyone's being real tight-lipped. I heard there's some big pow-wow with the detectives on Monday."

"Good. I think I need to see the file on the other dead prostitutes and Gillian Mathers."

"Uh-oh. Someone's caught the Nancy Drew bug."

"Driscol has me thinking. I just want to know what I'm dealing with."

"You can get the main reports online, but if you want to see the crime scene photos and stuff, you'll have to go to the Pit." The Pit was the building that housed Vital Records, affectionately termed the Pit due to its somewhat recessed architecture, kind of like a bunker.

"I need a reason to go there and get a look."

"Hmmm... leave that to me."

IF I EVER COMPLAINED about the décor in the morgue, I only needed to come to the Pit to realize we had it good. Old army surplus furniture filled the space, and avocado-green tiles decorated the walls. Once I was in the lobby, the only place to go was forward to the main window. A salt-and-pepper-haired lady with what looked like an excruciatingly tight bun perched on a barstool in the window, rummaging through files.

"How are we going to get past her?" I whispered.

"She has a thing for me. She thinks I'm cute."

"Kimi okay with you flirting with old ladies?"

"The things I have to do for the cause, I tell ya. Have you ever noticed that she keeps her hair pulled back in this really tight bun that makes her look like her face is being pulled off? I think it interferes with her brain. If I ask, she won't question why we need the files."

He stepped up to the window. "Sweetheart," DC said, opening his arms.

"Daryl! My word, it's been so long. How come you don't come see me more often? You aren't secretly seeing another record keeper on the side, are you?" she asked and then giggled.

"Oh, honey, you know I could never do that. My poor cats have been having the worst time."

"You poor thing."

"Sorry to interrupt," I said, approaching the window. "I just need to grab some copies really quick." I waved around a copy of the order, hoping she wouldn't look too closely at it.

DC pulled out his phone and started showing her pictures of his cat-a-ciser.

Without looking up from the phone, she said, "No problem," and buzzed me back. "Take your time. Head toward the right."

As I disappeared through the door, the receptionist and DC were deep in conversation about his cat's woes.

The warehouse of files reminded me of the stacks in the law library at Harvard, only these were not as well organized. I went toward the right as the receptionist had instructed, but I thought she was messing with me to get more time with DC. After doubling back, I stopped first for the file we needed for Dr. Hawthorne. With that secured, I looked for files on the prostitute and Gillian Mathers.

I didn't know what I expected to find. I had read through all the news coverage online. For the prostitutes, it wasn't much. With the exception of the stories from Gillian, the news outlets didn't seem to care about the dead girls. Once Gillian was killed, the coverage stopped altogether.

In Gillian's case, the police speculated that a simple robbery had gone terribly wrong. The stabbing happened in her home, and the perpetrator had stolen her jewelry. Burns thought otherwise, but maybe guilt clouded his thinking.

After locating the files, I moved to a reading table at the front of the warehouse. There were four prostitute murders, and Joy would make number five. A few times since Dad's arrest, I had been made painfully aware of how much our previous privilege had bought us. Reviewing the deaths of these girls, I had the same thoughts. Had they been four socialites from my former neighborhood, their files would have been piled high. Nancy Grace would be leading nonstop news coverage. Instead, the files were as thin as a rail.

All of the girls had been brutally beaten to death. The ash white of their faces contrasted with the dark red of the blood. No DNA or other forensics had been collected. All the bodies were dumped in dumpsters in the alley of the old warehouse district and not found for days after their deaths. The final police report in the file of the last girl killed speculated that the murders were committed by a "cranky john." Four women were brutally beaten to death, and the police had decided the killer was someone "cranky."

Next I pulled out Gillian's file. The top page of the report was stamped with the county seal—Office of St. Louis County Medical Examiner—and then it proceeded to her vitals—female, white, twenty-eight. The report continued as expected. Manner of death, homicide. Cause of death, exsanguination due to multiple stab and incised wounds.

An extensive write-up of the injuries came next. "Overall, most of the incised wounds on the trunk suggest a single-edged, thin blade, although a double-edged blade cannot be excluded. Multiple injuries of the hands and forearms are consistent with defensive injuries."

She fought back.

But the rest of the file was empty. There should have been a whole slew of reports detailing toxicology, X-rays, DNA, and trace evidence. But it was all missing.

As I scanned the list of clothing and valuables, the fact that a ring and a necklace were left on the body struck me as odd. If this were a robbery, those would have been taken for sure.

Finally, near the end of the report, I saw the photography line. "Instant print and 35-mm slide identification pictures. Instant-print photos were also taken of the scene and of many of the injuries. See attached."

I flipped the page to examine the pictures of the scene. I thought those might have disappeared, too, but there they were. The photos were startling in their depiction of brutality. They also showed items that were at the scene. A flat-screen TV and a Faberge-style crystal egg collection I'd have priced at about three grand. And a gold and crystal clock, things not usually left behind in a robbery. The murder had taken place in her home office. Papers were strewn everywhere.

Something familiar caught my eye. Sticking out of a corner of a pile of paper on her desk, there it was—the list:

6587245DCIX 15,22

3298134BDIS 22, 29
8735910XTOM 9, 15
5061992APG...

I looked closer at the surrounding information. The pile the numbers poked out of detailed research on the prostitute killings—times, dates, and profiles of each girl killed. A notation above the handwritten codes read *Mob money*. I had seen that exact sequence before—not something similar but that exact sequence of numbers. And then it hit me.

Grand's scrapbook!

My heart beat hard in my chest. My breathing grew faster as I tried to find a reasonable explanation for how something from my grand's scrapbook about my dad had ended up on a reporter's desk two months before his arrest, tying him not only to the mob but also to the prostitute killings. This was not happening. I refused to accept that my dad was a criminal and I was actually a mob princess.

I had to be wrong. I had been under a lot of stress lately. Numerous studies had shown that stress negatively impacted memory. I needed to get to that scrapbook.

After copying everything, I burst out the door to find DC still yakking with the receptionist. "We have to go."

"Right, you have the benefit," DC said, looking at his watch.

"Oh God, I have Mom's benefit!"

Chapter 10

"I'm not wearing something that makes me look like a peacock." Grand was arguing with my mother as I erupted through the door. She wore a blue-and-green paisley gown with feathers sticking out of the collar. She totally looked like a peacock.

"You don't look like a peacock," Mom replied, trying to be reassuring.

"I'll be lucky if someone doesn't try to put me in a zoo."

"Don't be so melodramatic, Mother. Besides, it's the only gown I could get on loan. There you are, Katherine. You're late."

Maybell waddled up wearing a beautiful blue halter dress and rhinestone collar. Of course, the collar was fake. I'd hocked the real one to cover the retainer for Dad's lawyer, but Maybell understood. She still looked beautiful. I knelt to give her some affection.

"I know. I'm sorry." Petting Maybell always made me calm. Given how late I was, it was going to take some finagling to get a look at Grand's scrapbook before we left.

"You need to tell Maybell she can't come. She wouldn't leave me alone until I got her dressed, which I didn't mind. She does look lovely in blue, but pigs aren't allowed at the benefit. And yes, I asked, so don't start on me." Mom pulled on the strap of her heel.

"The world's so unfair." I patted Maybell's head.

"What's unfair is looking like this. You owe me one," Grand said, turning to me. "I did a shopping trip to the old house and scored that green Vera Wang you always look so lovely in. I'd have had my dress, too, if it weren't for that stupid rent-a-cop."

"What rent-a-cop?" I stood up to face her and was attacked by feathers.

"Someone's posted a security guard at the house to keep intruders out. Imagine, accusing me of being an intruder in my own house."

"You're lucky you weren't arrested. Now, can we please stop talking about this unpleasantness and get going?"

Despite being knocked several rungs down the social ladder because of my dad's incarceration, my mom still threw a better charity event than anyone in the upper crust of the county. This benefit was her first one since Dad's arrest, and she was counting on me for support. Otherwise, I would have skipped the whole thing. Especially now. Mom worked to get her earring through the hole.

"Fine with me. We'll just keep pretending no one's in prison like we're on an episode of *Dallas*." Grand blew at the feathers sticking out of her dress. "Ready, Claude?"

Claude was a short, wiry man, with thick horn-rimmed glasses and a large nose that took up the majority of his face. My family owed Claude more than we could ever repay. Without him, we wouldn't have had a place to live, and I wouldn't have a job. It was his contacts that landed me the morgue job. He never took anything in return, and he continued to show up with flowers for Grand. For a man of his age and stature, he looked fabulous in his vintage tux, complete with his signature bow tie.

"No, we're not ready!" I said a little too loudly, startling everyone in the room.

Maybell let out a snort. Claude blinked.

"I mean, it would be nice, Grand, if you could stay and help me get ready." I couldn't go to the benefit with this on my mind. Plus, if the page in her scrapbook matched what I'd found in Gillian's file, I would need information from Grand.

"Don't be ridiculous, Katherine. We're already late," Mom said.

I looked at my grand with a pleading expression, trying to signal with my head that I needed her to go to the bedroom.

"Did you get a neck twitch stealing that body?" Grand asked.

"Oh, please!" Mom said, throwing her hands up in the air. "Under no circumstances is anyone allowed to talk about the morgue tonight. I don't have to tell you that tonight is very important for our family. Now, Katherine, get yourself dressed."

"I'd get dressed a lot quicker if Grand helped me." I bit my lip. "Mom, why don't you ask Claude to take you now and help you get set up," I said, smiling my best pageant smile, impressed with my brilliant idea not only to get Grand alone but also to seem like a helpful daughter. "We'll be right behind you, and this way, we'll have two cars there in case Grand needs to leave early." With an arm looped through one of Claude's and one of my mother's, I led them both to the door.

"I suppose that is a smart idea, and as you seem allergic to proper decorum these days..." She sighed.

I knew I had her when she sighed.

"I guess it makes sense."

Claude pulled his arm from mine and turned around. He gave Grand a little wave, then they went out the door.

"What are you up to?" Grand asked when we were finally alone. This was the tricky part. I needed to get a look at the book and find out what she knew about it without getting her worked into a frenzy.

"I'll tell you, but it's a secret." We moved to the living room, Maybell following, past the gaudy chair and to the corner with the antique cupboard. The cupboard dated from 1870, and Grand swore it used to be in Mount Vernon. Under the drawer, two ornate cabinet doors opened to a single shelf. This was Grand's workspace. The inside of the cupboard looked like a Hobby Lobby had thrown up.

"I'm working on a special case at the morgue, and I think you might have accidentally picked up something related to it when you were researching Dad's stuff."

"I did? Hot damn! I knew I'd make a great detective," she said, doing a little jump. Maybell danced in a circle.

"I need your scrapbook." I rifled the cupboard for it and wondered how she ever found anything in there. Finally I spied it in the back under a collection of new scrapbooking paper.

The scrapbook was as much a creative endeavor as a chronicle of the events of my dad's arrest. Grand had collected various scrapbook kits, specialty paper cutouts, paper frames in various shapes, and a host of special stamps and letter sets. I wasn't sure what paper collection said, "Congratulations, your son's heading for the slammer."

"What are you looking for?" she asked as I pulled the book out to look at it.

The craftsmanship of the book amazed me. Each page was exceptionally coordinated in color and style, not only with the content of the page itself but also with any accompanying pages. If I hadn't known better, I would have thought the scrapbook celebrated a great accomplishment or the birth of a child.

"See this photo from a crime scene? I think there's something in here that might match."

The opening spread was a montage of famous trials where the defendant had prevailed. "If it doesn't fit, you must acquit." I thumbed through the pages, looking for the match of the crime scene photo. I flipped past the NASA story, and after the series of Fletcher Reid stories chronicling my dad's early business success, eureka, there it was.

Attached to a page lined in silver foil, a half-torn sheet of paper with a scrolling list of characters similar to the ones from the crime scene photo peered at me. The headline on the page, spelled out in stickers, read, "U.S. Missile Launch codes." I scanned the list.

6587245DCIX

3298134BDIS
8735910XTOM
5061992APG...

They were all there, and the list contained twelve additional sequences.

"Grand, do you know what this is?"

"I titled the page. See"—she pointed at the header—"they're missile launch codes."

"I don't think these are missile launch codes. Do you remember where you got these?" This was a tough question. Thanks to my grand's condition, every possibility existed that she wouldn't remember, and that might cause an episode.

"How the hell should I remember that? I can't be expected to remember every connection to the defense department that ever existed!"

Maybell ran to the other room.

"It's okay, Grand. I need to get ready for the event, anyway." I closed the book and hugged it to my chest.

"Not so fast, Missy. What does a crime scene photo have to do with your father?"

Uh-oh, I thought, trying to come up with a story. "I'm sure there's no connection. Like you said, this is from the defense department. I'm sure it's just a coincidence." At this point, telling her about the possible mob connection was not an option. "Dad was an important man. The reporter was probably doing a story on him or something, and the papers just got mixed up."

"I'm old. I'm not an idiot."

"Of course not. And this is an important discovery in another case I'm working on that will be very helpful. It's just not tied to Dad."

"I can take it, you know. Everyone walks around here on damned eggshells. Even the pig. But I'm not feeble or fragile. If you find something about Clarke, I want to know. Do you understand me?" She pretended to smoke one of her fake cigarettes. I knew her nerves were shot, and we still had a whole ball to get through.

"I promise," I said, lying. "Now let's get to that ball before Mom kills both of us."

I COULD BARELY CONCENTRATE on the road as my mind raced, trying to figure out what the codes meant and where they could have come from. There was no way around wondering whether this meant my dad really was mixed up with the mob. That led to a whole other set of questions, like "For how long?" and "How in the world did it happen?" Gillian's paper had clearly said "mob money."

I refused to believe it. Clarke Waters was not part of the mob. Period. It had to be some weird coincidence. I needed to pull myself together and find a way to get through this event.

The annual fundraiser for local charities was sponsored by many of the mayors in the county who'd pooled forces and dubbed it the Mayors' Event. Several of the mayors openly disliked each other, making Mom chief negotiator for weeks leading up to tonight. They didn't agree on anything, from entertainment to flowers to food.

I was originally supposed to attend with Martin. We had planned to fly in from Boston to help Mom and Dad work the room. Martin's family always appreciated being associated with these kinds of events, even ones in what they considered an inferior city like St. Louis. Martin had already backed out when everything with Dad came up. The reality was that I was now a single girl.

My logical brain knew that if I was involved with someone who wouldn't stand by me through something like this, the relationship wasn't meant to be. Still, Martin and I had been together for a while, time that felt like a big investment.

The local casino hosted the event. In Missouri, casinos could operate only on riverboats, as if it were any less sinful to gamble over water. I drove to the pier.

We made our way through the casino entrance, past the clinking and clanging of the slot machines, to the ballroom. It was a beautiful room, with its crystal chandeliers and modern architecture, but Mom had outdone herself with decorations that would put David Tutera to shame. The "All That Jazz" theme was everywhere. The room sparkled in red, black, white, and silver. The cello from the jazz band made the room thump. Grand left me standing in the middle of the room, taking it all in, while she went to find Claude and Mom.

MY DAD WAS A PRO AT people watching. He could absorb a room, remembering people, faces, couples, and outfits, even across a broad room like this one. Over the years, I'd picked up the habit, if not some of his skill. That was why I knew I was being watched. I felt the gaze on me from across the room. I looked all around but didn't see anyone watching me.

What I did see, standing near a wall and trying to look invisible while taking in everything around him, was Burns McPhee. Beautiful Burns McPhee, who couldn't look invisible even when trying. At least, not to me.

I wondered what he was doing here. His eyes locked on mine from across the room. He didn't smile or wave hello. He stood there staring. The ballroom suddenly felt small. A crowd moved in between us. When I looked back, he was gone.

Finding Mom and Grand was easy. All I had to do was look for the peacock feathers. Mom stood with another woman who seemed almost glued to her. When Mom moved, the woman moved too. The woman wore a diamond tiara in her shoulder-length gray bob. The tiara matched the ostentatious red-sequined gown that clung to her curves. While it did flatter her figure, the low-cut sparkles seemed out of place among the formality.

"Aren't you lovely, Katherine," Mom said. She looked stunning as always in a long silver dress. Her hair was in an updo, fitting for the occasion. No one would ever have guessed my mom was in her late fifties. She had beautiful skin and thin auburn hair, peppered with small streaks of gray that only made it look fuller and her younger. The current Hamburger Helper diet had helped her lose several pounds.

"What took you so long?" Grand swooshed at her feathers. "Let's go, Claude. We've got a rug to cut." Grand grabbed Claude's hand and pulled him through the ballroom and toward the dance floor. Feathers flew up over the heads of the crowd.

"My, look how grown-up you are, Katherine," the woman in red said. "The last time I saw you was at your DAR initiation."

Our membership in the Daughters of the American Revolution had always been a point of pride for Mom. We had a pirate on her side of the family who had been in the Navy. The events always felt stuffy and political, but I went because I did support the troops. I didn't, however, recognize the lady in red.

"Oh, you probably don't remember me. I'm Greta Scott."

"Mayor Scott's wife," Mother added.

"Oh, a pleasure to see you. Your tiara is divine."

Mrs. Scott patted her bob and flashed the staged smile of a tiara model. "Thank you. It cost Richard a small fortune, but I rewarded him appropriately." She let out a loud cackle and, apparently realizing no one else had laughed with her, took a drink of her champagne. "I trust you're settling in well since your move back home."

"I've been practicing Master Tahkaswami's advice on managing change, but it hasn't been easy without access to his herb blend. I do think I'm starting to get a rhythm."

"Oh, isn't he splendid? I can't help but want to run my fingers all over that beautiful bald head. I'm sure all of the unpleasantness at the hospital hasn't helped you, though."

Mother's jaw clinched as a look of horror came over her face at the mention of the morgue.

"It's all just another misunderstanding," Mother said on cue.

"Honestly, I hadn't realized anyone knew much about that." I had been shocked that the body snatching and my involvement in it weren't front-page news. Apparently Grand had managed to charm Fletcher Reid into not printing the story. Or maybe it had been our body-tangling collision. Either way, I had been more than happy when my picture wasn't on page one. It was odd that Mrs. Scott had picked up on the incident.

"Richard and I are hospital trustees. The news has made the rounds with the board. You're lucky you weren't hurt. Do the police have any leads?" She took another big swallow, eyeing me intently over her glass.

"I'm really not at liberty to talk about an ongoing investigation. The detectives get cranky."

"I just want you to know that Richard and I have made it abundantly clear that our donations will not continue if you are fired over this whole nasty business."

"That's quite generous of you," I said, contemplating. Maybe Mrs. Scott could help push the makeover plan through the administration.

"Really, it's all just a big misunderstanding that I'm sure will be worked out in no time. Like with Richard and those donations." Mom smiled brightly at Mrs. Scott. Richard Scott had owned several successful businesses before becoming mayor of an affluent city. Even before his election, talk had swirled about the legality of some of his political donations. I always found it fascinating how smoothly rich people could throw insults at each other and still seem so polite.

Mrs. Scott let out another big cackle. "He's lucky his wife is so persuasive with the police commissioner."

"Well, it was so lovely catching up with you, Greta, but if you'll excuse us, now that Katherine is here, I might be able to squeeze some more donations out of these men." Mom pushed me in the opposite direction of Mrs. Scott.

With another loud chortle, Mrs. Scott downed the last of her champagne. "I'll call you for lunch soon."

For the next half hour, we shook hands, smiled, and made mindless small talk, managing to stay away from embarrassing subjects such as stolen bodies and fathers in prison. We met four mayors, three company presidents, and a congressman.

It was on the introduction of the congressman that I came face-to-face with Burns. He stood just off the shoulder of the man who was enthralling my mother with some story about Washington politics.

His eyes moved over me from head to toe as if he wanted to take in every inch of me. "You look beautiful."

What I looked was surprised. "What are you doing here?"

"Because riffraff like me don't belong in a place like this?" he asked with an easy smile.

"First, I'm pretty sure your bank account trumps mine in spades, but second, I'd think you would be more prone to throwing these types of events for Ingenisys than attending them."

"Occupational hazard," he said, nodding at the congressman. "We run his security for events like this."

"McPhee, how can you look so unhappy when you're in the company of such a beautiful woman?" the congressman asked, turning toward us. "I'm getting a drink. Flynn's at the bar, so I'll be fine. Ask Katherine to dance. That's an order." We watched as he disappeared into the crowd.

"You heard the man," Burns said, offering his arm.

"We can pretend we did," I replied.

"You're afraid to dance with me." He grinned. "I'll stay off your feet, I promise. Besides, you wouldn't want to get me in trouble with my employer, now would you?"

Before I could answer, he was pulling me through the crowd, onto the floor. His hand went up my back, and he pulled me to him. I shivered at the caress of his thumb as he traced the scoop back of my dress.

Boy, the man could dance. We glided through the crowd, and he twirled me like a pro.

"See, we're naturals."

The warm air of his whisper in my ear made my already-racing pulse surge. I let my head rest lightly against him and tried to decide if that was his heart beating fast or mine.

"You're good. Where did you learn?" I asked.

"My Bohemian poetry-loving mother was also very fond of dance and determined to make sure her son could hold his own on a dance floor," he said.

"So thanks to a great mom, you're as cultured as you are well traveled."

"I have to give all the credit for travel to the United States Army, but Mom is great and was determined to make sure I had broad exposure to all the good things in life."

Skillfully, he spun us through the crowded floor to a spot where we had more privacy. I caught Flynn watching us from the bar across the room, scratching at his collar as if he were allergic to the tie. "There's a sight I never thought I'd see, Flynn in a bow tie."

Burns laughed. "He comes off a bit gruff, but I owe him my life a couple of times over."

"Afghanistan?" I asked.

"Yes, but not just then. My dad died when I was in middle school. Car crash. I didn't take it well. I was angry and lashing out at anyone I could. Flynn found me behind school one day, surrounded by a bunch of older guys I'd pissed off. After he took care of the situation, he hit me in the head and told me to stop being an idiot. From then on, he was just always there. Got me through Gillian's death too."

The song changed, and Burns spun me with the tempo. We both laughed.

When I was in the tenth grade, my school had performed *My Fair Lady*. As I felt the rhythm of the music move through us, and the warmth of him next to me, all I could think was that this must be how Eliza Doolittle had felt. At that moment, I could have danced all night.

Until I felt the cold shiver up my spine again.

Burns noticed instantly when I lifted my head. "What's wrong?" he asked.

"It's nothing. I'm being silly."

He kept his eyes locked on mine. He wasn't going to give it up.

"I think we're being watched."

He spun me around, not in the rhythmic, romantic sway from earlier but in a practiced, deliberate move. His body changed from soft and enveloping to charged and rigid. His eyes darted about the room. "All units, report," he said.

That was when I noticed that the flag on his tie was really a microphone. Great. My ramblings were now on tape. "I'm sure it's nothing," I said.

"Of course it's not nothing. Between what you've been through the past couple of days and those great people instincts of yours, we'd be foolish not to pay attention to that feeling. I'm going to do a perimeter check."

He dropped me back with Mom and Grand and made me promise I'd stay with them the rest of the night. Before I knew what had happened, he was gone. I suddenly felt even colder.

"Rule number four. I need chocolate," Grand said, approaching with Claude. "All that booty shaking left me with a hankering. As expensive as this thing is, they should have good chocolate. Let's go check out the dessert table while Claude gets some drinks."

Mom frowned. "Katherine?"

She didn't need to say anything else for me to know I was on Grand-sitting duty. "Okay. I'll go."

Before I could object—not that I wanted to, since chocolate sounded like a good plan— Grand had disappeared into the crowd. I turned to follow her and, instead, ended up with a drink all down the front of me.

"Oh my gosh, I'm so sorry, miss," a tall man said and then began laughing. "Kat? We have to stop meeting like this. How can I help you?"

Fletcher Reid stood in front of me with that same casual smile that he'd worn the other morning. Only he was wearing a tux this time. I'd seen a lot of men in tuxes in my life, and he was the only one I'd known who could make a tux look comfortable and lived in while not appearing informal.

"I'll figure it out. Back away slowly. I didn't think reporters made enough money to come to these society things." I flagged down one of the servers to get me a towel. I looked up from my drying. "Sorry, I didn't mean that as rude as it sounded."

"My date is covering it for the paper."

"Date?"

"Yeah, she writes for the society pages. Why? You jealous, Stretch?"

"No, I'm not. Isn't she, like, sixty?"

"Ask your grandmother. I have a thing for older women, ya know."

"And my name isn't Stretch."

"Those long, gorgeous legs of yours seem to keep getting us tangled up."

With all my current problems with men, I didn't need Fletcher Reid thinking my legs were gorgeous.

"Any luck finding your missing body?" he asked.

"No. Not yet. But I'm working on it." I tried to wipe the drink off my dress with my hands. I grabbed some cocktail napkins from a nearby table, but they just pilled white balls onto the dress.

"With Burns McPhee?"

"How did you know that?" I asked, now less interested in cleaning up than in Fletcher Reid's conversation. Maybe he had seen us dancing.

"I'm a reporter. I know things."

"Do you know him?"

"We have a history."

"Because of Gillian Mathers?" Maybe Fletcher knew what she had been working on. Maybe his reports in the paper about Dad and the mob actually came from information she had passed him. Maybe he knew more about those poor dead girls.

"She and I were friends, yes."

"Were you working on the prostitute story with her?"

"No. She was working a story on her own. Said it was big."

"But you're covering it now?" The waiter was taking forever. I started to get cold. I opened my bag and searched for something more substantial to clean up with.

"Officially, there is no story. The cops keep saying Gillian was just in the wrong place at the wrong time."

"But you don't believe the cops have it right?" I started taking things out of my bag so I could find my packet of handy wipes. I'd forgotten how much stuff I'd put in there yesterday before I went looking for Burns.

"I know Burns doesn't."

"You're evading. Is he right?" I asked.

"I know he feels guilty." Fletcher glanced at the growing pile I was removing from my purse. "Can I help you with that?"

"Yes, thanks." I handed him half the stuff I'd taken from my purse. "Because Gillian asked him for help, but he didn't help her?"

"Burns helps everyone, which you should know, since I believe he's now helping you."

"How do you know that?" I asked, pausing my search. "Never mind. After the day I've had, I don't want to know."

"He wasn't just helping her. The night of her murder, she'd planned to meet him to tell him that she had uncovered something connecting him to her story."

"Him and the prostitute murders? That doesn't make any sense." I found the wipes packet and took some out. I began to reload the bag, taking things from Fletcher.

"Since her murder, I haven't been able to put the pieces together. She had a file name in her notes on the prostitute murders with an arrow drawn to Burns's name and circled. Covana."

I searched my memory of the photos of the crime scene. I didn't remember seeing that. "What's Covana?"

"That is the ten-thousand-dollar question. I haven't been able to turn up anything on it. I'd guess Burns hasn't either. Your body is the first lead any of us have had in months."

"Is that the only connection you've made? Have you made progress on the prostitute murders?" This, I knew, was dangerous territory. I didn't want to directly bring up the mob and a possible connection to my dad. That would trigger Fletcher Reid's alarm bells. His champagne was soaking through my two thousand dollars' worth of designer silk that I really couldn't afford to dry-clean, much less replace, but I needed answers. I stopped drying myself to study his reaction.

"No. After Gillian's death, there hadn't been any other deaths. Until your body."

"It's terrible what happened to those girls. And no one really seems to care. The last police report filed actually said the murders were due to a 'cranky john.' It's disgusting."

"You've been doing your homework."

"I know what it's like to have your life turned upside down in an instant. I'm lucky. We have resources. Those women had nothing and no one to fight for them."

"Then you should be careful, Stretch. If it wasn't a 'cranky john,' you could push some wrong buttons. You've already been targeted with that anonymous tip."

"So you believe my story? I appreciate that you didn't run it in the paper."

"You don't strike me as that easily paid off."

"You're awfully forthcoming with information to a virtual stranger."

"You're mixed up with McPhee. You should know what you're getting into. If someone had been more open with Gillian, maybe she wouldn't be dead." His eyes went cold for the first time since I'd met him. The talk of his friend's murder had clearly upset him. "Besides, I'm hoping we won't be strangers for long."

The server brought me a towel, and I returned to my cleanup.

"Can you believe it? All this money and not a single bit of decent chocolate," Grand said, joining the group. "They have some froufrou strawberry cream thing and something that tasted like pumpkins. Don't they know it's spring? Who has pumpkin in spring?" Her eyes sparkled when she noticed Fletcher. "Hey, handsome, are you following me?"

"Hi, gorgeous. Love the feathers," Fletcher said, putting her at ease about the gown. She smiled and stood a little taller on Claude's arm.

"Claude says they match my eyes."

"That Claude's a lucky man. Now if you'll excuse me, if I keep hanging out with you, beautiful, my date will get jealous," he said and kissed Grand's cheek. "Stretch, nice seeing you again."

Grand blushed. "What the hell happened to you? You look like someone peed on you."

"No one peed on me, but I do need to go to the bathroom. Can I trust you to stay out of trouble while I go clean up?"

"Do Claude and I look like Bonnie and Clyde?"

"You don't want me to answer that. I'll be right back. Behave."

I kept trying to pat the stain, but it seemed hopeless. I didn't know how one small glass of champagne could do so much damage. The waiter directed me to the bathroom outside of the ballroom.

Moving from the event to the quiet of the hotel lobby felt like going from the inside of a noisy blender to a library. I took a deep cleansing breath to steady myself. The last few days had felt like a whirlwind.

The sound of raised voices jolted me out of my own thoughts. Across the lobby in front of the bathroom were two men in tuxedos. As I approached, I heard them arguing.

"Even if I had it, which I don't, giving it to you would be a death sentence."

From where I stood, I couldn't quite make out the identities of the men, but I'd recognize that barking voice anywhere.

"Dr. Jaffe? Is everything okay?" As I reached them, the men jerked up, both seeming to realize they weren't in a private location. The man Dr. Jaffe had been arguing with did a quick scan of the lobby as if checking to see who else might have noticed them.

"Waters. What are you doing here?" Dr. Jaffe pulled at his collar.

"Katherine Waters?" At the mention of my name, the other man settled his gaze on me. He looked considerably older than Dr. Jaffe, distinguished, with salt-and-pepper hair. He wore an impeccably tailored tuxedo with diamond-studded cufflinks and a matching tie clip. Everything about him exuded wealth. "You must be Lauren's daughter."

I always found it strange when people referred to my mother by her first name. He stretched out his hand for me to shake. "Charles Montgomery. I'm CEO of Teradyne Defense and an old friend of your parents."

"Nice to meet you, Mr. Montgomery." I returned his gesture. Even his handshake radiated perfection—not too hard, not too soft. Firm for the exactly correct two-second, two-pumps timing.

"Katherine's mother organized the event. I'm surprised you didn't recognize the name, Jeffery."

I tried not to chuckle; I never would have pegged the taciturn Dr. Jaffe as a Jeffery, but standing in the shadow of Mr. Montgomery, he looked more like a scolded child than a cutthroat gambler who had potentially set me up. As he tugged again at his collar, Dr. Jaffe looked a little green.

"I should have seen the resemblance right away. You're as lovely as your mother. She's managed to charm me into a sizable donation tonight."

"I would feel bad about you parting with your money if I didn't know it benefited such a worthy cause."

"I see your resemblance to your mother doesn't stop at good looks. How exactly do you and my godson know each other?"

"We work together at the hospital," Dr. Jaffe managed to squeak out.

"That's right. I'd forgotten that you were embarking on a new career, Katherine." Mr. Montgomery made it sound so wonderful.

"I'm still considering all my options."

"There's our committed socialite." Dr. Jaffe obviously didn't mind being snarky in front of his godfather.

"No reason to be harsh, Jeffery. Not everyone can match your level of obsession." Mr. Montgomery's tone had a bite to it, and he glared at his godson.

I couldn't help wondering whether Mr. Montgomery knew about Dr. Jaffe's gambling problem.

"Well, it's been lovely meeting you, but we'll let you get on your way." Mr. Montgomery gestured to the ladies' room then took my hand and shook it again. "Please give our regards to your mother on her fabulous event. Jeffery, shall we?"

As they walked to the ballroom doors, I wondered exactly what Dr. Jaffe didn't have but that could get him killed if he gave it to Mr. Montgomery. I also wondered whether it had anything to do with the missing body. Once safely out of sight in the bathroom, I pulled out my notebook and jotted down everything I'd learned from both Fletcher Reid and Dr. Jaffe.

I cleaned up and headed to the ballroom. I started looking for Mom and Grand in the crowd when I realized the crowd had thinned, parting as I moved through. And then I saw why.

On one side of the room stood Grand and Claude, a fake cigarette dangling from Grand's mouth, her head slightly down, a wad of towels in her hands.

On the other side stood Marge Van Hollister, a tall woman, much taller than Grand. Her silver-blue hair was styled in a 1950s bouffant, and tonight she wore a powder-blue matriarch gown with sequins that matched her hair. She looked like a tall disco ball—a disco ball covered in strawberry cream cake. My mother stood next to her, trying to clean her up.

Some feuds were legendary—the Hatfields and the McCoys, the Capulets and the Montagues, Sherlock Holmes and Dr. Moriarty. And Grand and Marge Van Hollister. Their feud had been going on for forty years, since they were classmates at the same prep school.

As Mom headed toward us, Marge was muttering to whomever was near that this was what should be expected of criminals, and I saw the flashbulbs of cameras.

"I think it's safe to say we'll make the papers tomorrow" was all Mom said.

As we walked down the ramp to the car, I felt the chill of an icy glare. Someone was watching us.

Chapter 11

I stepped into the tiny kitchen, scooped up one of the packets of coffee I'd taken from the morgue, and put it into the secondhand coffeepot.

"Katherine, can you please ask your grandmother not to slurp her milk so loudly?" Mom asked. She was six inches from Grand but refusing to speak to her, casting me in the role of Cold War emissary. When I didn't respond, she continued to give Grand the eye.

"Do you think it's hard to find green skin dye that will leave a permanent stain?" Grand asked. She was too busy plotting revenge against Marge Van Hollister to notice that Mom was giving her the silent treatment. Grand had started a new scrapbook, devoted to possible revenge plots against Marge. Options ran the gamut from dying Marge's skin green the next time she went in for a facial to other possibilities that involved the purchase of small munitions. Each option had a color-coordinated scrapbook page, complete with co-ordinating stickers from a disaster-themed collection. She affixed the green gas bomb sticker next to an unflattering picture of Marge.

While it would have been refreshing to have a morning off to catch my breath from all the investigating, I was thankful to have to go into work the day after the benefit. I didn't think even Master Tahkaswami could unwind the tension in the household.

I would have thought, though, that Mom would have been happy. At least we only made the front page of the society section and not the whole paper. Marge Van Hollister glared at me from her picture above the fold. Her mouth agape, she stood covered in strawberry cream cake, positioned in mid-launch of aiming a dish toward a woman with her back turned, instantly identifiable as Grand, her peacock feathers on prominent display.

To top it off, Maybell had been up half the night with a stomachache from licking strawberry cream from Grand's peacock dress.

"Katherine, can you please tell your grandmother—"

Everyone jumped at the sound of the doorbell.

"That's probably a courier delivering papers expelling me from the Women's League," Mom said.

"It can't be my fireworks delivery. I just ordered them last night," Grand said, looking up from her book.

I opened the door to a large bouquet of red and hot-pink roses.

"Delivery for Katherine Waters," a kid said from behind the large display.

I took the flowers from him. Grand gave him our leftover pizza as a tip.

"Aren't those lovely," Mom said. "Do you have a new young man, Katherine? You and Fletcher Reid seemed awfully attractive together at the benefit."

"I am not attracted to Fletcher Reid." I plucked the card from the overly large bouquet.

Passionflowers for my passionflower. You looked beautiful amongst the gold of the casino, a jewel amongst jewels. As I promised, we'll meet soon, my love.

Victor

I dropped the card as if it were on fire and tried to process getting flowers from a crazy body-snatching Russian. I shivered as I realized this meant he could have been watching me. If he was, at least I'd know who had been watching me at the benefit. The downside was that I also now knew that a crazy Russian named Victor knew where I lived.

"Do we know a Victor, Katherine? Is that the senator's son?"

I took the flowers, dumped them into the trash can, then headed to work without a word. I needed to process the fact that I was possibly being stalked by a crazy body-snatching Russian.

Thankfully, I could escape to the morgue. The day looked more promising with the party-planning meeting before me. Nothing perked up my spirits more than the opportunity to spend someone else's money creating a happy experience for others. Plus, it would give DC and me another look at all of the suspects.

While we were still waiting on final approval from the administration, word of our plan had spread through the hospital grapevine. Everyone seemed excited. With some pushing from some of the others, Dr. Hawthorne had tentatively agreed to let me hold a planning meeting. I would soon need to figure out what was making him so nervous about this whole thing if we were going to move forward.

By the time I arrived, everyone was already sitting around the conference room table.

With a cozy glow about him, Sam Allen Winston looked happy to be there. He'd obviously brought a paper and pen for writing notes, and it looked like he even had recipe cards. Not what I would have expected from a potential Russian-colluding serial killer.

Dr. Jaffe sat with his arms crossed, looking disgruntled as usual. I was surprised he had even bothered to come. I'd convinced Dr. Hutchinson to volunteer Dr. Jaffe to help us. When I told him that getting Dr. Hawthorne to agree to county-funded autopsy requests might become easier if he pitched in, he offered Jaffe up in an instant. Jaffe made it abundantly clear to anyone who would listen that he thought the party would end in disaster and cause the morgue even more indignity.

Henry and Meg sat next to him. They doodled together in Meg's pad. DC had the two of them engaged in some chatter about the decline of bumblebees.

"Oh yeah. Without the bee, we're all doomed. Mass famine, crop failures of epic proportion."

"Good morning, everyone!" I took the handouts from my bag. "I'm thrilled you've all agreed to help with the planning and execution of the morgue makeover party. While planning can be difficult, it need not be boring."

"Well, thrilled for most of you, anyway," DC snarked as he passed the handout to Dr. Jaffe. DC and Kimi were still having trouble. I doubted anyone else could tell, but I noticed his usually sunny disposition wasn't shining quite as brightly today.

"I'm not here to participate or have fun. My role on this committee is to ensure that nothing happens that would jeopardize the reputation of the morgue any further than it already has." Jaffe set his planner aside without even looking at it.

"You don't have room to be accusing anyone of misconduct, do ya, Jaffe?" Sam glared at him from across the table.

Dr. Jaffe twitched in his chair without responding.

"Wow, there's so much to do," Meg said, looking at the list.

"Yeah, but you're great at this kind of stuff," Henry said.

"Only because you're such an awesome partner," Meg replied.

Henry's tan cheeks turned crimson.

I stood at the head of the table and cleared my throat to deliver a speech I had given at countless sorority meetings. "The most important decision in any party-planning process isn't about the food or the decorations or who to invite. The biggest decision is 'why.' Why are you giving a party at all? All of a party's details flow from the answer to that one question of how to best connect your guest to your 'why.'"

"The why is because Dr. Hawthorne has lost his mind." Dr. Jaffe pushed his chair slightly away from the table and crossed his arms.

"If we hear one more negative word out of you, it might be your last." Sam banged his fist on the table, and his face flushed red. This was more than his usual disdain for Dr. Jaffe. The happy glow Sam had entered the room with seemed to dim with each interaction with Jaffe, and Jaffe refused to even look at Sam. Dr. Jaffe looked like he might run out of the room. In my book, that gave Sam points, even if he was in cahoots with the Russians. When he realized we had all noticed his strong reaction, Sam relaxed and sat back in his chair. "My 'why' is to get a damn coffee maker that works out of this deal."

"That's good, Sam." I gave a small clap to show approval. "As we're making over the morgue, it's good to identify some of our priorities. But the 'why' for a party should also be tied to the message you want your guests to come away with."

"Like the divorce party my mom threw." Meg sat up straighter in her chair. Her dress today featured black and white polka dots. "Her theme was a good end to a bad beginning, all designed around the featured drink, 'Rum, Baby, Rum.'"

"Exactly. I bet your mom's party was a big hit."

"I, for one, would like our guests to get the message that morgue work is important," DC said.

"That's true. I'd like my mother to know that I'm not wasting my talents," Henry said.

"Your mother wouldn't know talent if it bit her," Meg said.

Henry beamed.

"Without us, no one would know why someone died. That's important," Meg added.

Henry nodded.

"It's a place people need, but no one likes to think about that." Sam rubbed his goatee.

When Jaffe grunted as if in agreement, I knew we were on to something. I went to the board, picked up the whiteboard marker, and wrote, "Taking the Mystery Out of Your Neighborhood Morgue—The Last Place You'll Ever Need."

"Great job," I said. "I think we have our 'why.' So now all we have to figure out are fun ways to help our guests experience that."

"We did the autopsy of the actress Morgana Grable," Meg said.

"And the brewery kingpin, Adolph Miller," DC added.

"And Mario Granaldi," Sam said.

I didn't recognize the name. Granaldi sounded Italian. The last thing I needed was for us to be celebrating mobsters. I wasn't the only one who didn't recognize the name. Everyone around the table looked at Sam with confusion.

"You know, the famous chef," he said.

With a sense of relief, I wrote on the board the idea of the famous-autopsy montage. Meg and Henry agreed to be in charge of compiling and presenting the information.

For the rest of the hour, we filled in the party-planning worksheet around the theme of celebrating the morgue's work. The last task was to assign duties.

Along with Meg, I took the job of handling the decorations. That would give us some bonding time. Maybe she knew Henry's secret.

"Uh, I'd be happy to help with the food," Sam said, standing up.

"Okay, but no rattlesnake," DC said.

Sam grinned, and Jaffe huffed.

Thanks to the additional business Mom's caterer had gotten from other guests at the benefit last night, she had agreed to cater the morgue event for free. I gave Sam her contact information. He also agreed to head up the construction crew for the morgue makeover.

Surprisingly, Dr. Jaffe agreed to put together a tour of the morgue to help guests get a feel for what happened during an autopsy.

I put DC in charge of the cake and the auction of all the leftovers in the evidence room. That would be one way we could raise money for the new spectrometer Dr. Hawthorne wanted.

Now all that remained was the shopping.

"BABE!" A RASPY WHISPER came from behind me as I stood at the morgue's coffeepot, praying that coffee would drip from it eventually. Someone had taken the wrench.

"I'm really not in the mood, Marshall." I turned around to face him. His body twitched, and he shuffled from one foot to the other. His wide eyes looked like they might pop out of his head.

"I read the paper. I'm sorry you had a rough night." He looked over his shoulder, probably to make sure no one was around. "But you have to come with me."

DC had left early to take his cats to their shrink appointment with Kimi. Thankfully, Dr. Jaffe had worked only a short day today. Henry and Sam were working a suicide with Dr. Hawthorne, and Meg had finished up and headed home to get ready for shopping later. I mentally growled at Marshall's invasion of my first quiet moment all day.

"Even if my night had been stellar, there aren't enough handbags in all of Italy to convince me to go anywhere with you."

"Babe, I'm wounded." He brought his hands to his heart. "But seriously, you have to come with me." He started pulling on my arm. "I have something for you."

I jerked my arm away and wiped the grease from where he had touched me. "All right, I'll come with you. But we don't need to touch."

Marshall continued to look around as we moved through the hospital.

Instinctively, I looked over my shoulder too. "What are you looking for?"

"I'm making sure we aren't followed. You aren't exactly inconspicuous in those things." He pointed at my lovely Stuart Weitzmans, the most comfortable heels for work, in my opinion.

"It's not like I can go barefoot. These floors are filthy." We went up two flights of stairs—making me even happier I'd chosen the Weitzmans for today—through a nurses' station and to a long hallway of patient rooms.

Marshall stopped in the middle of the corridor. "We're here."

"If by 'here' you mean a janitor's closet, then yes. What are we doing at a janitor's closet?"

Marshall looked around again as he knocked on the door. "They prefer the term 'custodial engineers.'" He tapped a code on the door, alternating long and short knocks three times.

"That's not the right code," a husky voice said from behind the door.

"Open up. It's us." He pressed his face tightly against the door as he spoke and breathed heavily, as if the person on the other side had X-ray vision.

"How do I know it's you if you don't know the code?"

"Max, open up before someone sees us."

A click of the lock sounded, and a crack opened in the door, allowing a sliver of light to illuminate the pitch-black inside. The light reflected off the plastic of Big Max's knee brace. Marshall went in, pulling me along.

"Why are we meeting Big Max in a dark jan... custodial engineer's closet?" I batted Marshall's hand away and began looking for a light switch.

"Hey, how does she know it's me? You said she couldn't figure out it was me if we met here."

A hand groped the back of my leg near the bottom of my skirt. "Move your hand, Marshall, or something bad is going to happen to you."

A loud crash sounded behind me, and Marshall yelped.

"Get off me, dude," Max cried as I turned on the light.

"What in the blazes is going on here?" I asked.

Marshall sat tangled on the floor with Max's knee brace and a stray mop bucket. "Max has some information that could help you, but he was afraid to say anything." Marshall rolled back and forth on the floor, trying to get enough momentum to push up.

"If it'd been anybody but you, Kat, my lips would be sealed. But I figure I owe you after what you did for me, not reporting me for what we was doing. That would have been my third offense. I would have lost my job. Plus, you helped me get fixed up." Big Max patted his leg brace. "If the information would help you, it was the least I could do."

"Aw, that's so sweet of you, Max."

"Yeah, yeah, he's a gumdrop." Marshall's voice strained as he pushed himself onto all fours then stood. "Now, can we please get on with this before someone walks in and wants to know why the three of us are in a broom closet?"

"That night you found me and Tilani doing the deed down in the morgue? That wasn't our first visit that day. We'd been in there earlier."

"Dude, impressive," Marshall said.

"Did you see something when you were there?" I could use a break. A bunch of strange clues were all I had to go on in figuring out who might be a backstabbing murderer. When I threw in the new information about Burns possibly being tied to Gillian's murder and my dad maybe being mixed up with the mob, I was more confused than that time I had tried to make my own at-home facial.

"Mostly it was hard not to see it," Max said. "The two of them were arguing pretty loud. I was afraid they were gonna come to blows and I'd have to come out of hiding to break it up. Which would have been unfortunate, since I didn't have any pants on."

"Trust me," I said, "no one wants to see that. Were you able to hear what they were arguing about?"

"I heard the whole dang thing. This skinny know-it-all guy threatened this big biker guy that if he didn't make the call, he was going to tell everyone the biker guy's secret."

"He said 'make the call'?" My voice cracked.

"Yeah, like, you know, a call to Dr. Hawthorne that maybe someone we all know and love is on the take."

Marshall made a kissy face at me. My stomach turned.

"Did he actually say the call was to Dr. Hawthorne?"

"No, and that's when it got heated," Max said. "The biker guy came at the other guy and put a choke hold on him with one hand. I've never seen anything like it. It was one fell swoop. The biker was on him like white on rice and, with one hand, had him lifted in the air. Told him if he breathed one word of anything, he'd end him."

"The biker's obviously Winston," Marshall said. "The other guy, I'm not sure if it's Jaffe or Henry."

"Henry would make sense, given what Wiggins told us. But Sam and Jaffe were going at it pretty heavy today. Did the guy look more like Beaker from *The Muppets* or more like Fozzie Bear?" I asked Max.

"Definitely Beaker. He had a long skinny head."

"Jaffe!" Marshall and I said in unison.

As we left Max to head back to the morgue, Marshall reminded me no less than six times that he had now delivered on his end of the bargain, so I needed to show up with bells on for bowling on Thursday. When he hit attempt number seven, I finally shouted at him that if he said one more word about it, I'd stuff a bowling ball up any number of available orifices. Marshall finally got the hint and left.

Since the disappearance of the body, I'd felt like the whole world had spun upside down. I sat at the morgue computer desk and took a deep breath. I took out my lucky pink feather pen that matched my notebook and reviewed my list. In addition to the notes on the prostitute who didn't look like a prostitute, and notes about Burns and his team, I added all the new information about my potentially nefarious coworkers:

- Victor: A maybe-crazy stalking Russian body-napper with a weird creepy crush on me.
- Dr. Jaffe: Gambling addict with angry godfather who was also head of the country's largest defense contractor. Why had he exploded at the mention that he might be mixed up with Joy? Was it related?
- Henry: On the take from the morticians. At least 3 grand a month. Where does the money go? Threatened by parking lot lady with the bad Mary Janes.
- Sam Allen Winston: Fight with Dr. Jaffe about a secret call. Was it about me? If not, what was it about?

And I still hadn't quite absorbed the possibility that my daddy could be mixed up in all of this. At the very least, Gillian seemed to have the same clue my grand had that somehow ran through the mob. It just didn't seem possible that Clarke Waters had any more of a connection to the mob than watching *Goodfellas*. Maybe the clue was somehow linked to the misunderstanding that had landed him in jail in the first place. If I could find the information Gillian had, it could help get him out.

I hadn't quite figured out what, if anything, I'd tell Burns about the "missile launch codes" and my dad. If he had investigated my dad's case, maybe he had something that could clear him. On the other hand, he could also freak out and conclude my dad had something to do with Gillian's murder, and then Burns might go back on our deal. Without his help, I didn't see how I would get out of the suspension. Maybe it was better if I didn't tell him about my dad.

After all, Burns hadn't felt it necessary to tell me about the mysterious Covana and his possible connection to Gillian's murder. If I didn't tell Burns about my dad, I'd only be leveling the playing field. Of course, thanks to Fletcher Reid, I now knew one of Burns's secrets, so the playing field wouldn't quite be level. Plus, my indecisiveness had the side effect of making me a bad liar.

But I did have a slew of new clues to share with him. And as a bonus, maybe he could help me with my Victor problem. I'd agreed to go back and help with a sketch of the man who had stolen the body to see if they could identify him. With a first name now, maybe they could.

Plus, it would be nice to talk to Burns again. He was such a study in contrasts—poetry-reciting, orphan-saving Fred Astaire on the one hand, gun-toting, secret-keeping special ops guy on the other.

Also, I had made a date with Meg for shopping later. Given the current state of my bank account, and the fact that the feds had all of our credit cards, seeing Burns had become a necessity. He was, after all, the party sponsor. Whether I wanted to or not, keeping in good graces with one's sponsor was a party-planning necessity. I'd just have to try to avoid any conversation about my dad.

As Master Tahkaswami would say, "A journey to confidence begins with a single tenuous step."

Chapter 12

When the Bumpit-wearing Stepford receptionist had said that Burns was unavailable, I'd had mixed feelings. The whole drive over, I'd gone back and forth about what I would say to him. By the time I pulled into the parking lot, I still hadn't figured it out. So I was relieved when Neutron finally appeared to collect me.

"Let's get started," Neutron said and led me to a set of chairs in front of a giant computer monitor.

I watched as he pressed several buttons and typed a bunch of strange lines into the computer. Neutron looked much more confident behind his computer screen than he had in DC's greenhouse, shooting at a wayward plant.

He pulled up a computer software program that gave me a series of choices for facial features like eye color, eye width, and facial hair then asked me to look at the drawing and make recommendations by feature, like "make the nose bigger." The program was almost exactly like the one my friend Kate Simmons's plastic surgeon had used to show her what her new face would look like.

By the time we were done, the picture on the monitor looked exactly like the body snatcher, evil gaze and all. Even his picture gave me chills. In DC's defense, the man did kind of look like a Russian Tom Cruise.

"That's it. That's amazing. I always thought an artist had to come and do that."

"These days, software can do amazing things. This is the program the FBI uses for sketching terrorists and kidnappers."

"You stole the program?"

He smiled big. "It's more like borrowing. Now let's see if we can find your guy in one of the federal databases with their facial recognition." He typed more strange lines of code.

"Why do people call you Neutron?"

"It's my hacker name. Ya know, the glasses, Jimmy Neutron and all. My real name is Harold, but no one named Harold gets taken seriously as a hacker. I'm a very good hacker."

"Is that how you met Burns?"

"Sort of. He sprang me from the psych ward after a hack gone bad."

"Is that a good thing? Did you need to be there?"

"Maybe a little but not enough to worry about seriously."

"Did you hack anyone good?"

"I sent Chief Justice Roberts a lifetime supply of Viagra using a credit card number I stole from a retail site." He typed more lines then pushed the enter key. Pictures and records zoomed across the screen.

"Did he need Viagra?"

"I don't know. But I thought someone important should know how easy it is to steal credit card numbers. Someone stole my mom's and ran up this huge bill, and the company wouldn't help her. The courts ruled against her. So I thought if I proved a point, it would help."

"At least they didn't put you in jail."

"I think the judge thought it was funny. So he sentenced me to community service and a psychiatric evaluation. When Burns heard about my story, he helped get my mom's credit card fixed and hired me as lead tech here."

"Do you like working here?"

"I know we look a little crazy from the outside, but we're family here. Burns has a knack for recognizing hidden talent, and while he's not the emotional type, he takes care of his own."

The computer made a loud *bing,* and a mug shot with a dossier popped up next to the computer drawing. His photo was even more ominous.

"And we have a winner," Neutron said, printing the profile of the man I had identified, Victor Chentinko, aka The Chin.

"I was shot at by a body part?"

"Ha. No, this is all Russian mob. Rap sheet a mile long."

"So I was right. But what does the Russian mob have to do with any of this?"

"It's weird, really. The Russians tend to stay out of the prostitution game. It's just not their thing."

"What is their thing?"

"Smuggling, drugs, gambling. Anything with a heavy money component where they don't have to worry about the product running off or flipping out. I suppose it could have something to do with human trafficking, but that seems like a stretch. A lot of the dead girls were local girls who'd been around for a while. A lot of them had regulars. These don't seem like snatches gone wrong or girls trying to escape a ring. The pieces just don't fit right for that. The Russian trafficking operations tend to be more hit-and-run. They don't like to stay involved. This seems like something else."

Great. I'd spent weeks trying to convince everyone my family wasn't involved with the mob, and now here I was, potentially involved with the mob. It seemed the only thing I had gotten right while defending my dad was that it wasn't the *Italian* mob.

"I'll start running background and let Burns know we have something. He's with a donor." Neutron pushed some buttons, and the picture of Chentinko started reproducing itself on the nearby printer.

Before too long, Burns emerged through the fake door of the conference room. Today he wore an exquisite pinstriped suit. He looked like he could own Wall Street and was just as dangerous in a suit as he had been as a lumberjack.

Burns took in the images of Chentinko on the screen before he said anything. "It looks like you've made some progress since we last talked."

"I just don't get why he's stalking me." Even the photos of Chentinko were enough to make me shudder.

"Stalking you? Who?" Burns looked alarmed.

"Chentinko," I said, pointing at his eerie mug shot. "He called me. And sent me flowers. Said I looked beautiful in my dress last night and that we'll be meeting soon."

"He sent those to your house?"

"Yes. And called on my personal cell. I assume it's information that someone from the morgue gave him."

He walked over to a phone on the conference room table and dialed. "I need a full package for Kat. Car, home, work. She sneezes, I want to know." He hung up.

"What are you doing? I'm perfectly capable of taking care of myself." I didn't even believe me when I said it. I was quite sure he didn't either. He smiled at my effort.

"We made a deal, remember? You collect information, and I provide security better than the police could. There's a body-snatching murderer running around. This is me upholding my end of the deal."

Burns moved closer to me. "Any idea why Chentinko has taken a liking to you?"

"I have no idea. He said it was because I've gotten in his way, but that doesn't really explain his weird affection. Maybe he thinks we're soul mates because we both like expensive shoes." And perhaps he thought we were connected because of something with my dad. But I wasn't ready to share that with Burns yet.

"Maybe he has a thing for sexy morgue workers."

"Sexy?"

He took another step closer, and my pulse quickened.

"Funny, loyal, smart, great dancer. He might be a psycho, but you did look beautiful last night." He ran his hand through my hair. The warmth of the touch was mesmerizing. His breath warmed the side of my neck as he leaned in.

And then the door opened. Burns stepped back slightly. The cold rushed in, filling the space between us. Neutron strolled through, head down and focused on some new electronic gizmo. He returned to his computer.

Burns put his hands in his pockets. "When I saw in the paper this morning how your night ended, I thought you might have your hands too full on the home front to bother with our pesky Russian problem." His teasing lightened the mood.

I grinned. "I was a bit preoccupied trying to decipher what 'Covana' could mean."

Without lifting his head up from his computer, Neutron looked over the top of his glasses at Burns, then at me, then back at Burns as if he were watching a tennis match.

Burns moved to the cabinet for water. "And how is Fletcher Reid?"

"How do you know I got it from Fletcher?"

"Because he's the only other one who knows about it. We didn't even tell the police," Neutron said then went back to typing on his computer.

"Why did he tell you?" Burns asked. He leaned against the cabinets and drank.

"He thinks you're dangerous."

"Do you think that?"

"Twenty-nine million people visited emergency rooms last year for 'accidents.'" I didn't know what I believed. "Do the police have any other leads on Gillian's murder?"

"No. But I think the police have it wrong about the burglary."

"Me too. No one would have left that crystal egg collection."

Surprise flashed across his face. "You did some homework."

"You're right that it doesn't seem to be what the police claim it is. We could try Madame Rosa, my personal astrologist. She might be able to point us in a direction."

"That's about the only thing we haven't tried, Burns. Maybe Kat can give us a recommendation."

"Funny." He screwed the cap back on his water. "The cops think Gillian surprised the burglar in the middle of his break-in, causing him to panic and kill her and then run with whatever he had, leaving the rest."

"I suppose it's plausible." I mentally turned over the crime scene photos of Gillian.

"I ran every pawnshop in St. Louis. The jewelry never turned up. If it were a run-of-the-mill break-in, someone would have fenced the stuff," Neutron said.

The receptionist appeared in the door with a tray of coffee, water, and pastries. She had a snooty attitude, but her bold green gingham A-line skirt was to die for, and she had brought pastries. I could overlook snooty for pastries. They looked incredible. I couldn't remember the last time I'd had pastry.

"Thank you, Amber." She set the tray down and left.

I perused the pastry plate and took a muffin. "Maybe the robber's smart and didn't want to be connected to the murder."

"Maybe," Burns said. "But then they would have dumped the body somewhere and someone else would have picked it up. Burglars aren't known for their self-control. I'd be surprised if the perp was sitting on it. Too much temptation."

I contemplated while I let the sugary goodness of the pastry cream hit my system. "Maybe we do need to see Madame Rosa. It all seems to be so cosmically connected—Gillian, my dad, Dr. Jaffe, the Russians, the mob..."

"What do you mean 'connected'?" he asked.

I wasn't sure I meant to say that out loud, but here we were. I liked Burns, and I didn't want to keep secrets from him. After all, he hadn't freaked out about me knowing about Covana. Maybe he wouldn't freak out about this either. "When I looked into Gillian's case file at the morgue yesterday, I found this." I took the photo out of my bag and passed it to him. I guessed I had decided to tell him.

"Okay." He looked relieved and put the photo down. "Kat, just because the mob is connected to the prostitute killings doesn't mean it's connected to your dad. Reid only runs the speculation stories about your dad and the mob to sell papers. He doesn't care whether they're true at this point. In fact, if it were true, he'd be quiet until he had an exclusive with real proof."

"You don't understand. I haven't bought in to some hype. See those codes on that piece of paper sticking out from the corner? My grand found a matching set of numbers in my dad's papers."

"What do you mean?" Burns asked.

"An exact match. Not something like them, but those specific codes."

He picked up the photo again. From the look of surprise on his face, he didn't know a connection existed until now. Good news. I could see him trying to calculate what this meant.

"Your dad is an insurance broker, right?"

"Yes. Wills, estates, insurance, some occasional estate planning. These codes don't match anything I've ever seen attached to the business. Grand thinks they're missile launch codes. You deal in defense. Do these look familiar?"

"No, why would you think that?"

"Ordinarily, I wouldn't give Grand's crazy connections much thought. When you've run the social circuit as long as I have, you learn that there is no such thing as a coincidence in networking. Yesterday I learned Dr. Jaffe"—I pointed at Dr. Jaffe's photo on the board—"is a gambling addict. Like a cash-business gambling thing." I looked at Neutron and pointed up at the screen to Chentinko's photo. "Last night at the benefit, I discovered that he's the godson of Charles Montgomery."

"Montgomery? Teradyne Defense Montgomery?"

"Yes. They were arguing and were not at all pleased that I had overheard them."

"You're sure?" Burns asked.

"I've been a socialite in high society since my sweet sixteen ball. I'm an expert at subtext." I searched the board until I found the photo I was looking for. "You spent a lot of time investigating Gillian's case. Do you know what those are?" I asked and pointed at the photo that matched the codes from Grand's scrapbook.

"No. Neutron pored over them for weeks, and we always came up empty."

Neutron pulled up the photo of numbers on the big screen and said, "They aren't bank account numbers or credit cards or anything else we can match. From the way they're put together, I thought they might be serial numbers for products, but it might take months of searching manufacturers' databases to confirm."

"Maybe it's just a coincidence that these numbers are the same," I said.

"Or maybe that's why Chentinko is stalking you."

I breathed out heavily. I hadn't wanted to believe that my dad was actually connected to all of this. It had to be some mistake. But Chentinko was calling me. He'd sent me flowers. There was a connection, whether I wanted to believe it or not. "Yes. I had considered that. I just didn't want to say it out loud yet."

"There is an obvious solution to our problem." He poured a cup of coffee but failed to look casual, eyeing me. "Go visit your father and ask him."

"I can't."

"'Can't' as in 'don't want to' or 'can't' as in 'don't have that option'?"

"So far, my mom and Grand's requests to visit have all been denied, supposedly for his own safety. It's driving them nuts." I hated to admit it, but I had been trying to avoid the whole visiting thing, as if my not acknowledging his imprisonment made it less real. With such a good reason for needing to see him, I couldn't keep sticking my head in the sand. "The lawyer's filed an appeal for them, but that could take months. I can put in a request. Maybe his unassuming daughter will have more luck, but with this problem at the morgue, I can only imagine I'll be denied too."

"And you don't find the denials a little suspicious?"

"I didn't until this week. Now I find everything suspicious." We were told that it wasn't that unusual in mob cases for visitation to be denied, but still, they hadn't seen him in months, and it felt like an eternity. He sent letters when he could and sounded okay. The lawyer said he was fine, but still. "Suspicious or not, without a way to see him, we can't get any answers. My grand might know more than she's said. She got this paper from somewhere. There might be more."

"Okay, you work that angle. Neutron can take another run at these numbers, but I don't know that we'll make any progress. Our best bet is to focus on your friend here." Burns pointed at Chentinko.

"Any more on your side?" I asked.

"We got a hit on the partial plate of the van that picked them up. A warehouse in Midtown. It's new but not tied to the Russians."

"Are you going there?"

"Yes."

"I want to go."

"No."

"What do you mean, no, just like that? If you really want to find out what happened to Gillian, that photo proves my family is connected to this somehow. Look, this isn't about making sure I can hold on to my job anymore." I pushed the half-full plate away and stood. "This is about someone needing to stand up for these girls. And this is about my family. I need to know what's really going on. My whole life, I've thought I was this one thing. Now I learn I may be something different. An awful something. You want information? So do I. Like it or not, we need each other."

Burns sat there for a long time, looking up at me. I could see the gears turning in his head, running tactical battle scenarios, each to its own conclusion, like a bad simulation from the movie *War Games*. Eventually, I knew he'd ended at the same place I had. His face softened, and he smiled gently at me. We were stuck with each other.

"Fine. But I'm in command. When I give you an order, you follow it, unquestioned."

"Great. Then it's a date. I have more." I told him all about Sam, Henry, and Jaffe.

"Wow, I thought it might be a myth that only nutjobs worked at the morgue," Neutron said.

"If DC were here, he'd tell you it's not good for your karma for you to label people. But I have to admit, I'm a bit surprised that we have so many angles to run down." I took a last bite of pastry and stood up. "The only person we don't have anything on yet is Meg." I pointed at her picture on the board. "And thanks to you, I'm going to be taking care of that today." I held out my hand.

Burns looked at it. "Thanks to me?"

"Yes, as our party sponsor, you're covering Meg's and my shopping trip. If I'm lucky, in addition to some lovely accessories that will make the morgue feel way less like a morgue, I might be able to get us another lead."

Burns opened his wallet and handed me his credit card.

"Ah, the power," I said with a maniacal tone.

"Ha. Just like a real girlfriend," Neutron said.

It made me warm inside to hear that.

"You've never been shopping with DC, or you wouldn't stereotype so blatantly," I said, putting the card in my wallet.

MEG PICKED ME UP OUTSIDE of McPhee's in her adorable little yellow Smart car.

I slid into the passenger's seat. "Great car."

"Thanks. I live too far for public transportation, but that doesn't mean I shouldn't still try to be nice to Mother Earth."

"I have a hybrid." I clicked my seat belt into the buckle. "No. I guess that's not right. More like the repo man has a hybrid."

"Those are cool, too, but you're better off with something that doesn't have such a big footprint, anyway."

I could still smell the fresh leather of the seats. The car wasn't new. It took a lot of care to keep that new-car smell going once it wasn't new anymore. "And you're proof that environmentally friendly doesn't have to be unfashionable. It's so sporty."

Meg had pulled her short bob into two tiny pigtail buns that looked like alien antenna. She wore a black silk button-down over a dark plaid mini with knee-high leather boots that had four-inch heels and ten buckles up the back. I wondered if those boots would be comfortable for a shopping trip. "Did you want to change before we go?"

"I already did." She smiled at me and put the car into gear.

"I'm sorry. I don't seem to be able to keep my foot out of my mouth."

"All things considered, I think you're doing pretty well. At least you don't hate us anymore." She looked across traffic and turned as she spoke in a steady, casual tone. I wondered how such a confident person could be so tentative around Henry.

"Hate you? My goodness, no. I've been way too self-focused to bother with hating anyone."

Meg laughed, but I was serious. One reason that I hadn't gotten to know any of my coworkers was that I'd been busy trying to pretend that any minute, my life would go back to the way they had been. With the appearance of Grand's launch codes or the mob codes or whatever they were, I couldn't keep my head in the sand any longer. "I don't know what your family situation is like, but my father was our rock." I looked out the window at the passing people as I thought about him. It had been so long since I'd heard him laugh. "I've been running around trying to manage my eccentric grandmother and stunned mother, neither of whom appreciates being managed. I suppose I figured if I kept busy enough, maybe I wouldn't notice I wasn't in Boston anymore." I turned my attention back to her. "Rule number eighteen—Avoiding things takes a lot of energy."

"My family is pretty tight too. I can't imagine what I'd do in the same situation. I think you're dealing with it the best you can. And I still give you props for the way you handled Marshall that first day. Henry still talks about it."

"He does?"

My first day at the morgue, Marshall had decided to initiate me by having me fish through some poor old man's intestine to recover his wife's wedding ring. The widow had given several stories of how the ring ended up there, but none of them changed the fact that it had to be retrieved. I had barely seen blood before, let alone someone's intestine. Things with my family were bad enough, though. I would not be intimidated by a reject from a grease farm.

Marshall looked stunned when I walked over and untied his cheap loafer, removed the shoestring, and fashioned a makeshift fishing pole from it, aided by one of DC's hook earrings.

"Simply brilliant," Meg said.

"That Dr. Jaffe can be pretty maddening, that's for sure. Did you see how mad Sam was at him? It was like he stole his Harley or something."

"I think everyone noticed. Do you have any idea what they're fighting about?" I kept mum about what Big Max had witnessed. I wanted to know what she knew and not spook her.

"No. I asked Henry about it, but he didn't know. Only that Dr. Jaffe had done something to make Sam want to pound him into little pieces."

The moment we walked through the doors of the Galleria, I felt better. I took a deep breath of the money-filled air and let the shopping endorphins fill me. We hit all the biggies, filling bags with accessories for the new coffee bar and the employee lounge. At first, Meg had been a little reluctant to spend someone else's money, but once she loosened up, she surprised me with her terrific eye.

From the mall, we headed to one of my favorite boutiques. I hadn't been back to my neighborhood since I'd watched the police cart away my life in several boxes. It felt good to be somewhere familiar, even if I did feel out of place in the midst of the obvious decadence. Even the planters framing the entrance were plated in gold.

"You'll love it here," I said to Meg as I opened the door. The store's soft lighting offered a refreshing contrast to the bright spring sun and accentuated the crisp, neutral décor.

"May I help you?" A short, older man with glasses approached us. He must have been new. I didn't recognize him. He moved his glasses down his nose and looked at us. "Hmmm."

Meg looked around. "Some of the lighting pieces here are spectacular." She picked up a Schonbek French gold and crystal table lamp and traced its shape.

"Excuse me, miss. Please don't touch that." The little man, whose name tag said Barney, hurried over and took the lamp from Meg.

She looked at the floor and tugged on her mini.

"I don't think we'll have what you're looking for," Barney said as he set the lamp back down.

"Oh, and what exactly is it that you think we're looking for?" I asked, crossing my arms and giving Barney my best hairy eyeball.

"It's okay, Kat." Meg headed quickly for the door.

He grimaced at me then took a towel from his back pocket and began to clean the lamp as if Meg had contaminated it.

"Let me tell you, Barney"—I pointed my finger at his bald head—"you're going to regret that."

I ran after Meg, who was already outside. "I'm so sorry. Some people are just boobs."

"It's not your fault. I know I look different."

"I don't think bald Barney, with his horn-rims, is one to be calling anyone out for how they look."

She smiled. "Can I take you somewhere? I want to show you something."

We drove to a part of town near the university and pulled into the driveway of a restored Victorian.

An acorn-and-leaf iron fence framed the walkway to the beauty. The fine metalwork continued up the steps leading to the door. Italianate features such as curved window caps and corner boards in an exuberant, eclectic style caught my eye first, but it had a Neoclassical Revival front porch with Ionic columns and an open staircase turret in Queen Anne style. The three-story tower and elaborate iron ridge board suggested Second Empire style. Whatever its story, the detailing was impeccable, and the remodel had really done the house justice.

A sign planted in the lawn read "Too Good to Be Threw."

"This place is gorgeous, Meg."

"Wait until you see the inside."

I wasn't disappointed. Not only had the detailing of the restoration continued in the interior, but also the store inside the house had the most charming and eclectic accessories. I ran my hand over a beautifully stitched tablecloth made from what looked like antique wedding dresses and fawned over a collection of hand-embroidered pillows.

"Over here." Meg motioned from where she stood in front of a table. It contained a collection of dazzling lamps fashioned from old piping, gears, and other industrial parts. They looked more like art than light but were wonderfully functional. A small card on the table read "Megathons."

"Did you make these? They're wonderful."

"You're not just saying that?"

"Gosh, no. First, we have to have some of these for the morgue. They're perfect. And second, I know how I'm going to get even with Barney."

Meg smiled big. "How?"

"It's a surprise, but you'll love it. Now, how about some of that ice cream from that shop on the corner? Burns is rewarding us for our hard work." I giggled as I held up McPhee's credit card.

Once we were situated in front of a bowl of Jamocha Almond Fudge, I figured it was time to get down to business. "Thanks for doing this with me today. I really had a lot of fun."

"Me too."

"Most of my close friends don't live here anymore, and the ones left don't exactly want to be seen with me these days."

"Well, that just makes them boobs, and you now know who your real friends are. It's for the best, anyway, not to have cling-ons who only love your money." Meg patted her head repeatedly. "Brain freeze."

"I need to ask you something personal."

"Okay. I don't think I really have anything personal."

"It's about Henry."

"Oh." She sighed and took a drink of water.

"I know you like him. Why don't you just ask him out?"

"Is it obvious?"

"Maybe not to Henry. No offense, but he seems a bit dense."

"None taken. Henry is my best friend. We tell each other everything. It was his idea for me to try to sell the Megathons, and he's always helping me. But that's the problem. I've been friend zoned. Do you have a boyfriend?"

"I have... complications. Men can be very confusing."

"Right on to that." She dug into the ice cream with a new zeal. "I've tried everything I know to do. I've hinted that maybe we could be more. I've tried to make him jealous. I've tried to point out all my girl features, and still he acts as if my name could be Mike instead of Meg."

"We'll just have to find a way to change that. Do you know if he has a girlfriend?" The direct approach was sometimes best.

"*My* Henry?" She laughed. "I'd claw their eyes out if another woman got anywhere near him. Why are you asking?"

"I saw him with a strange woman. Do you know if he's having any money problems?"

"What do you mean?"

"Wiggins, the mortician, told me something that made me worry a bit, and then I saw Henry giving this mean woman some money."

Meg's brows furrowed. "I've seen Wiggins give him money before, but I didn't really want to think about it. Do you think he's okay?"

I didn't think someone's eyes could get that big.

Meg sat back in her chair and clenched both sides of the table. "What if someone's out to get him or blackmailing him? You don't really think he's seeing that woman and just trying to spare my feelings?"

"I don't know if he is or not, but you have to admit, it's a bit odd. I think we should try to figure out what Henry's into."

"You have to help me." She grabbed my hand from across the table. "I can't be in love with my best friend if he's hiding another woman on the side. Or what if poor Henry needs us?"

"If you're open to it, I have an idea."

Chapter 13

For the second time in a row, when I walked through the door of our apartment, the smell of brewing coffee greeted me. But this time, it didn't stop there. Someone had cleaned. Gone was the organized clutter that usually filled the space, which now seemed almost stark. Before I could contemplate where in our tiny apartment someone could have possibly stuffed all of our—mostly Grand's—stuff, Maybell waddled up, snortier than usual. She wore her red party dress, another sign of trouble.

As I bent to greet Maybell, my eyes traveled across the newly polished terrain. I found Mom and Grand sitting at the dilapidated thrift store table, now covered in fresh linen. Even from my crouched vantage point, I could see the light glinting off the china, china that hadn't been in the apartment when I left.

A flash of red sequins adorning a woman's pudgy back roll poked out of the side of the Queen Anne. Because of the height of the chair, I couldn't make out more than her glittery back fat, other than the matching red feather that protruded from the top of the chair—and, I imagined, whatever headpiece the woman wore.

"Katherine, right on time as usual." Mother wiped her mouth with an antique ivory linen napkin, another accessory that hadn't been in the house earlier. "She does such important work at the hospital," she said to the mystery guest.

I rose from the floor to move toward the table, curious to know what visitor I owed a thank-you for the miracle of getting my mother to recognize my morgue work as something other than an embarrassment.

"When I go, I'm going to donate my body to science." Grand wore what she termed her "formal visor" for the occasion. It was made of bright-blue cloth and had fake crystals on it. When the sun shone through the window and reflected on them, it made her head a prism, directing rainbow sparkles everywhere.

By the time I'd made it to the other end of the room, I found Greta Scott sitting in the Queen Anne, her unmistakable laugh at Grand's comment giving her away. "And they'd be lucky to have you too." She raised her wineglass in a toast.

"Wasn't it nice of Mrs. Scott to come visit us in our new house for a late lunch?" Mom took a big swig of her drink. "She brought wine."

"The table looks beautiful." I recognized only some of the china. They must have hit up a thrift store when they found out Mrs. Scott was coming. The salad plates were a French pattern that went well with the light-blue lace tablecloth. A beautiful bouquet stood on prominent display near the fourth chair at the table.

My stomach tightened. My mind raced, trying to figure out if Chentinko had been there and if he knew I'd chucked the first flowers. I could not receive two stalker bouquets in one day. I put my bag on the breakfast bar, which had been covered with doilies to act as a serving station.

"I couldn't get the silverware when I went shopping at the hou—"

A thud sounded from under the table.

"Ow!" Grand squealed.

"Oh my, is everything all right?" Mrs. Scott asked.

"Grand must have hit herself again on that darn table leg." Mother smiled. Whether the wine or the company had caused it, I felt grateful the cold war between Mom and Grand seemed to have thawed. At least temporarily. "I'm sure Greta understands that we still have so much in boxes from the move, Mother. Please, won't you join us, Katherine?" She motioned me to the open chair. I felt like I had been summoned to a meeting with an auditor. "You'll have to move the flowers. They're for you, anyway, and these, I don't think you'll want to throw away." She lifted the bouquet to me.

"I'll save you the suspense," Grand said. "They're from that devilishly handsome reporter, that's who." A glint came into Grand's eye.

I took the card from the flowers.

Stretch,

Sorry about your dress. Hope this makes up for it. Dinner? Tell Grand I said nice pie to Marge Van Hollister's face and give her a kiss for me. I'll call you.

Fletcher

"Are you dating a reporter?" Mrs. Scott asked.

Even though I was busy studying the card from Fletcher, I could feel her gaze.

"Oh, heavens no. We had a bit of a run-in. They're a peace offering." I tucked the card in my purse, determined to forget about Fletcher Reid's desire to further complicate my life. I didn't care if he could charm a banana from an angry horde of monkeys. Three days ago, he was the enemy. Of course, a lot had changed in three days. Three days ago, I still had a job. Three days ago, I wasn't being stalked by some psycho mobster. Three days ago, I wasn't questioning my entire upbringing.

"I think you should take him up on it. You need a rebound guy so you stop sulking," Grand said.

I turned my head, hoping she wouldn't notice my cringe. With everything going on lately, I hadn't had two minutes to dwell on the implosion of my relationship with Martin. It had been almost four months since he'd called off the engagement. The breakup still felt recent, though. It hadn't helped that when I received my belongings in the mail, his mother had included a picture of Martin and a brunette at a society function.

Martin Eldridge was a nice man from Boston with a family my parents approved of. Martin was sensible. No one shot at him. He didn't carry a gun or track down deranged killers. He owned pastel polo shirts and wore only Brooks Brothers suits. He ordered chicken and drove a Mercedes. We had been dating for two years and engaged for only a month before my dad's arrest. I was angry at his meddling mother, but I supposed it said something about the relationship that I didn't feel angrier at him. He was the one who didn't stand up to her, who dropped me like a bad habit at the first sign of trouble. We had never been all that passionate, but I'd thought we shared values, like putting family first and being loyal.

As I looked at Fletcher's flowers and the blinking security light of Burns's surveillance tracker, I thought perhaps Martin had done us both a favor. Fletcher and Burns were both putting it all on the line to avenge their friend. Burns would never consider abandoning any of that ragtag group he had assembled.

"It's important these days to find a man who respects your independence," Mrs. Scott said.

"So true. I'm lucky Claude appreciates a strong woman," Grand replied, a twinkle in her eye. I hated that twinkle. Old ladies shouldn't be so perceptive.

"You must try some of this gourmet noodle stroganoff." Mrs. Scott scooped some of the casserole onto my plate. To make it "gourmet," Mom must have used the name-brand Hamburger Helper instead of the store brand.

"This will help." Grand poured me some wine from a bottle on the breakfast bar.

Maybell parked her bottom on my feet. DC had helped me find her a new piggy Medicaid vet for low-income pig owners, and the vet had recommended that we not allow her to eat any food from the table. She had become quite a pill at mealtimes.

"I have to admit that now that we're more on our own, I am quite enjoying experimenting in the kitchen."

By "experimenting," Mom meant learning to put different things into the microwave.

"And I'm intrigued that you're able to fit so much charm into your new downsized space," Greta said.

"Yeah, that's us. Aren't we quaint?" Grand flicked the brim of her visor.

"I feel fortunate that Katherine was able to find us a place in such a cultured part of town. Did you know, Greta, Tennessee Williams used to live near here?"

"You don't say. I have to tell you, Lauren, when I first heard the news of Clarke's... troubles, my heart was worried for you. But you really do seem to be taking it all in stride."

"Smooth as pudding." Grand took some of the spilled salt on the tablecloth and threw it over her shoulder.

"This thing with Clarke is just a big misunderstanding. I'm sure we'll be back to normal in no time. But with this lovely new home and Katherine's budding career, we're really doing well."

"And don't you worry, Katherine." Mrs. Scott put down her fork and covered my hand with hers. "Richard and I are in your corner."

"Thank you. I'm sure it will all get worked out soon. But actually, there is something you could do to help." I explained the morgue makeover plan and party to her.

"What a marvelous idea. You can certainly count on Richard and me helping you get this approved. Do the police have any idea who murdered that poor girl and stole her body?"

"As I told you at the benefit, I'm really not supposed to talk to anyone about the investigation."

"Surely the police don't mean hospital board members, Katherine."

I didn't even have to look over at her to feel Mom's frown.

"I wouldn't tell a soul, dear. I'm merely worried about the hospital's reputation. I can't believe someone snuck in there and stole a body right out from under everyone's noses."

"That's not quite how it happened." I couldn't decide whether Mrs. Scott was just a bored housewife looking for juicy gossip or if more was going on here than it seemed. This was the second time in two days that she had pressed for information. And this time, she'd driven all the way to a less than stellar part of town to do it. I figured if I gave her some details, I might get a better feel for her motive. "A Russian man took the body, and I chased him."

"Goodness gracious, a Russian?"

When someone had as many years of experience influencing people as I did, they became an expert at reading body language. Mrs. Scott's hand clenched around the tablecloth, the corner of her eye began to twitch, and her face turned as pale as one of Grand's linen napkins. The mention of Chentinko had nearly caused a panic attack.

"Thank goodness you weren't hurt," she managed.

"She comes from a long line of detectives," Grand said, watching Mrs. Scott intently.

"With the outdated and broken security system, it's really no wonder something like this hasn't happened sooner. That's why I'm sponsoring a morgue makeover event."

"I'm so proud to see you put your upbringing to good use. Maybe you could get the board to chip in some money, Greta?" Mom asked.

"Oh, that won't be necessary. I've already procured a sponsor. McPhee Security. Maybe you've heard of them?" I took a sip of wine and watched Mrs. Scott.

"McPhee?" she asked.

I caught a tiny crack in her voice even though her mask was firmly in place.

"Yes, do you know him? I understand that in addition to his security work, he runs an organization that builds schools and roads in Afghanistan. You might have donated?"

"Ingenisys. Yes, I believe we have." Mrs. Scott wiped her mouth and took a breath before picking up her wineglass and pasting her smile back on. "The hospital is lucky to have such a resourceful employee as you, Kat. Dr. Hawthorne snagged a great hire. You make sure we're on the guest list for this event."

I could tell she would find her way onto that guest list one way or another.

"Do you plan on taking a position somewhere, too, Lauren?"

"Yes, once we're settled in here. I'm being a bit particular."

By "particular," Mom meant that she had refused to apply to fast-food places.

"Of course you are. Progressive women like us can't be expected to sit around and keep watching our men screw up the world, now can we?" She threw her head back and let out one last loud cackle.

After a nouveau chic dessert of Twinkies, doing our part to help rescue an American icon, we were finally able to get Greta Scott out of our apartment.

"What the hell was that?" Grand asked as the door closed behind Mrs. Scott.

"You tell me. And where did you put all of our stuff?"

"I thought it was very gracious of Mrs. Scott to check in on us." Mom cleared the plates to the kitchen.

"Sure, if by 'gracious' you mean she totally had an agenda. My Nancy Drew instincts are in an uproar." Grand tugged on her hat.

"I have no idea what the two of you are talking about. Don't open the cupboards, Katherine." Mom shooed me away from the cabinets.

That answered part of the question.

"Also, you might want to stay out of your closet for a while."

"And the shower," Grand added.

Maybell snorted. The shower had become her favorite place in the apartment. She hadn't been allowed in the one at the old house.

"You know I love you, Mother, but I think you're being a bit naïve. Greta Scott is up to something. And maybe this thing with Dad isn't just a big misunderstanding."

Grand wiggled up onto one of the breakfast bar stools and poured herself another glass of wine. With her condition, she shouldn't have had any, but I always found it hard to tell someone who'd lived as long as Grand that she couldn't have something.

"You've ignored the whole issue of your father for months, and suddenly you're an expert?"

"I haven't been ignoring it."

"That's what I love about our family. Steeped in honesty," Grand said.

"Fine, maybe I've been ignoring it. But I'm not acting like an expert. I'm merely suggesting that maybe we need to start considering that this thing with Dad isn't temporary. How much do you know about why Dad's in prison?"

"I know what your father's told me, that it's all a misunderstanding and will get cleared up eventually." Carrying the tablecloth, Grand headed for her bedroom.

"And what if it's not?" I yelled to her in the other room.

"Then we're pretty much screwed," Grand said, returning to the room.

"Stop talking like this. I won't have you disparaging your father. Is it that job making you think all these sinister things?" Mom asked.

"Funny, an hour ago I was brilliant and my job was important."

"Someone's got to help the dead people." Grand lifted her glass to me.

"It's time for us to face some facts, Mom. We need to start preparing ourselves for the real possibility that Dad is guilty, that maybe he's not who we thought for all these years. Or at the very least, that this may not blow over."

"Katherine Marie Waters, you look at me." Mom squared her hips and stood up taller. "I understand that you have been through a lot lately, that adjusting has been difficult. But the one thing I know unequivocally is that your father is a good, honest man. I know you think I'm all about appearances, and perceptions do matter. But so do insides. And your father's insides are, without question, honorable. With all the moments you've spent with him, you should know it too. Now, I'm taking Maybell for a walk." She put Maybell's leash on her halter and left, slamming the door on her way out.

"Amen," Grand said. She slid off the barstool and came over to me. She patted my face. "We can't lose faith."

I took her hand in mine and kissed it. "I suppose. It's all been a bit overwhelming."

"And you've handled it like a true Waters woman. Don't blow it now." She gave me a slight hug and then, stepping back, tugged on her hat. "Now, how are we going to figure out what Greta Scott is up to? Your mother may not want to admit it, but there is something going on with that woman."

Chapter 14

"If you're going to credibly pull off this fake relationship thing with Burns, the two of you actually need to look like you know something about each other," DC said as he paced around the war room.

We had put a picture of Mrs. Scott on the suspect board, and I relayed the events of the luncheon to everyone. When I mentioned that my hearing date had been set for a week from Thursday, DC went into planning mode.

"I don't see how my fake relationship status is going to be relevant to my suspension hearing." I looked between Burns and DC.

"We need McPhee Security to have access to the morgue. You partly sold this whole plan as your boyfriend helping you clear your good name," DC added.

"We didn't sell it as just that," I said.

"No, the other half of the argument we made was that he's a security expert with deep pockets who you just happen to be close to. Don't you think the other board members who helped push our remodel plan funded by one Burns McPhee and Ingenisys are going to ask you about him? Make sure it's all legit? They're already worried you're on the take."

"Plus, we'll be starting in on the main security installation and getting ready for the party soon. It will look weird if you two aren't at least comfortable," Neutron chimed in.

"I agree with both of them," Flynn said to McPhee while pointing at Neutron and DC. "You know how I hate that."

"Besides the fact that she has an unhealthy attachment to shoes, what else is there to know?" Burns teased.

"You should have an origin story," DC said.

"I don't suppose we can tell people we met at *Invasion of the Body Snatchers*," Burns said with a smirk.

"You need to know each other's favorite color," DC added, exasperation growing in his voice.

"Is camouflage a color?" I asked Burns, joining in the teasing.

"And who leaves the cap off the toothpaste when you stay overnight," DC yelled in a last gasp.

I spurted my water.

"Oh no, don't you look at me like that, Ms. I'm-on-the-rebound-and-all-men-suck. I will not have my security compromised because you two can't swap a first grade *All About Me* book."

DC could be rather over the top. It was part of his charm. At times like this, when he had latched on to something, he could also be as strong and stubborn as a mule.

"Fine," I conceded. "We'll find time for a 'getting to know you' date."

"In the meantime, we've caught a break on Chentinko's getaway van," Burns said, standing. "Gear up."

"What kind of break?" I asked.

"Owner of the chop shop we tracked the van to is an old friend."

Neutron and Flynn loaded the SUV with supplies, and we all climbed in. We drove for several miles into a more industrial part of town and turned in to the driveway of a large multi-door garage. One of the doors floated halfway open, but we didn't try to drive in. Instead, everyone got out of the SUV in the driveway.

The inside of the garage was much larger than I had anticipated. It was a long, deep square and much cleaner on the inside than outside. Several cars in the center sat in various states of dismantling. The whirring of power tools filled the space. Two guys were working on a shiny black Lexus with missing doors. Another guy was under a sporty BMW. To the right stood a square folding table with four guys engrossed in a card game. Stairs in the back led to a second-floor glassed-in office.

Off to the far left side, I spied the white cargo van that the corpse-napper had jumped into with my body. I gasped, causing the four men at the card table to quickly turn to me.

"A little early to be cheating at cards, ain't it, guys?" Flynn asked.

"This is a private garage," said a large black man in a gray sweatshirt that had the arms cut off, his muscles bulging and an air of confidence about him as he sized up our numbers. He wore a Chicago Cubs cap.

"Anyone who roots for the Cubs doesn't deserve any privacy," Flynn replied. There weren't many things that St. Louisans agreed on, but hating the Cubs was one of them.

"For someone who's trespassing on private property, you're awfully mouthy," the man said, leaning back in his chair, apparently trying to decide what to do about us, Flynn's confidence causing him some uncertainty.

"Now, Flynn. It's not nice to insult our hosts. Go get your boss," Burns said to the skinny guy who had crawled out from the Lexus and was quietly approaching us from the side.

I was happy the man went without any questions. Burns, Flynn, and even Neutron all seemed calm, but I wasn't so sure about all of this.

"There's no reason to be all twitchy, guys. We're all friends here," he added.

I was glad to see he wasn't letting the situation get out of hand. These guys were scary.

"So, while we're killing time, how's the body-snatching business treating you?" Burns asked.

So much for not pushing the situation.

Everyone tensed, but before anyone could answer, two men descended the back stairs, the one from the Lexus and another man. The new addition to the group was of medium build, a little stocky, slightly older, and had bits of gray in his dark hair. He was clean-shaven and better dressed than the others in his tan slacks and sport shirt. The group parted to allow him to the front of the circle.

"You entertaining company on work time now, Nathan?" the new man asked the muscle man in a measured voice, his eyes never leaving Burns.

"They want information on transporting dead bodies."

"Oh, is that right?" A big smile came across the new man's face, still fixated on Burns.

"I had to let Flynn play with them a little," Burns said, also smiling. The new man and Burns embraced in a man hug, which didn't look like much of a hug because it involved a lot of backslapping, but the action did lower the tension in the room.

"Last I'd heard, you'd gotten your ass kicked by a bunch of Arabs and were still looking for payback," the man said.

"We're about even now," Burns said, stepping back. "It's been a long time, Duff."

"Not so long you've forgotten how to make an entrance. Flynn, how goes it?" Duff asked, nodding toward our group.

"No complaints."

"Since when do you run with women?" Duff asked, pointing at me.

"It's a long story."

"Still taking in strays, I see," Duff said with a big grin.

"I'm not a puppy," I answered, crossing my arms in a huff.

"Back to work, you candy-asses," Duff ordered, and his men began to return to the cars. He led us to the card table, and we sat down. Neutron and Flynn kept a distance.

"How's your ma?" Duff asked Burns, somewhat sheepishly.

"I would have thought you'd been burned enough by that flame," Burns replied with a chuckle. "She's doing okay."

I knew he'd said she was Bohemian, but still, I was surprised that Burns's mom had dated a car thief.

"Bet she's glad to have you back home in one piece. I thought she turned crazy when you were runnin' cars for me, but that was nothing compared to how nuts she went when you left for Afghanistan."

"I appreciated you looking out for her while I was gone."

"Wait, you stole cars?" I asked.

"Best key charmer I had," Duff replied.

Burns actually blushed but tried to cover it by straightening in his chair.

"What's a key charmer?" I asked.

"With all the new tech, you can't steal a car with a screwdriver and a rubber band anymore. You have to boost the key if you want the thing to drive," Burns answered.

"We usually set up fake valet stations or search lines, but with Burns, we didn't bother, as long as the owner was female."

"Some women find me compelling," he said, wiggling his eyebrows at me.

"Ha! You're lucky you didn't get caught, although statistically, car thieves are the least likely of all criminals to serve any time," I replied.

"Anyway, what brings you looking for bodies, Burns?" Duff's expression turned serious.

"Gillian," he answered with some force, and Duff absorbed it, looking down at the table, quiet for a while as if that one word conveyed all he needed to hear.

"If I'd known it was connected, I'd have come to you. You have to know that," Duff said, almost apologetically.

"How'd you end up with a gig like that, anyway? That's not really your style," Burns asked.

"See the skinny guy over there?" Duff pointed at a young guy bent over a car. "He's new. About two months ago, his first night out, he goes out with Joey and Nathan. They decide he's doing fine, so they left him by himself. Figured they'd turn more cars that way. Before anyone knows what's happened, Louie Fingers's new bright-blue Trans Am is sitting in my bay."

"Louie Fingers?" Burns asked.

"You'd think the kid wouldn't be stupid enough to go shopping at the mob's favorite restaurant."

"No one told him to stay off the Hill?"

"Apparently not."

"What'd you do?" Burns asked

"I put on my best apologetic face, marched into Manny Guido's like I owned the place, and returned the car to Nino Marino myself. In return for the favor, he promised Louie Fingers wouldn't kill me. What else could I do? I explained the kid was new and dumb and that I'd educate him."

"You're lucky you're alive." Burns laughed.

"Extremely lucky. A couple of days ago, three mean-ass-looking Russians show up telling me Marino's calling in his favor."

"Russians? Since when does the Family mix with Russians?"

"My thoughts exactly, but their story checked out. A body they wanted had been picked up by the cops before they'd had a chance to dispose of it."

"So that's why they stole her from the morgue," I said.

"They didn't want the coroner to get it, and they didn't want anyone knowing the Family's involvement. I was supposed to call in an anonymous tip to the mayor's office that some chick in the morgue took a bribe and stole the body."

"As part of the original instructions?" I asked.

"Yeah. After leaving the call, I was supposed to pick up the Russians with both bodies and take them wherever they wanted to go."

"Both bodies?" I asked.

"He means you and Joy," Burns replied.

I was overwhelmed by the thought that I could actually be someone worth killing.

"No shit? You're the morgue chick? I thought I recognized you from somewhere," Duff said.

"Less than ten percent of all employees working in a morgue are female. I'm an anomaly."

"You can say that again. They mostly spoke Russian, but I gotta tell ya, it was a little creepy. One of 'em had all kinds of pictures of you." He pointed at me. "Looked like he'd been following you for a while."

"Did he say what they wanted with her?" Burns asked.

"No. Just to bring her alive and be prepared to take care of her when they were done."

That made everyone go tense.

"Uh, sorry," Duff said, looking at me. "They said the plan changed because you had company."

"That would have been me," Burns said.

"Good thing you don't have a hero complex or anything." Duff grinned. When Burns didn't look amused, Duff continued, "We dropped the Russians and the body in the West End. I'll get you the address, but they're likely long gone." He got up from the table. "But Burns, these are nasty guys. You two be careful."

"Thanks, Duff. I appreciate it."

We got the address from Duff and headed to the SUV.

"Why don't the Russians and the Family mix?" I asked.

"Oh!" Neutron's eyes grew wide. "The Italians and the Russians don't like each other."

"Russians working with the Family? Great," Flynn said. "This just keeps getting better and better."

Burns sat silent, texting on his phone.

"When are we going to the address of the Russians?" I asked.

"*We* aren't. Right, Burns?" Flynn said, clearly still miffed that I existed.

"You don't just stroll in and find a body at the Russians'. We need to do some surveillance first," Neutron added.

Before Neutron had even stopped the car, Burns jumped out and opened my door. After I got out, Burns closed the door behind me. A single look from him had Neutron and Flynn heading upstairs, leaving the two of us alone in the garage. He started pacing, his body rigid.

"You're upset," I said.

"They had your body bag picked out." Burns stopped pacing and turned to me. "Do you think for a moment any of the people we're dealing with would bat an eye at slitting your throat and tossing you aside like yesterday's trash?"

My head spun from the enormity of it all. I could feel the toll the last few months had exacted. The initial chaos surrounding my dad's arrest was followed by the realization that my whole identity might be a fraud, and I was now the target of a madman. The life I had worked so carefully to put into neat little boxes had spun out of my control. My head pounded.

"It's nice to know you care." I smiled, trying to lighten the mood. It wouldn't do either of us any good to turn maudlin.

"Yeah, well, maybe I'm growing a little fond of all your froufy shoes," Burns said, smiling back.

"There's one thing I can't figure out," I said. "Why would anyone want a dead body so much that they would call in favors to steal her? If she's not the girl you're looking for who was working with Gillian, who's the dead girl, and why do they want her? Maybe it's just a coincidence that she's a prostitute."

"I suppose it's possible, but it doesn't seem likely. One thing's for sure, something's not right here. The mob isn't this sloppy. They don't off prostitutes in a serial killing spree, and they don't lose bodies. They don't stalk witnesses and send flowers." Burns rubbed the back of his neck and pulled his hand through his hair. "Plus, he had pictures of you. Lots of pictures. *Before* you were even involved in this, Chentinko had surveillance on you."

"Which leads us back to my dad and what's actually going on with him."

"Maybe. Maybe it's as simple as Duff said, that they think you found something on the girl and tipped me off. Either way, you're not safe." He spoke calmly but forcefully.

"I'm not completely helpless, ya know. I've had three years of self-defense training."

"Which will not serve you very well when someone's holding a gun or a knife on you." Burns blew out a big breath he seemed to have been holding for a while. He took out his phone and started texting. "Okay, I know where this 'getting to know you' date of ours is going to be."

"You do?"

"I do, and no shoes with pointy heels."

AT THE CURB, NEUTRON and Flynn waited in the front seat of the SUV. I slid into the back. Flynn grunted what I assumed was the closest thing to a pleasantry that I was ever going to get from him.

"Hey, this isn't the way to the range, moron. Where are you going?" Flynn asked.

"We're making a detour," I said. I had texted Neutron last night about needing to pick up DC, who was dealing with his own tragedy.

"Oh no," Flynn said, raising his voice upon realizing where we were heading. "We are not letting that freak show get anywhere near me and a gun."

"Have a heart. DC needs the distraction. His girlfriend broke up with him."

"I thought this was supposed to be 'getting to know you' time for you and Burns," Flynn said.

"We're doubling. You can decide whether your partner is DC or Neutron," I said with a smile.

Neutron pulled into the driveway of Momma Claiborne's. DC had spent the night there because he didn't want to be alone in his hour of need. Apparently, when Kimi found out about Momma's house getting shot up, she said that between being a marked woman and the psycho kitties, they couldn't live together anymore. Sitting on the porch, DC's momma held tissues in one hand and iced tea in the other. She seemed fairly emotional.

"Oh, Miss Kat, have you heard the terrible news? I'm never going to get grandbabies now," she said and sniffed into her tissue.

"DC's quite a catch, Momma Claiborne. I'm sure he'll find someone to settle down with soon. Maybe he should try a dating service."

"You mean like one of those internet porno magnets?"

"There are classy ones too."

"He says he's too depressed to meet anyone new, that he'll never love again."

"It's still a fresh wound. I'm sure it will fade in time. Going shooting should help."

"You're such a good friend. As soon as you invited him, he started feeling better. Of course, he didn't have anything to wear shootin', so he had to go shoppin.'"

DC emerged clad head to toe in black leather. His boots looked like rejects from Army surplus and didn't quite seem to fit him right. He had to step very high and pronounced in order to move his feet forward. His leather pants were most likely women's. There was no way he could have found man pants that small. He topped off his outfit with a biker jacket, which made him look like he could pass for one of the Harley guys from the River Road, as long as they looked at him only from the waist up.

When DC opened the car door, I jumped out and gave him a big consoling hug.

"Hurry the hell up. You can do social hour on the way," Flynn snapped.

DC tried to climb into the SUV. It took a bit because he couldn't bend in the pants, and the boots were so clunky he could barely lift them into the car.

"What the hell are you wearing?"

"Isn't it fabulous? Even Momma thought I looked badass. Don't I look badass, Kat?"

"The only one who thinks you look like a threat is the cow who wasted its poor life so you could wear that ridiculous thing," Flynn answered.

"I can't believe you said that to me," DC said with an almost sob. "I've been through a horrible ordeal. You should have more compassion."

"Flynn wouldn't know compassion if it bit him in the ass," Neutron chimed in. "I'm terribly sorry for your loss, DC. I brought you White Castle," he said and handed a bag into the back seat.

"For me? You did that for me? Now that's true friendship. See, that's what family's all about. I bet *he* wouldn't leave me just because my cat peed in his ostrich briefcase or because a bunch of mobsters showed up and tried to kill me. No, sir. He'd buy me a treat, that's what he'd do."

We pulled into the driveway of a long white building. On it were painted large red stripes that ended in nested circles. The sign on the front read, "The Bull's Eye—It's a blast. Call 785-GUNS for All Your Party Reservations."

From the back, Neutron unloaded a bunch of hard cases that I assumed carried guns.

The front door opened directly before a counter. A stereotypical redneck stood behind it, reminding me that stereotypes existed for a reason—beard, ball cap, and a belly that had obviously done its part to support the local beer business. He was reading a tabloid. I couldn't see which one, but the article had something to do with aliens. When the bell rang, signaling that the door had opened, he looked up.

"Been a while," he said, barely glancing away from his paper. He eyed DC and me curiously. "I won't ask. Sign them in under you. Burns is already here. You'll have the place to yourself."

"Thanks, Marv."

We walked into a long space with separate lanes, like in bowling, but instead of pins at the end, there hung targets. Some were round with circles. Others looked like outlines of bodies. As I looked around, the gunfire startled me. Burns stood in the far lane, his arms outstretched and aimed at a target quite a distance down the lane. As he continued to fire, a black hole formed over the paper target's heart. When he finished, he holstered his weapon, took off his hearing protection, and pulled in his target.

"You're gonna teach me to shoot like that, right, Burns?" DC yelled.

"You finally made it," Burns said, walking up to us.

"We had a detour," Flynn said, rolling his eyes. "You'll be lucky if I let you anywhere near a gun today. The first thing we're going to cover is gun safety."

"That's ironic coming from people who shot up my greenhouse. Don't you think that's ironic, Kat?"

"You can go sit in the car," Flynn said.

"Okay, okay, gun safety, but only because I'm a marked man who needs to defend myself."

For the next half hour, Flynn and Burns explained how guns were put together and all the possible ways they could fire accidentally. Flynn emphasized these points with DC, strangely not his usual rude self, full of passion for the conversation. We practiced taking the safety on and off several models, and he taught us how to put together one of the automatic weapons that Burns kept standard. Finally, we were ready to try our hand at firing something.

Burns went to get the guns, and Neutron handed me a pair of what looked like old 1970s headphones. He started to hand a set to DC.

"Oh no. I am not putting that thing on my handsome head."

"Why not?"

"It will make me misshapen."

"Misshapen?"

"People of my persuasion don't have the cushy bush on top of our heads that you whiteys do."

"You have to wear something. You don't listen now. I can't imagine if you went deaf."

"You're gonna have to figure something out, because I am not wearing those things."

Neutron went to the front and talked to Marv. When he came back, he was holding two giant blue marshmallows.

"What am I supposed to do with those?"

"Stick 'em in your ears."

"I can't put those in my ears. My ears are dainty. Momma always said I could never wear wire glasses on account of my dainty ears."

"You can stick 'em in your ears, or I'm gonna stick 'em somewhere else," Flynn finally chimed in, his patience completely gone.

DC proceeded to put them in his ears, but they stuck out at least an inch. He was right— his ears were dainty. The blue marshmallows sticking out of his head made him look like a Blue Man Group reject.

Neutron handed me a pair of safety glasses.

"Now this, I'm prepared for," DC said, pulling out a pair of shades from his leather jacket.

Once we all had hearing and eye protection on, we headed to the alleys. In a nod to Flynn's already-frail patience, Neutron shepherded DC over to one of the alleys several stalls down, and Flynn took his own.

Burns came over and handed me a gun. "The Glock 19. Good gun for lightweights like you. Better safety than a .38, has a slim profile, which eases concealment, a mild recoil, and with sixteen rounds of 124-grain ammo, you are well armed for any confrontation that you might run across. If you can't defend yourself with sixteen rounds, you'd better turn and haul ass."

I held it in my hand for a moment, amazed at how heavy it was.

"It's a five-point checklist. Every time you pick up a gun, you need to run through the same five things in your head—stance, grasp, grip, sight, trigger. You do it over and over until it's muscle memory. Aim at the target."

I looked at him for a moment, not really understanding the request.

"Number-one rule in shooting—don't think. Your head will get in the way. Aim at the target, and we'll adjust your feet." He looked down at them. I was wearing my exceptionally sparkly Giuseppe Zanotti tennis shoes. He rolled his eyes, but I was sure I saw a smile.

I took the gun, squared my feet like they do on TV, and stuck my arms out in front of me. Burns came behind me and moved one of my feet back and shifted my hips to a forty-five-degree angle. His breath was warm on my neck. I inhaled to control the electricity flowing through me.

"It's a fighter's stance. This needs to become second nature." He then pushed my back so that my shoulders moved forward. "Nose over toes. It will help you manage the recoil and allow you to fire quicker."

Next he adjusted the gun in my hands. First he pushed the gun way up the top web part of my hand, then he turned my thumb down.

"The higher the hand, the lower the bore axis. That means much better control of muzzle jump and less movement when it recoils. If it moves, you won't hit the target. Now, grip. Squeeze the daylights out of it. If you hold it soft, you're likely to try to grip harder when it goes off, and then you'll move. Imagine it's my neck," he said with a smile. "Now, when you go to shoot, stop looking at the target."

He whispered it in my ear. The flutter of air was so soft I instinctively closed my eyes.

"Once you know where the thing is you want to shoot, you don't look at it anymore," he said.

"How on earth can I hit anything if I'm not looking at it?"

"You want to be looking at the front sight"—he pointed at a place on the gun—"not the rear sight and not really the target, although you need to be target aware," he said, pointing at the target as well. Next, he put his hand over mine. "Finally, you pull the—"

And before I could blink, he squeezed my finger back on the trigger. The gun let out a loud bang, and I let out a loud squeal, jumping closer into him. His embrace tightened around me. I was surprised at the sound, given the hearing protection.

He kept his hand over mine for several more shots, each time letting off the pressure so that eventually, I was pulling the trigger all on my own. Each time we squeezed, I squealed. I sounded like I had the hiccups. We reloaded the gun a couple of times. I still wasn't getting anywhere near the target.

"You're thinking about it too much still. You have to turn off that big brain of yours and let the motion take you." He wrapped himself around me, holding the gun along with me. "What's your favorite color?" he asked softly in my ear.

"What?" I asked and tried to turn my head toward him.

He pushed my head back toward the target with his chin. "Getting to know you. Mine's green. Close your eyes and tell me what your favorite color is."

"Bright blue," I replied, and I felt him let go a little. I squeezed the trigger. I opened my eyes to see that I had hit the target. Not a bull's-eye, but I was on the paper at least.

"Yes!" I yelled and turned in his arms, looking up at him.

Burns looked proud, causing my anti-man defense barrier to slip.

"Better," he said, giving me a squeeze before he let go. "Do it again."

"Did you see me?" DC came rushing over, Neutron in tow, holding one of the targets. It had a tiny hole in the top right corner, nowhere near the picture on the target. "I'm a natural."

After another hour of my hiccup squealing, I started hitting the target. Although it was still unlikely I would kill anyone coming at me, there was a good chance I wouldn't kill anyone else by accident and that I could at least inflict some damage. Although, given my compulsive squealing, it was a safe assumption that I wouldn't have the element of surprise. I signed up to come back and practice some more.

Neutron took me home and walked me to my apartment.

"I can take it from here, Neutron. Thanks for your help today. Mom and Grand are inside."

"Boss's orders. I promised I'd make sure you were in safe and sound."

"Who's the twelve-year-old?" Grand asked as we came through the front door.

"Maybe I should grow a beard," Neutron said.

"They let twelve-year-olds grow beards? Do you need shots for that?" Grand asked.

"This is Neutron, Grand. He's a professional hacker."

"I think the internet's another way for the government to steal our souls," Grand said.

"Nine million people a year have their identity stolen," I said.

"These days, it's everywhere. Even coffeepots have IP addresses," Neutron added.

"They can spy on me through the coffeepot?" Grand asked, eyeing the kitchen.

"Cool, huh? I can show you how to dodge Big Brother if you're interested. Excellent statue," he said, pointing.

I didn't know when it had happened, but sometime in the last couple of days, Grand had gone shopping at the old house. This large, ugly statue of a dog that doubled as a side table—the table's surface atop the dog's head—sat perched next to Grand.

"You should have seen us trying to move this baby on the moped. They won't let me have a dog here. With Claude going away on business, I need companionship."

"Where's Claude going?"

"He didn't say, but he might be away for a bit. Oh, you got a package today. Some new messenger service brought it. He was a bit rude."

"What kind of package?" Neutron asked.

His tone told me that warning bells were going off in Neutron's head.

"It's on the table."

The package was a small white Styrofoam cooler. It didn't have shipping labels on it or anything else like a normal package. "Is it ticking?"

"Ticking? We're going to get exploded?" Grand asked. "Take it in the bathroom, away from my antiques. No one cares if the toilet blows."

"It's not ticking," Neutron confirmed. "Bombs don't tick these days, anyway."

"Then maybe we shouldn't open it. Do you have any of that FBI bomb-checking stuff?" I asked.

Neutron took out his pocketknife and slit the tape that secured the lid to the body of the cooler. Slowly, he lifted the lid. Steam came out of the cooler.

"Boiling witches' brew?" Grand asked.

"No, it's more like dry ice," Neutron replied.

The smoke from the dry ice cleared. Inside the cooler was a rectangular white card.

Katherine, I thought of you when I saw these. I'm sure you can see why.

Neutron lifted the card out of the box. Underneath it, staring at me, were two bright-blue eyeballs sitting in a pool of blood.

Chapter 15

"Thank you for coming in, Ms. Waters." Detective Lambert sat down across from me at the table in the interrogation room. She carried a file with her.

Burns and I were still debating whether to turn over the eyeballs to the police. Currently they were in Burns's freezer. He was adamant that they get any forensic evidence that might be on them, that Neutron hack any DNA or fingerprint-matching database, and that neither Burns nor I needed any more police attention until we both had a better idea what the heck was going on. I found it hard to argue with that logic.

"My family is always happy to assist St. Louis's finest. You know, not many women can carry off the pantsuit as well as you, Detective." I hadn't been pleased to get the summons that the detectives wanted to see me, but I was determined to make the best of it.

"Uh, thanks. I think."

"Will Detective Driscol be joining us?"

"He's not available at the moment."

Her eyes shifted. She was lying. I turned around to look at the two-way mirror. When I turned back, she grimaced.

"I understand they've set a date for your suspension hearing."

"Yes. Next Thursday. I'll be glad to get it behind me."

"From what I hear, you don't have any worries. Some members of the board are even calling for the hearing to be dismissed."

"Really? I'm preparing diligently and am confident of a successful outcome. My former meditation specialist, Kindar, says proper visualization is important for creating positive outcomes."

"Does that preparation involve Burns McPhee?"

"Of course."

She looked surprised at my candor. They were obviously following either me or Burns or both of us. So there was no sense in denying we were working together. "He's the sponsor of the morgue makeover and community open house that I've planned as a good-will gesture. You and Detective Driscol should come. The morgue is an important partner for your department."

"I'll see if we can fit it in. Seems like an odd use of your time, under the circumstances."

"Part of the reason I'm in this mess is because the elevator that leads from the morgue to the main hospital wasn't properly secured. And you have to admit, the incident involving Billy Idol and the security footage has further complicated my situation. You're aware that Mr. McPhee runs a robust security firm?"

"We're aware, yes. I have no problem with you and McPhee teaming up to better secure the hospital facilities. I have big issues with you interfering with an ongoing police investigation."

"Oh, Detective, I highly doubt that a socialite throwing a party would be considered interference by either the hospital board or a jury." I shot her a coy smile.

Lambert took a deep breath. "Should we consider you suddenly wanting to visit your father 'interference'?"

Then it dawned on me—my request to visit must have triggered a call to them.

"Are you close to your parents, Detective?"

"You have to admit that from our perspective, the timing of your desired visit is... interesting."

"It's terribly kind for the department to be so concerned with how I'm spending my time these days."

She smiled.

"In a way, all of my recent trouble has been a bit of a catalyst."

"How so?" she asked.

"It's made me realize I've been avoiding. I had hoped everything with my father would go away on its own and I would magically get my life back. Mom's rule number five—We have to embrace our right-now moments."

"I see. Do you know this man?" Lambert took out a photo from her file folder and laid it in front of me.

I wondered what other goodies she had in there. "Of course. This is Sam," I said. "He works at the morgue."

"Did you know that he has ties to Russian organized crime?"

"I'm aware he had some youthful indiscretions. I'm sure a lot of us have things in our youth we'd rather forget as adults. Mine involve a Miss Southern Belle contest."

"We wouldn't be having this conversation if Mr. Winston's affiliations were in the past, Ms. Waters."

Hmm. So they had something to show that Sam was working with the Russians again. I wondered whether Burns knew. "So you have proof that Sam is working with the Russians? I wouldn't know anything about that, but that must mean you've decided to give some credence to my belief that the body snatcher was Russian mob."

"I'm not at liberty to get into that," she said.

"I've been thinking about you a lot lately, Detective."

Her eyebrows knitted together. "You have?"

"Do you do much party planning? We had our first party-planning meeting for the morgue community open house earlier this week. I'm a master party planner. I inherited the skill from my mom."

"I got my mom's nose."

"It fits your face really well. Anyway, as I was giving my spiel on the key to creating a successful party being all about the why—why this party is needed and how to connect to your guests—I thought, this is what Detective Lambert needs."

"Okay, I'll bite. What do party whys have to do with Winston, Russians, or the missing girl?"

"Everyone involved in this has been entirely focused on the who. Who was the girl, who are the suspects at the morgue, who is the Russian... but no one is really asking why. Why steal the body of a dead woman? You're all obsessed with the invitations and the guest list, but no one's thinking about the purpose of the event."

"And you think you've come up with the answer?"

"I can think of only a couple of reasons someone would steal a body from a morgue. One, maybe she had something on her person, or two, someone doesn't want her identified."

"That seems reasonable. You said that when you first checked her, none of her effects were that remarkable."

"Nothing worth stealing. She could have had something on her insides. But I can't stop thinking about her manicure."

"Her manicure?"

"Not just her manicure. Her salon-perfect hair. Her gold cross. As you can imagine, Detective, I know people from money when I see them. If I was in charge of looking for this girl, I'd be checking in with other police departments around the nation for reports of missing persons who match her description."

"Other departments? You don't think she's from around here?"

"Rich people get noticed when they go missing, don't they? If there was a missing socialite around here, my grand wouldn't have made the front page for throwing pies."

Detective Lambert left me with a warning to stay out of their way then let me go. I was relieved that another trip to the police station hadn't resulted in newspaper headlines. As I climbed into my wagon, the phone rang.

I never could have afforded a phone. Claude had been worried about getting me a message if something happened to Grand, so he had graciously supplied me with one.

"It's Tony," a gruff voice said into my phone.

"I'm sorry?" I didn't know a Tony.

"You know, Sheila."

"Oh, hi. I'm sorry, but I'm at the point that I think it would be harmful to my psychological health if I parted with any more of my shoes right now."

"I'd imagine. That is some collection. But that's not why I'm calling. I think I've got something for you."

"Really?"

"Can you meet me at Roxy's, Third and Main?"

"That's not the best neighborhood for this time of night." I wanted the information. I just didn't want to get mugged in the process of retrieving it.

"It's a strip club. What other kind of neighborhood do you think it'd be in?"

"All right. I'll grab DC and be there soon."

I called DC as I drove to the club from the police station. I was glad to have something to take my mind off things. Plus, I'd never been to a strip club before. Those women always seemed so exotic.

"I can't go to a strip club with you," DC said.

"Of course you can."

"Momma wouldn't like it. Neither would Kimi."

"I thought you broke up?"

"I'm hoping for reconciliation, and anyway, I try not to get them both angry at the same time. Why don't you get Burns to go with you? It would be good practice for you two playing boyfriend and girlfriend."

"I can't believe you even suggested that. I'll be there to get you in thirty, and wear something appropriate."

I had decided not to go home to change. I knew I looked like a prissy prude in my double-breasted gray Donna Karan pantsuit that I had chosen to wear to the station. Detective Lambert hadn't said what the visit would be about, and I had wanted to look presentable if reporters were on the scene. Going home to change, though, would mean answering questions I didn't want to answer.

First, there would be questions about what the detectives wanted. Both Mom and Grand had been nervous about Detective Lambert's call. Then there would be questions about where I was going. Whatever I would wear to a strip club would be sure to solicit inquiries.

Plus, Grand would want to come. She had said she hadn't been able to investigate much lately and was worried her skills were getting rusty. While I applauded her ambition, I wasn't prepared to take Grand to a strip club. The Donna Karan would have to do.

DC emerged from his apartment in his black leather shooting-range outfit. He stood on the sidewalk.

I reached over and rolled the window down. "Why are you wearing that?"

"You didn't say if we were going as customers or dancers. And you should park. We are not taking a vehicle that screams 'steal me for parts' to that section of town," he said.

"All right. I'll park. We can take the boat."

We drove DC's car, and he pulled into a crowded parking lot. Glittery, curvy letters blinked one at a time to spell out Roxy's. We went around to the back as Sheila had suggested.

In front of the door stood a large bouncer in a black uniform with hot-pink curvy lettering that matched the club's sign. He watched as DC and I approached. DC tried to pretend he didn't notice him.

"You can't go in there." The bouncer pushed the door closed.

"Why the hell not?"

"I'm pretty sure neither of you are dancers," the bouncer said, looking us over.

While DC argued with the taciturn bouncer, I texted Sheila. The bouncer's insults continued as I typed.

"I'm going to have my lawyer file an NAACP lawsuit on your ass," DC said.

"Sheila's waiting for us at the other door." As I pulled DC along with me, he continued to bark at the bouncer around the corner.

"Don't you look stunning," Sheila said as we approached the back door. I couldn't tell if the compliment had been meant for me or DC.

"You must be talking to Kat, because I look badass." DC smoothed his leather.

As we got closer, I realized I didn't recognize Sheila—or Tony, I supposed—out of drag. He'd traded in his spiked wig and short skirt for a black silk button-down and nicely cut slacks.

"I can't believe you let your woman work in a place like this. That bouncer was either sexist or racist or maybe both," DC said.

"She likes it here. The pay's good, and she gets dental now."

"I get that you can't underestimate the power of a good dental plan, but sheesh. This isn't the fifties."

"I almost didn't recognize you. Do you prefer Sheila or Tony?" I asked.

"It's Tony when I'm with my lady. Come on in."

The back area of the strip club was part pageant, part Moulin Rouge. Beautiful scantily clad women ran around putting on make-up, changing costumes, and practicing dance moves.

"Wait here a minute. I need to see if she's ready," Tony said.

"What's this all about?" DC asked.

"Trust me, I wouldn't have had you come if it weren't big. You need to hear this." He looked back and forth as if to make sure no one had overheard him and then disappeared.

He left us by the stage opening. A woman in a Cleopatra outfit was down to her tassels. The bright lights beamed off her gold-chain headdress. Two more women worked poles that stood on opposite ends of the bar top. A bachelor party took up most of the front row. It looked like a pretty good crowd for a Wednesday.

"Hey, I think Meg has that outfit," DC said, pointing at someone on stage. "You don't think Meg's really a stripper, do you?"

"No, that's just a great outfit. Maybe Henry is, and that's why he's being blackmailed." I smiled.

"Or cranky-ass Jaffe. Can you see him in sequins and pasties?" DC asked.

I could, actually, which made me giggle.

"Okay, come this way, but I'm warning you, she's scared, so go easy," Tony said.

I was surprised when Tony took us down the stage entrance and out into the crowd. DC almost fell down the stairs in his shoes.

"I didn't think places like this were usually busy on a weeknight," I yelled to Tony.

"Oh, yeah, usually it's quieter, but it's the Jell-O-wrestling Olympic tryouts tonight." Tony pointed ahead at a large, quivering vat. It glowed under the black light.

He took us to a side room. Its door had an outline of a champagne glass next to the sparkly VIP lettering.

Inside, a blonde wearing four-inch hot-pink stilettos paced back and forth while knocking together her two pink-boxing-glove-covered hands. She looked like Rocky Balboa in heels. Raised black letters that spelled Rocky protruded from her butt.

"There you are, baby," Tony said.

Another woman appeared out of the far dark corner. She had long, curly black hair and wore a leopard-print bikini. Tony embraced the woman, so I guessed she was his girlfriend.

The blonde pushed aside her flyaway hair that had been cut sharp at the ends, revealing dark eye makeup that would have given Meg a run for her money. "Jesus, Tony, Sasha and I were starting to think something had gone wrong." She shook her arms as if trying to shake off her nerves.

"We had an issue with Alex."

"Is that the name of the sexist, racist bouncer?" DC asked.

"That's him. How you doing, DC? Love the leather."

Sasha and DC exchanged a quick embrace.

"Adrian, this is Kat, the woman I was talking about. We'll leave you two alone," Sasha said, pulling DC toward the door.

"Oh no, we won't. I am not going back out there. I think someone grabbed my butt." DC rubbed his leather.

"It's okay. He don't look like no threat," Adrian said.

Sasha and I both laughed.

"If I didn't think it'd get me kicked back out into the man mob, I'd protest your snickers," DC said.

"Adrian, why don't you tell us what you saw?" Sasha said.

"All right, but you didn't hear it from me. I don't want to end up dead like that other girl."

"You saw her get whacked?" DC's eyes went wide.

"No. But I saw her get dumped."

"Really? You're sure it was her?" I asked.

"Look, lady, we might be hard up, but we don't have dead bodies being dropped outside our dumpsters every day."

"Of course not. Did you see who dumped her?" I asked.

"No, but I heard her. I was sitting on the side of the dumpster."

"What are you, Supergirl with X-ray hearing?" DC asked.

"Don't make fun of me, or you can go back into the man pack. Her suit makes a sound."

"Suit?" I asked.

"Yeah, you know, like DC's pants," Sasha said.

"Before I got this job, I briefly worked at one of the local dungeons," Adrian continued.

"She doesn't mean kings and queens, Kat. She means whips and chains." DC smiled.

"I guessed that." I hadn't, but okay.

"The madam's rubber kink suit made this loud, strange squeaking noise. The woman who dumped the body made the exact same noise. I'm sure it was her."

"Do you know who she is?" I asked.

"Not her real name. But I can give you the address of the dungeon."

We got the address and said our goodbyes. As we walked across the club floor, my mind raced, trying to figure out what in the world a madam had to do with the missing body and the Russian and why they had stolen her from the morgue.

"I'll go pull the car around. That way, we won't have to deal with the bouncer from hell again," DC said.

I waited for him, watching all the strippers get ready for the Jell-O contest.

"What are you staring at? You got a problem with me?"

I gulped. I had been staring at a beautiful woman with long, straight platinum-blond hair and a perfect nose and lips. "I'm sorry. I didn't mean to stare. Do you always go without foundation when you put on your makeup?"

"She always this nosy?" she asked Sasha.

"Ah, she's okay, Jen." Sasha nodded at me.

The woman waited for me to continue.

"If you must know, I haven't been able to find a foundation that won't run in the lights and that doesn't clog my pores."

"Oh! Have I got a product for you," I said and pulled out a tube of my friend Carrie's foundation. "It's organic and fantastic for stage lights, and best of all, it's super cheap because the 4-H kids in Farmington make it. I'll get you the info if you're interested."

Jen took off the cap and sniffed. "Smells nice."

"What's that, Jen?" Some other ladies had joined us.

In my best pageant-circuit teaching voice, I said, "Even women as beautiful as Jen must use a foundation before applying stage makeup. And you might have been told to match the color to your skin tone, but the truth is, for stage wear, you should really apply a foundation one or two shades darker than your natural skin tone. That way, you won't wash out under the lights. This product is custom-made for just that purpose."

"What are you, some Broadway queen?" Jen asked, looking at me.

"Ladies, you are in the presence of Miss Missouri's two-time"—Tony held up two fingers—"award winner for best makeup."

"No shit?" Jen said.

"You got any other tips you could give us?" Sasha asked.

"Sure. The two most important tools in any pageant girl's toolbox are her can of hair spray and her petroleum jelly."

"We got lots of jelly around here," one of the girls said from the back.

Everyone giggled.

"Great. Put a dab on your teeth before you go on stage, and you'll be able to smile for hours, effortlessly."

"For real? I'm going to have to try that one."

We swapped a few more tips, and I began to wonder whether DC might have found some trouble with that bouncer. Sasha sent Tony to find him.

"Do you like stripping?" I asked Sasha.

"It's okay for now. I like to dance, and I like the costumes. I know how to get people to pay attention to me now, and I don't just mean by taking off my clothes. There's a real art to engaging a customer for something intimate like a lap dance and making them feel like they're the only one in the room, like you're excited to be with them even though it's your fiftieth dance of the night."

"Do you think you could teach that to someone?"

"Honey, I don't think you need lessons in how to get people to pay attention."

"Oh, it's not for me. I have a friend. There's a man, and he's kind of dense."

"Do I know that type! You bring her by here, and we'll take care of everything."

Tony came through the door.

"Tell me the police aren't involved, baby," Sasha said.

"No, but DC might need a new outfit."

Chapter 16

Burns: We talked about this. I'm the muscle, you're the info collector. You shouldn't go there alone

Kat: I wasn't going to

Burns: DC does not count as backup

Kat: Spoilsport. You're stuck with a client all night. This could be our big break.

Burns: Exactly. Big breaks come with big bad guys

Kat: It's a madam. She can't be that dangerous, and you taught me how to shoot, remember. We'll only scope the place out. Get information. I promise

Burns: Why do I have a bad feeling about this?

"What did he say?" DC asked once I'd finished reading the texts and pulled out of the club's parking lot. He tried to wipe the gunk from his pants. He had injured his driving foot in the fight with the bouncer, twisting it in a sewer grate and landing in a scary puddle of goo, so I was driving. I'd never driven a car that big.

"That we should wait for him. I don't want to wait. There could be information in all of this that would free my dad. I've been wrong. And I don't mean white-pants-after-Labor-Day wrong. I've been cheap-foundation-left-on-overnight-no-moisturizer wrong. I've been so wrapped up with my own worries, I haven't been the most supportive daughter. This could be my chance to help him."

"So you think we should go check this out?"

"Consider it an opportunity to prove to Kimi what a hero you are."

"What do you mean?" DC asked, sounding wary.

"We'd be like superheroes, saving the city from the bad guys."

"I do look good in tights."

"Plus, if we rescue the body from this kinky house, people will stop shooting at you, and then Kimi won't have a reason to break up with you anymore. So really, this is as much for you as it is for me."

"You might have a point." He was quiet for a few minutes. He wiggled his ankle round and round on the car dash. "Okay. If we're going to be superheroes, I need to change."

"Excellent! That will give you a chance to get us some weapons and things to make a diversion," I said.

"What kind of things?"

"I don't know. I'm not that far in the *PI for Dummies* book yet."

"I'll improvise," DC said.

A few minutes later, I pulled into a space in front of DC's loft. "Don't take forever."

Twenty-five minutes later, a masked man emerged from the door of the building, dressed in a black spandex shirt and black tights. A cape spread out behind him. He carried a man purse and struggled with the weight of it.

"What are you wearing?"

"A superhero has to be properly attired. Plus, my shooting outfit's ruined."

"The mask has to go. You look like a burglar."

"It's too hot, anyway," he said, ripping it off. "I need one of those half face masks like Batman has." He eyed my attire. "Maybe you should change? I could put something together for you too if you want."

"I'll be the well-dressed yet plain-clothed sidekick. I wouldn't want to overshadow your ninja prowess." I was thankful for the excuse.

"I understand. Remember, there are no small parts, only small actors."

We drove to the address Adrian had given us.

"That's a kink house?" DC and I both stared at the cute ranch bungalow in the middle of the quiet suburban neighborhood. It had maroon shutters and several lawn gnomes.

"I guess they can't really have signs that advertise it. A hiding-in-plain-sight kind of thing. Like the contraband Grand steals from our old house."

"I don't see any cars," he said.

"Adrian said it emptied out around dinnertime. The madam only takes private appointments on some nights. The front is that it's a private therapist's in-home office. That way, the traffic coming and going isn't conspicuous. So, no nighttime appointments. Less risky. First task will be to break in. What did you bring?" I asked.

DC dumped out his backpack, and a menagerie of As Seen on TV products emptied onto the seat.

"Good gosh, I said bring weapons. What is all of this?"

"I'm not a mob princess like you. I don't have any weapons, so I improvised."

I lifted up the first thing that looked remotely weapon-like. "What does this do?"

"It's a cucumber cannon. It's supposed to be the ultimate in vegetable-slicing preparation. The first time we used it, we almost put a cucumber hole in the side of the kitchen. I thought it would be perfect for today. I even brought ammo," he said, pulling two cucumbers and a small frozen chicken from a grocery bag.

"What's with the chicken?"

"Electric turkey fryer. It'll set off a small explosion."

"That's a myth, you know. They don't really explode. But it will make a nice fireball."

We went through all of the other items. The Bun Builder was a U-shaped thigh squeezer we could use to squeeze someone's head. Vac storage bags, designed to shrink a whole wardrobe of sweaters down to the size of a tissue box, would hold a body if she was there. The Forearm Forklifts would help us move her. DC had also packed various other devices, from a gel massager to a dozen Insta Bulbs, and we'd figure out how to use them as we went.

We parked the car on the next block over and snuck through the alley toward the back of the kink house. Nothing looked familiar. The streetlight overhanging the grassy alley wasn't working, making it even more difficult to figure out where we were.

"We need some light," I said.

DC rummaged around in his bag and pulled out a stuffed penguin. With the click of a switch, the penguin began to illuminate brightly from its belly button.

"What happened to the Insta Bulbs?" I asked.

"You don't like my Flashlight Friend? I was afraid the Insta Bulb would be too hard to hold on to. Hang on. I have another idea." Rummaging around some more, he pulled out two baton-like objects. He peeled off a plastic backing and stuck them to his costume. With another click, his forearm and chest both lit up. Between the costume and the lights, DC looked like Lantern Man. "Stick and Clicks. You can keep the penguin."

"Okay," I said. "But if we think someone is coming, we can't forget to click you off."

We cut around a chain-link fence and crept up to the patio of a redbrick ranch. The house sat on a hill, causing the back of the house to be higher off the ground than the front had appeared. That made it difficult to look in windows to see if anyone was there. Still, it didn't look like any lights were on inside.

"You're sure this is the house?" I asked.

"I'm positive. I have an impeccable sense of direction."

I opened the screen door leading to the back door and tried the handle. Locked.

"How do you think we should try to get in? The windows all look too high."

DC went into his bag and took out what I first thought were drumsticks. He connected the sticks to create a good-sized rod. A metal pincher perched at the top of the rod. "Extendo Sticks."

I didn't think it had much chance of working, but DC went window to window, using the rod to push up on the window lips until he found an open one on the far side of the house.

"It opened! I did it!"

We fashioned a grappling hook out of the expandable pocket hose and a shake weight and tossed it through the opening. I gave it a tug. It felt solid, but I couldn't believe something so light was really going to hold our weight.

"It has a lifetime guarantee," DC said.

"That won't do us much good if we're in the hospital or, worse, jail because the thing broke."

We didn't have any other options, though, if we wanted to get a look inside the house. DC went first. He looked like a comic book character, his cape flapping in the wind as he scaled the wall of the house up to the window.

On my turn, I ripped my pantyhose on the brick but otherwise made it through the window uneventfully and fell on top of DC, who hadn't gotten off the floor.

"Why are you still on the floor? Do you hear someone?" I whispered.

"Uh. You could say that." He had clicked off his lights, so the room was dark.

A low growl came from the doorway. My heart stopped. There was a reason I had a pet pig.

"She didn't say anything about a damn dog. How come she didn't tell us?" he asked.

"Maybe she didn't know. Maybe it's new."

"We need the chicken."

"It's down in the bag still." The bag had been too heavy for either of us to carry up. Instead, I'd loaded my pockets with as much as I could carry, and we planned for one of us to go out and get it as soon as we cleared the first floor.

The growl grew louder.

I pulled the things I had grabbed out of my pockets and held them up. "I've got the cucumber shooter with one round of ammo and the tummy tucker. One of us can use the stretchy belly wrap of the tummy tucker to muzzle it while the other one covers with the cucumber shooter."

"I'm not muzzling no Cujo. I'm a cat person," DC said.

"Fine." I handed DC the cucumber Uzi, clicked on his lights, and opened the tummy tucker wide. Crouched close, we slowly crept toward the growl.

Until we came face-to-face with the cutest Chihuahua ever.

"I can't believe you were afraid of that," DC said.

The Chihuahua yipped.

"Shh. That's a good boy," DC said.

It didn't stop yipping.

"We have to get it to be quiet," I said. I looked around but didn't see any toys. Finally, I threw the penguin into the room. The Chihuahua pounced after it, and I closed the door.

"Our first casualty," DC said.

I aimed DC's forearm around the space and into the next room, which looked like a leftover from a salon. Beauty stations complete with reclining salon chairs, hair-washing bowls, and dryer domes filled the room. But they were all dusty and looked unused. Not exactly what I had expected of a sex dungeon. Boxes covered the floor.

"I thought this was supposed to be a therapist's office," I said, pulling out a wig.

"Maybe it's some kind of kink room for a weird makeover fetish," DC said.

We peeked around the corner and made sure the coast was clear. The rest of the house looked the same. We found more dusty beauty supplies. Through the darkness, I could just make out that chairs filled the main living room, which looked more like a waiting room.

A desk had an appointment pad on it. The file drawers were locked.

"Psst. This way." DC had found a door that led to the basement. "It has to be down here."

As we descended, black-and-white photos of naked women in various states of bondage lined the stairwell.

"I think we found it," he said.

The stairway opened up into a large main room complete with stripper pole and trapeze. A collection of paddles and whips had been arranged like an art installment above the fireplace. Several pairs of shackles hung from the ceiling above leather benches. Across the room were two doorways.

"This is like that Hannibal Lecter basement," DC said.

"It wasn't Lecter's basement. It belonged to the serial killer."

"Because being in a serial killer's basement is supposed to make me feel better."

"At least we haven't found a body yet."

"Yet."

A door slammed above us. DC swung his cucumber shooter toward the stairs. "Someone's here. We have to hide."

"In here." I grabbed DC's hand and pulled him through one of the doorways. It was a hallway that led to several rooms. Each door had a cute nameplate hanging from it. We passed the medical exam room, the shower room, and Daddy's bedroom. I pulled DC into the tickle room.

Inside, a purple crushed-velvet comforter covered an extra-large four-poster bed prominently displayed in the middle of the room. Shackles in the headboard protruded from the top of a bevy of luxurious pillows. An array of feather dusters lay on a bench at the foot of the bed. Several pairs of handcuffs covered a nearby nightstand.

"Holy *Fifty Shades of Grey*. What the hell were we thinking coming here?"

"You're a superhero. Stay calm. Master Tahkaswami would advise you to mentally prepare for a potentially difficult encounter by visualizing what success looks like."

"Success looks a lot like me eating at the White Castle and never seeing this freaky place again."

"Shhh. Someone's coming."

"How on earth did you get locked in that room? My poor brave baby." The voice sounded slightly high-pitched and somewhat familiar, but I couldn't place it.

The dog yipped.

"Oh no. What if he remembers our scent?" DC asked.

The voice said, "Everything seems fine. I only have a little work to do, and then I'll be there."

"There's more than one. We only have one weapon," DC said.

"We have the cuffs. I'll stand by the doorway, and when they come in, you shoot them with cucumbers, and I'll get them into cuffs." It sounded like a better plan in my head.

"I only hear one voice. They must be on the phone."

"I know you've had a long day. I promise to take good care of you when I get home," the voice said. Then came the cackle.

"Oh my gosh!" I said. "It's the mayor's wife."

"The mayor? Are you sure?" DC asked.

"I'd know that cackle anywhere."

Before I could decide what to do, the door flew open. Mrs. Scott stood in the doorway in a latex suit complete with a hood that cov-

ered her face. The suit squeaked when she moved. She looked like
Catwoman.

And she was pointing a gun at us.

Chapter 17

"Cool outfit," she said to DC. "Is that a cucumber shooter?"

"You'd be amazed what damage a high-velocity vegetable can inflict," he said.

"Cucumbers can be lots of fun." She winked at him, and his eyes got very big. "I suppose that puts us at a bit of an impasse, then, doesn't it," she said. "Although, I'd be willing to wager on my bullets over your cucumber."

"There are two of us. You probably couldn't get us both," I said.

Her apple-red talons wiggled around the gun's trigger. Her nails were so long she had trouble getting one through the opening. I was afraid she might accidentally shoot one of us.

I needed to make a quick decision. My stomach tightened. "Mrs. Scott, we only want to talk. I promise you, I have no interest in harming you or revealing your secret dungeon."

"I should have known you would figure it out. Such a clever girl. How do I know I can trust you?"

"Think about it. Outing you does nothing for me other than tie my family name to yet another scandal. Trust me. That is something my family is not in the market for."

She lowered the gun. "That makes sense, I suppose. All right. We can talk. But I'm keeping the gun. Richard knows where I am."

"He knows you run a sex dungeon?" DC asked.

"Of course, honey. He's a very bad boy." She let out a loud cackle.

We moved the conversation into the main room. "Hey, what's with all the salon stuff around here? I thought your cover was a therapist's office," DC said, sitting down in a stylist's chair in the corner.

"Damn bureaucrats. You'd think being married to the mayor would have some perks, but I guess not. The county passed an ordinance last year forbidding in-home salons, so we had to switch our cover to providing psychotherapy." Mrs. Scott sat on top of one of the cages. She peeled off her hood as if she were peeling a grape. Her gray hair shook free down her back. She crossed her legs and laid the gun in her lap.

"It's closer to the truth, anyway," I said, smiling and taking a seat on a spanking bench.

She laughed. "We did keep the name of the place the same, for branding and all." Her expression turned more serious. "What gave me away?"

"The short answer is your squeaky suit. We'll have to work up to the longer answer," I said.

"I told Richard I needed to get a new one. At least now he'll believe me. They're a bit expensive, and it's hard to write them off as a business expense." She winked at DC.

"I'm taken," DC said.

"Ooh, the more the merrier." She blew him a kiss.

I had never seen someone out-flame DC before. Under different circumstances, I'd have enjoyed the show.

"I'm sorry, but I can't think of a tactful way to ask this," I said.

"It's all right, dear. We're all friends here. For now, anyway."

"Did Gillian Mathers call you Joy?"

"Oh my, you have pieced together quite a lot, Katherine. The men in your life underestimate you. Present company excluded. Yes. Gillian knew me as Joy. She was helping me solve a sticky problem."

Sitting across from Mrs. Scott at lunch, I never would have guessed she was a professional dominatrix, let alone someone capable of murder. Even now, watching her try to flirt with DC, it seemed like a stretch.

"I can't tell you how awful I feel about what happened to her on account of me," she said.

"Then you didn't kill her?" DC sounded gleeful at the revelation.

"Heavens no, darling. Gillian was my friend by the end of things."

"She's a reporter. Wouldn't exposing the mayor's wife as the city's madam be a big scoop?"

"It would have been, if I hadn't had a bigger scoop for her."

"The murders."

"Yes, although by the time of her death, I think I had grown on her. I don't think she would have given me away."

"Do you know who did kill her?" I asked.

"Until a week ago, I was convinced the Russians had done it."

"Chentinko," I said.

"Yes, but now I'm not so sure."

"Because of the dead girl?" DC asked.

"Beauty and brains. Delicious." Mrs. Scott's face went serious, accentuating the wrinkles. Her near-constant, joyous persona had been better than any anti-aging cream on the market.

For the first time since I'd met her, she looked like the older lady she was.

"It's important to me that you understand that I didn't kill that girl either. I only disposed of the body."

"Maybe you should start from the beginning," I said.

"I've been running the dungeon for over fifteen years. I have a tacit agreement with all the organized crime families in the city that I'll stay out of their business if they stay out of mine."

"But someone forgot to tell Chentinko the rules?" I asked.

"He's naughty and not in the good way. To get a leg up the family corporate ladder, he started leaning on me for part of my take. Of course, I refused and threatened to have him taken care of. I have a diverse clientele." Her smile returned.

"Instead of backing off, that's when he started killing the girls?" I asked.

"Uh-huh. As you can imagine, I panicked. So did my clients. My business plummeted. I thought about just folding, but it seemed so unfair. For one, I'd miss it too much. But all those girls. I couldn't let him get away with it."

"And you can't exactly go to the police," I said.

"No. So I hit back where it counts. My girls and I set a trap to steal the records for his business. He keeps them on a laptop."

"You took the laptop?" I asked.

"We sure did. I told him if he didn't back off, intimate details of Russian Mafia operations would begin to leak to people he surely didn't want them leaked to and that I'd go out of my way to make sure everyone knew they had him to thank."

"Wicked," DC said.

"So how did Gillian Mathers get involved?" I asked.

"I didn't trust Chentinko any farther than I could throw him. I wanted him to pay for what had happened to my girls."

"You struck a deal with her. The laptop in exchange for her keeping your secret?" I rolled it around in my head, wondering if that laptop could be where Gillian had gotten the missile codes I found in Grand's scrapbook. Maybe that was where Burns's mysterious Covana could be found.

"Like I said, I don't think she'd have given me away, anyway, but I did entrust the laptop to her to help deal with Chentinko. When she ended up dead, I assumed Chentinko had figured it out and taken back what was his. The police never recovered the laptop. But then that girl who works for him broke in looking for it."

"The missing girl from the morgue? The one you dumped at the dumpster?" DC asked.

Her hand shook. "Yes. I came home and found her lying dead on the linoleum with a note pinned to her."

She walked over to a cabinet full of sex toys and rummaged around. She handed the note to me. I read it out loud.

Dearest Madame,

As your humblest servant, I leave you this gift. She said she was sent by that bad Russian man you are at war with and was looking for a laptop. I would never take such an action without your permission, but it was an accident. I surprised her, and we struggled for her gun. Her head hit the fireplace.

We all looked toward the fireplace.
"I swear I didn't kill her!" Mrs. Scott said.
I went back to the letter.

I knew you would know best what to do, so I have left her here for you. It was an accident, but I did it for you. I hope you are pleased.

Yours with devotion

"We believe you. Don't we, Kat?" DC asked while I contemplated the lack of a signature.
Maybe DC was starting to warm up to her.
"Yes. I think I do. But if you didn't do it, you must know who did. It has to be a client."
"Not really. I didn't have any scheduled appointments that night. So it could have been any of my customers. It's not exactly something I can go around asking. Besides, I'm sure it was an accident like the note says."
"So to keep your cover safe, you disposed of the body?" I asked.
"The hardest part was having to hit her in the face after she was dead. I thought if it looked like another one of my girls had been

killed, no one would pay any attention. This is really Chentinko's fault. He never should have sent that girl to do his bidding."

"So you think Chentinko stole the body from the morgue because he didn't want her tied to him."

"Probably," she said.

"Do you know why he would try to make the police think I was involved or if he has someone working at the morgue?"

"No. I was as surprised as you. Maybe he thought that given your father's troubles, if they were focused on you and your family, they wouldn't go looking anywhere else."

"Of course, the bigger question is, if you don't have the laptop and Chentinko doesn't have the laptop, where the hell is it?" DC asked.

"And who killed Gillian Mathers," I said.

Chapter 18

"We can't just go barging in there and scare all the madam's clients," I said to Flynn. We had added the latest information to the board and were trying to decide what our next move would be. Flynn wanted to interrogate all the dungeon clients.

"Besides, the note said it was an accident," DC added.

"Because murderers are such an honest lot," Flynn quipped.

"Mrs. Scott thought it was true, that Chentinko sent the girl to steal his missing laptop and ran into a client," I replied, my mind racing through all the connections on the board.

"So *if* that's true, does that mean Chentinko didn't kill Gillian?" Neutron asked.

"Mrs. Scott had assumed Chentinko somehow figured out she'd given the laptop to Gillian, but I don't know how he could have. Gillian hadn't done anything with it yet that would have tipped him off that she had it," I said.

"So Chentinko didn't kill the girl, and he didn't kill Gillian," Burns said and threw his cup into the trash with a little more force than necessary. "We're right back at square one."

"Not completely," I said. "We know who Joy is now, and we think we know she was killed for the laptop."

"Didn't you guys realize her laptop was missing?" DC asked.

"It wasn't hers, remember. Reid said hers was at the paper. Neutron didn't find much on it," Burns replied.

"We need to find that laptop, which will lead us to Gillian's killer," I said. "We could interview all the dungeon clients to see if one of them knows more about the girl, but I'm not sure that even if we found that person, it would give us much more information."

"And if Chentinko didn't kill Gillian, it means he probably isn't responsible for stealing her forensics from the morgue," Burns said, walking up to the pictures of the morgue suspects.

"So we're back to who at the morgue did, because they have to be connected to the laptop," I said.

"Time for you two lovebirds to put this plan in motion," DC said, sticking his head between us and clapping one hand on each of our shoulders.

I DIDN'T HAVE TO WAIT for someone to badge me into the morgue the next day because the door stood propped open. Sporting tattoos that matched Sam's, biker guys in construction hats passed by me as they carried wood into the morgue. Volunteers were everywhere. The makeover and party setup for tomorrow were in full swing.

"Get your foot off my nose, you moron!" Flynn clung to the rungs halfway up a ladder with one hand and had his other hand steadying Neutron. Neutron stood at the top, one foot partially in Flynn's face, as he stretched to reach a camera on the wall.

"Good morning." I waved up at them.

"Hi, Kat. The place is really starting to transform." Neutron bent and waved back at me.

"Keep your balance pointed to the ceiling!"

I spied Marshall out of the corner of my eye. "Keep up the good work. I'll catch up with you later."

Marshall carried a box out of the evidence room.

"Marshall! Just the man I wanted to see."

"Babe? What's wrong with you?"

"Nothing's wrong."

"You're not trying to weasel out of bowling tonight?" He set the box down. He breathed heavily, in desperate need of a breath mint, as he straightened back up. "You can't bail on me now." He clutched my arm, his face almost white.

"No, no. It's nothing like that. Quite the contrary. I'm looking forward to bowling tonight."

"You are?"

I wasn't, actually. Not the bowling part, anyway. But I needed Marshall's help. I linked arms with him and headed toward the employee lounge to put my stuff in my locker.

"Of course. Communal sport, cute shirts... what more could I ask for? That's what I wanted to talk to you about. I want you to bring Henry with you."

"Henry? No way. He can't be my date." Marshall threw up his arms and grabbed both sides of his pudgy head. "That would be a disaster."

"I'd still be your date. I promise. I just need you to get Henry to the bowling alley tonight." I opened my locker and noticed a nicely wrapped package. "Otherwise, if you can't get Henry there, I may not be able to come at all." It was time for some hardball. I was tired of being nice to him.

"You have to come. You made a deal!"

"I'm altering it slightly. If you want me there, you figure out a way to get Henry there too." I stroked his cheek with my finger. "I know you can do it, Marshall."

He nuzzled my hand. "Don't think a little attention is going to get me to cave."

I stroked his face again.

"All right. I can do that."

"Marshall, where's that damn box?" DC's voice came from the other room, and Marshall went to find him.

I took the pretty wrapped package from my locker and warily set it on the table. I couldn't find a card, so maybe it wasn't my Russian Secret Santa. I listened to the package, even though I wasn't sure it was possible to hear a bomb inside. I unwrapped the package and opened the box.

And let out a bloodcurdling scream.

Instantly the room filled with people. Burns rushed through the crowd to get to me. He looked at the dead rat sitting in the box. The pretty wrapping paper lay next to it. His hand went up my back, and he pulled me into a half hug. "There's a card." He reached into the box and grasped the card by its edges.

Cutout letters from a magazine had been glued to the plain card stock. Some were big and dark, some smaller but in vibrant colors. The message read, "I know what you're doing, and you'd better stop. Or ELSE!!!!!"

"Don't worry, Kat. That really is nothing," DC said as he came to my other side and pointed at the box. "You've probably got bigger rats than that in your apartment." He smiled big.

"We should get security," Meg said.

"That would not be advisable." Burns scanned the crowd, his arm still around me.

"Is that one of your 'complications' you told me about?" Meg asked. Her smile put me at ease.

Burns ignored her and signaled to Flynn to start moving people out of the room.

"All right, everyone back to work. Plenty to do today." Flynn directed the workers out into the hall.

Meg squeezed my hand before she left. It helped me shake off the awful feeling I had from the note and dead rat.

"What are we going to do with the rat?" DC asked. "And how are we going to find out who put it there? I can't start getting death threats. Kimi's barely speaking to me as it is."

"We should stick to the plan." I let out a breath and put down my arms. It was a good plan. We'd made someone nervous. "You'll get a good feel for the people today, and the big reveal DC and I cooked up will help smoke out whoever's behind this. Everyone needs to keep their eyes open. Someone will give themselves away. I'm sure of it."

"Stretch? There you are." Fletcher Reid glided in from the other room.

"I should have known you'd be close by when I saw the rat." Burns eyed him intently.

For a moment, Fletcher looked confused, then he peered into the box on the table. "You shouldn't be too surprised, Kat. Things do have a bad habit of turning up dead around Burns. You might want to share that with the cops." Fletcher ignored Burns and instead shot his electric smile toward me.

"I don't think so." Burns stepped slightly in front of me.

"Oh, that's right. You're above the law," Fletcher said.

"All right, I'm overloaded on testosterone now," DC said and furrowed his brow. "I have an auction to plan. Dr. Hawthorne's been twitchy about all the stuff in the evidence room since I started. I should go make sure he hasn't blown a gasket. I'll catch you later, Kat."

Despite the obvious tension of the situation, neither Burns nor Fletcher looked tense. Burns stood with his hands in his pockets, his usual intense but controlled look. Fletcher stood in the doorway, looking like he'd just strolled in off the beach, his casual air not fading even when Burns pushed his buttons.

Nonetheless, I had a full agenda for the day that didn't include male posturing. "Burns, would you mind terribly taking care of the rat? Fletcher and I will only be a minute."

"Which one?" Burns asked, smiling as he picked up the box by his fingertips.

"Cute," Fletcher said as Burns passed him.

I motioned Fletcher over to the couch in the small lounge area. By the end of the day, the torn secondhand monstrosity would be replaced with a sleek but comfortable new settee.

"When I requested the paper give us some coverage, I didn't think they'd send their ace reporter." I sank down into the ripped cushion.

"I asked for the assignment. Did you get my flowers?" Fletcher asked.

"Yes, they were very beautiful. Thank you. But they were also unnecessary."

"Flowers are pretty, not functional. They're never necessary." Fletcher looked as put together and casual as always. He wore a tan sweater-vest over a plain button-down and black slacks, giving off a sexy geek vibe. The dingy light from the overhead made his surfer mop look even more sun bleached.

"Don't get all logical on me. You know what I'm saying."

"I only understand you about half the time," Fletcher said. "But I'd like an opportunity to improve on that. You didn't answer my request for dinner."

"For a crack reporter, you sure are dense. Have you noticed what a shambles my life is currently in?"

"I'm aware." He didn't seem deterred by my protest.

"Aside from that, I could be dating someone."

"I don't think you are. Although I think you and Burns are considering your options."

I wondered how he could possibly know that.

"The average cost of a wedding in 2011 was twenty-seven thousand and twenty-one dollars, with West Virginia of all places being the least expensive state at fourteen thousand two hundred and three dollars, according to the top two internet wedding sites."

"Don't you wonder where the extra twenty-one dollars went?"

"What?"

"You said it was twenty-seven thousand and twenty-one dollars. What did the extra twenty-one dollars go to?"

"Why would I know that?" I shifted to get the pointy spring out of my butt.

"You seem to know pretty much every other useless fact."

I needed to change the subject from my love life. "Can I ask you a question?"

"Sure."

"What do you really know about my dad's arrest? Not the sensational stuff you run to sell papers but the real story?"

Fletcher squirmed into the lumpy couch. He tried to cross his legs but sank back instead. "Honestly, not much. Which, I would add, is strange."

"What do you mean?"

"None of my contacts at the feds knew anything about this. There was no months-long secret investigation or sting operation that led to your dad's arrest. It came out of the blue."

"So why all the mob talk?"

"Sells papers. Racketeering charges make it an easy target. But I can't find a single person who knows anything about what's going on. No one from a grand jury. No one in local law enforcement was in on it. That doesn't mean they aren't out there. If anything, it means it's a bigger case than we think."

"Does libel mean anything to you?" I asked. I could feel my blood starting to boil.

"I'm sorry. I know you and your father are close." Fletcher looked genuinely sorry. His arm was stretched over the back of the couch, and he reached toward me but stopped short of ruffling my hair. My man radar flashed red, and I moved away from him. He tried to change the topic and asked, "How's your grand?"

"If you're covering our big event tomorrow, you'll get to see her. She's running classes to teach people how to put together death scrapbooks."

"Of course." He laughed. "She clearly has skill. So are you going to tell me why someone's delivering dead rats to you?"

"Maybe someone doesn't like parties."

"Maybe someone doesn't like you and Burns snooping around."

"I can assure you, unequivocally, that Burns and I are not snooping together."

"I don't know if that's supposed to make me feel better or worse."

"Can I ask another question?"

"Maybe, if it gets me out of trouble."

I couldn't deny that Fletcher's charm had chiseled away at my staunch determination not to like him. "Actually, I need a favor. I need something run on the society page."

He looked puzzled.

"Don't worry. It's to help a friend, and it's something I'm sure you would approve of."

"Okay. I'll help you." Fletcher wiggled his way up off the couch. "In exchange for dinner." He stuck his hand out, offering to help me up.

Before I could answer, a loud chorus of voices sounded from the front of the morgue. I ran to the front and found a crowd of people. A paint roller on a large extension pole lay over Sam's shoulder.

The transformation of the morgue captivated me. "Wow, look at this!" Sleek desks with state-of-the-art computer equipment had been set up in the old administration area. A new wall with gray slate tile had been built to cordon off the new coffee bar area. The espresso machine shone in the light of Meg's beautiful lamps. I stood on a new engineered hardwood floor that would hold up way better under the demands of the morgue than the awful pee-colored carpet.

The walls had a fresh coat of a soothing moss-colored paint on them. "Sam, it's wonderful."

He beamed. "All that's left in here is to paint the accent walls." He twirled the paint pole. In addition to their matching leather and tattoos, Sam and his gang all wore matching tool belts.

"Pink. He wants to paint the morgue pink." DC's voice squeaked.

"It's not pink. You're blind. It's *rouge*." Sam took his pole and ran a stripe of paint down the back of the coffee bar wall, over Henry's head. He was right. It wasn't pink. And not red either. Somewhat like a salmon, but that didn't quite capture it. "Rouge" described the color perfectly.

"I like it," Meg said. "It's warm."

"But not too bright," Henry finished.

"And it matches the moss and gray perfectly," Meg added as Henry nodded.

For the next several hours, everyone worked diligently completing tasks for both the makeover and the celebration party tomorrow. Meg and Henry worked to mount the photo stories of the famous past "clients" for the autopsy walk down the hall that led to the autopsy room. Sam finished painting in the main area, and next, he and his crew tackled the employee lounge. DC and Marshall plowed through the evidence room leftovers, sorting, organizing, and pricing.

"Get away from that, Mr. Claiborne. That's not for sale," I heard Dr. Hawthorne yell from the room.

"What's going on in here?" I asked. The room looked like a yard sale had thrown up.

"Dr. Hawthorne doesn't want me to sell anything," DC said, pouting like an eight-year-old.

"It's a family-oriented open house. We can't sell that blow-up doll," Dr. Hawthorne insisted.

"He might have a point," I said.

DC looked as deflated as the doll.

"Do you really think anyone's going to buy all this junk?" I asked him.

"Oh, for sure. We're going to rake it. You only have to show up at an estate sale on a Sunday morning to know that people like dead people's stuff even more than church."

As I came out of the room, Dr. Jaffe grumped in behind them, carrying a paintbrush.

Burns was in peak form and worked the crowd like a pro, engaging people in conversations that would instantly make them comfortable. He hit Sam up for advice on his bike's carburetor. He got Henry talking about the upcoming World Cup soccer tournament. With Dr. Jaffe, it was horse racing.

He even managed to get Dr. Hawthorne to talk by mentioning how great the new equipment would be for the morgue and asking the doctor to tell him about it. For almost ten minutes, Dr. Hawthorne detailed all the new features of the spectrograph.

"For one, we'll be able to pass lab specimens back and forth electronically and not risk the issues we had with your poor friend Miss Mathers." Burns steeled himself and clenched his fist, clearly startled by Dr. Hawthorne's mention of Gillian. "Such an unfortunate accident."

"How'd you know we were friends?" Burns asked.

"The police told me when you started making a fuss. I don't blame you. I really felt awful about the whole thing. I'm sure the evidence is in the Pit somewhere. I haven't given up on finding it and bringing the perpetrator to justice."

"Okay, everyone. We're ready," Meg interrupted with a beaming smile. Henry stood next to her. "Follow me."

A group formed behind her as if she were a tour guide. The display looked like something I would have curated at the museum.

Gorgeous handcrafted frames captured the portrait of each famous St. Louisan engaged in the vocation that made them famous. Underneath each portrait was their story.

"Meg and I will lead the guests through the hall, pointing out facts about each mystery that surrounded the autopsy of the famous person," Henry said.

It was the first time I'd heard Henry say more than five words at a time. He stood tall. They walked us through the hallway, perfectly in sync as they told the story of each person. Finally, we made it to the autopsy room.

"At the end, we'll hand it over to Dr. Jaffe," Henry said.

"And I'll take each guest through the ins and outs of how we perform an autopsy."

"Keeping the graphic details to a minimum," Dr. Hawthorne added.

Although the main autopsy room hadn't been that transformed, even the minor touches had made a big difference. New X-ray viewers from this decade lined the walls. Burns's team had installed security devices at the sexavator to prevent another body snatching. They would also leave the Big Maxes of the world without a place for tonsil hockey.

"And when they're done, I'll take over." DC stood next to a large curtain in the area of the mobile gurney and floor scale. "I'll tell our guests about the latest mystery we're trying to solve."

He ripped back the curtain to reveal a gurney bearing a life-sized model of Joy—in cake. A perfect replica of her face was airbrushed onto the peach icing. A gasp came from the crowd.

Burns glanced at me as Dr. Jaffe knocked against the autopsy table.

"While I applaud the detail, Mr. Claiborne, do you really think people are going to want to eat parts from a dead body?" Dr. Hawthorne asked. He smiled down at her. "Stunning detail, really."

"I think it's totally cool. Plus, someone might recognize her. Right, Henry?" Meg asked.

"And the cake is delicious," DC said. "No one turns down cake."

As the buzz of conversation moved through the room, one voice was notably missing. Sam Allen Winston had completely vanished.

Chapter 19

Midwesterners had a long and strong love affair with bowling. We were the home of Brunswick, Dick Weber, and the Pro Bowlers Association. We loved for our pizza and beer to come with rental shoes and ten-pound balls. We wore with pride our weird-colored shirts with our names above the pocket and corny names on the back. That was, unless the shirt came from Marshall.

"I'm not wearing that, Marshall."

He held up a pink V-neck shirt that plunged practically to the navel and was trimmed with dark-pink fake feathers coated with silver glitter. On the back was the team name "Uncle Marshall and the Pimpettes."

"Babe, you have to do this for me."

"You're lucky I showed up." I spied Henry sitting in the corner. I'd really come to support Meg, but Marshall didn't need to know that.

"You owed me."

"I don't owe you that."

"Surprised you showed up, Dickwad." A voice came from behind us.

At the top of the stairs that led to the lanes stood a man who looked like a 1950s throwback. It was hard to believe he had gone to high school with Marshall. He wore tweed pants and a light-blue bowling shirt with the name Pete above the pocket. Diamond-shaped black patches ran down the sides of the shirt. His slicked-back hair contained so much oil that I feared I might get some on me if I got too close. His biscuit-toed black-and-white wing tips completed the outfit and made him look like he'd stepped off the set of *Grease*.

"Hey, watch your mouth in front of the ladies. Didn't your ma teach you any manners?" Marshall asked.

Pete looked left then right.

"What ladies? My girl's not here yet, and you don't have one, so... Oh, look"—he pointed at Henry—"I guess you did bring a date." He let out a smarmy chorus of "He, he, he," which I guessed was meant to be a laugh.

"Of course Uncle Marshall has a babe," he said, taking my hand and pleading with me with his eyes and mouth, begging.

For the first time ever, I felt sorry for him. Someone on this planet was more of a creep than Marshall. "All right, but we're square after this. And if I'm doing this all night, I want wine." I took the shirt and headed to the bathroom to change.

"Take your time in the bathroom, honey." He turned to Pete and pointed at me. "My date. My babe, right there."

The only thing more of a trip than Pete was his partner, Carla, whose throwback look rivaled his. She had a bright-red bouffant hairdo sporting a thick neon-blue, polka-dotted Minnie Mouse bow. A baby-blue button-down cardigan overlaid her bowling shirt and perfectly matched her poodle skirt. Even her ankle socks screamed 1950. Pete and Carla had appropriately named their team the "Rock-and-Bowlers." She obnoxiously popped her bubblegum.

"What are those?" Marshall asked when I took out the lovely red, white, and blue wedge bowling boots that Meg had loaned me.

"You don't really think I'm putting my feet into rented shoes, do you?"

"Who knew they actually made those?"

"If this were going to become a regular thing, I'd have to figure out how to get my hands on a pair of bowling heels I saw online. But Meg's knee-highs will do the job for tonight." Between the low-cut shirt, the feathers, and the knee-high leather boots, I had a bowling hooker look going. At least it was all for a good cause. Meg would be here soon.

Like most kids in my neighborhood, I'd grown up spending my Saturday mornings in a junior bowling league. While I wasn't a horrible bowler, I wasn't going to be hitting the pro tour either. At least I wouldn't embarrass myself with my bowling. The outfit took care of that. I looked like a reject from a strip club, and when I threw the ball, I had to be careful that my boobs didn't fall out.

The neckline of Marshall's shirt proved to be a plus. Every time Pete got up, I stood in his peripheral vision, shook my girls a little, and he'd blow the shot. We were up twenty-two pins. The bigger problem with the shirt was that the feathers made me sneeze.

After two games, Meg finally appeared. That was what I had been waiting for. It was time to get to the bottom of things with Henry once and for all.

"You'll have to take over for me, Marshall. I have some business to take care of."

"Babe, you can't abandon me now."

"Trust me, what is about to occur is bound to screw up Pete for at least another round."

Meg approached, seeming nervous despite how amazing she looked. Her dress was a sexy one-piece red-and-black corset that flared to a lace mini with a fluffy tulle petticoat. A big black bow accentuated her cleavage, and she wore matching bows at the top of her thigh-high stockings. She'd accessorized perfectly with a mini top hat that sported a half-sized black veil and fire-red spiked Mary Jane heels.

"You look terrific. Are you ready?"

"I think so. I practiced with Sasha and the other ladies from Roxy's all day." She pulled a black feather boa out of her bag.

"If this doesn't get you out of the friend zone, I don't know what will." I took her hand as both a gesture of support and to keep her from falling in her heels.

"Henry Braxton?" she asked as we approached Henry.

Thankfully, we had been given the end lane, and Henry had found the cornermost chair in back of the spectator seating. For a bowling alley, it had a surprising amount of privacy.

"Yes?" His voice cracked. He eyed Meg with big puppy-dog eyes and bit down on the small stir straws that had come with his drink.

Meg set a portable speaker on the table and clicked a button on her phone. "Timber" began to play. "Welcome to your night of confessions." She wrapped the boa around Henry's neck and put one heel up on his armrest.

"You see, Henry," I said as Meg began a sultry shimmy to the beat, "I know Meg would be perfect for you."

She pulled the boa across his neck. The beat thumped.

"Perfect for me?" Henry swallowed hard.

"Yes, as your girlfriend," I said.

"Would you like that, Henry?" She kicked her leg over his head and brought it down next to him with a stomp then reached down for her toes in a classic dip and swish. "Tell me I'm not the only one who feels this way." She stopped dancing, her face inches from his, and looked Henry in the eyes.

Henry sat quietly in his chair, his eyes downcast.

"It's time for some honesty, Henry," I said. "By tomorrow at this time, our Meg will be a rich and famous lighting designer, the talk of the society page, with lots of romantic options. Now, Meg's got it bad for you, so if you're truly not interested, it's best to let her know so she can find a man who deserves someone as great as her."

Henry looked up at Meg.

"I think you do like Meg, but something's holding you back."

"Wha... what?" was all Henry could manage.

"The money, Henry. I know you've been taking money from Wiggins," I said.

Meg flipped the boa around his neck and straddled him in his chair. "Look me in the eye"—she lifted his chin from her chest—"and tell me where the money goes."

Henry sat frozen.

"Are you in some kind of trouble? Because I can help you if you are." She pulled back from him, standing up to give them some space, taking his hand in hers. "It's true that I'm attracted to you, but first and foremost, you're my best friend."

"I am?"

"Of course you are. I would never want to jeopardize that, and whatever trouble you're in, we can solve it, together."

"I saw you with that woman," I said. "She put her scarf around your neck. You said you were taking care of things."

"It's not what you think. I'm not involved with that woman." Henry dropped his head into his hands, pulling away from Meg. "I'm marrying her sister," he groaned as he looked at the floor.

"What?" Meg and I exclaimed at the same time.

She pushed his head up, forcing him to look at her.

"But I don't want to! I swear, Meg."

"Okay, start talking," she said.

Henry took a deep breath and looked at Meg then me, then back at Meg before he let it go and said, "It's my mother. She's in trouble. That woman Kat saw me with is Ariel Rodriguez, and she's a horrible person. A few months ago, she caught my mother shoplifting in her store. But instead of calling the cops, she followed my mother to another store and watched her steal there too. Apparently my mother's been shoplifting her way through half the city."

"Over ten million people have been busted for shoplifting in the last five years, most of them grown adults, not kids," I said. Maybe if Henry knew his mother wasn't alone, he wouldn't feel so bad.

"But she didn't turn her in to the cops. Instead, she followed my mother home one night and met me, and that's when it all went downhill."

"She's blackmailing you," Meg said.

"Yes, but the money is only part of it. Her father won't let her get married or take over the family business until her sister is settled here and they're both financially secure. Her sister is in Spain, and Ariel said if I don't agree to marry her sister and bring her to America, she'll have my mother locked up."

"She can't do that!" Meg said, a determined look coming over her face. "We're going to fix this. I promise."

"You really think we can?" he asked, looking up at her.

"Oh, Henry Bear, of course we can." She ran her fingers through his hair, and he blushed.

I took that as my cue to leave. I was glad to cross Henry off the suspect list. He and Meg really were a perfect couple. I headed to the concession counter. All that heat and suspense had left me thirsty. Plus, DC had been buzzing my phone with texts for the last five minutes.

"Nice shirt. Love the boots." Detective Lambert sidled up next to me at the counter. Her steel-gray bowling shirt had a picture of crossed pistols over the pocket and "10 Pin Enforcers" in sharp black letters on the back. The color matched her dark bob perfectly.

"Detective. I didn't expect to see you here."

"We're in the league semis against the DA's Convicted Strikers. But I've been hoping I'd run into you."

"You were? How'd you know I'd even be here?"

"Your bowling partner isn't exactly discreet. Do you have a minute? I have something to show you."

I followed her to a small set of lockers away from the lanes. She took out a file folder and led me to a set of chairs where eager bowlers busily swapped out their street shoes. From the file folder, the detective produced a picture of a beautiful woman.

"Meet Stephanie Jackson."

I recognized her instantly. "My missing Jane Doe."

"You were right. Her father is an oil baron from Scarsdale. Apparently she's had some rebellion issues of late. She was last seen in Las Vegas about two weeks ago. Anything you want to share about why a debutante from Scarsdale might have ended up dead and her body stolen from a St. Louis morgue?"

DC buzzed again.

"Excuse me a moment, Detective." Replying to DC would buy me some time to figure out what to say to her. I pulled out my phone.

I froze at the message.

"GET HELP, they're going to kill me!"

Chapter 20

I made a graceful exit from Detective Lambert, promising I'd call her if I stumbled over anything else. I wasn't sure she believed me or even how graceful I had been. DC's text spun me into full panic.

"You're okay to talk?" I asked him.

"Yes," he whispered. "I'm in a storage compartment on a Russian boat."

"How on earth did you get there?"

"I followed Sam. I found him in the parking lot after the cake reveal, arguing on his phone about getting the package delivered and how they'd all be dead."

"The girl. Or maybe the laptop?"

"Right, that's what I thought. I still had my superhero costume in the car, so I figured I'd follow him. He stopped and picked up a set of knives."

"Maybe they're going to chop her up?"

"That's what I thought. So I kept following him."

"Did you find the laptop or the girl?"

"What I found was a Russian Mafia poker game. Winston has totally disappeared. He must be driving the boat or something. Although, I could swear I hear his voice every so often."

"Boat? Where are you?"

"In Lake St. Louis. The *Murmansk*. It's in the far boat slip at Lake Center. I don't hear the engine yet. I think we're still in dock."

"How did you even get into the marina?" The Lake St. Louis Marina required membership and a key card.

"I convinced some dude I was Nelly. He has a boat here. It's been in all the papers. I told him I had lost my key card on stage at my last concert."

"Good thinking."

"Now *you* need to do some good thinking. How the hell am I going to get out of here? What if we take off? I'm going to be shark bait."

"Why'd you follow him on board to start with?"

"I wasn't going to, but I tripped on my cape, and he almost saw me. I had to duck into the boat to keep him from discovering me. Then all these other Russians showed up. So I found a place to hide."

"You said they're playing poker?"

"Yeah, about six of them, maybe more."

"I have an idea. Stay put. I'll be right there."

"Where do you think I'm going?"

I clicked off with DC and made two calls, one to Burns and another to Sasha. I drove to the marina and waited for everyone to arrive.

The McPhee Security SUV pulled in first. Flynn, Neutron, and Burns filed out.

"Start unloading," Burns said. He eyed me. "Nice outfit." He flipped a finger at one of my feathers. I had been so worried about DC, I hadn't taken time to change. Plus, with my plan, the getup might come in handy.

Flynn dropped a trunk onto the ground. When he opened the lid, I could see that it was full of weapons.

"What are those for?" I asked.

"Not too bright for Harvard," Flynn said.

"You can't go shooting up a place with a bunch of Russians. For one, it will be a bloodbath. Not to mention, I don't plan on spending any more time in a police station."

"We weren't planning on sticking around to answer questions," Burns said.

Even though I knew I was right, I found it difficult to resist Burns's command-and-control mode. Lean muscle bulged out of his olive T-shirt, which blended perfectly with his dark olive skin. He had on camo cargo pants and black Army boots. The only thing missing were the dog tags, but he didn't need them for anyone to know he was standard issue Special Forces.

"Even if you don't get DC killed, you'll blow any chance we have of getting to the bottom of things with Sam Winston. Do you want to figure this out or not? You can't always go all storm trooper. Sometimes things require a little finesse."

"What do you think we should do, then? It's not like we can just march in there and get him, Miss Priss," Flynn said.

"Oh yes, we can. I have a plan."

As if on cue, Sasha pulled in next to us, and another car pulled in behind her. The Roxy's girls filed out, all looking the part I needed them to play. Sheila emerged, outfitted in full Tina Turner. A pistol holster peeked out from under her sequins.

"If I'd known we'd be working with military hunks, I'd have worn my red, white, and blue tassels," Jen said. She squeezed Flynn's bicep. His face turned beet red.

"All I need you to do is get us through the gate," I said to Burns. "And provide backup, of course, in case something goes wrong."

"The gate's no problem, Boss." Neutron carried several electronic devices over to the gate's keypad.

"Only you could come up with a plan like this," Burns said. "These guys aren't going to be terribly welcoming to party crashers, ya know."

"You leave that to us, sugar." A tall brunette named Carmen, who had on nothing but an emerald-green bikini and white leather stiletto-heeled boots, ran a finger under Burns's chin. "Play's our special-ty."

"When was the last time you heard from DC?" Burns asked.

"He texted me a few minutes ago. Thankfully, they haven't left dock. The game's going strong, and he's still safe in the closet."

"What if Winston recognizes you?" Neutron asked.

"Oh, we're going to take care of that, sweetie. Won't no one recognize her when we're finished," said a short blonde in a poofy *Alice In Wonderland* outfit.

"How are you going to get him out?" Flynn asked.

"That's where I come in," Sheila said. She pulled out a short evening gown.

"DC has great facial features. They won't even realize he's a guy," I said.

"What if things get rough?" Burns asked.

"Sasha's got that one," I said.

"A few drops of this into their drinks"—she held up a vial—"and they'll be out like lights before we finish with the first dance."

"And we've always got you." I patted his chest.

He stuck his hands in his pockets and went quiet. His eyes went smoky. Calculating. "You know how to use that thing?" He pointed at Sheila's gun.

"Yes, sir. Two tours in Iraq," Sheila answered.

He took my arm in his hands and squared so our eyes met. "All right. But you're going in wired, and I want to know what's going on every step."

"Sugar, you can be in any place of mine you want," Carmen said.

"If I get even a twitch that things are off plan, we're coming in."

"Of course." I stretched up on my tiptoes and kissed his cheek.

Jen and Sasha took over, preparing me. Before I knew it, the golden locks of a long, curly-haired wig flowed down my back. They had squeezed me into a tight sailor's halter that tied under my boobs.

A fake crystal was glued to the side of my belly button just above my matching blue sailor's skirt. I tugged on red platform boots. If Mom thought the morgue was bad, she should see me now. At least if we made the papers, no one would recognize me.

"Sailor Moon got an older crime-fighting sister," Neutron said when I emerged. "Not even Winston will be able to tell it's you."

"I like this even more than the feathers." A big, wide smile filled Burns's face. It was the first time he'd smiled since getting out of the SUV. In fact, it was one of the first times I'd seen that much pleasure in him since we'd met. It suited him. He came close and tugged on the bow in front of my cleavage.

"You can't look at me like that," I whispered. "I'll never get through this."

"It's not exactly easy on this side," he said.

Neutron wired Sheila and me. We were the only ones wearing enough clothing to disguise the wiring. He did his techie ninja thing and popped the gate. Like a bad car caravan, we headed to where DC had said the *Murmansk* was supposed to be. We found his Lincoln parked in the adjacent lot.

"I think I'm getting seasick. Hurry," DC's text read.

The *Murmansk* was a beast. More like a mini yacht and probably the largest boat on the lake. The shiny white hull stood in contrast to the dark-tinted windows. A few lights illuminated the deck.

We all climbed aboard. A husky guard stood in front of the door that led below deck.

"Let me do the talking," Sasha said.

When he saw us, the guard came to attention.

"Hey there, sweetheart," Sasha said. "Is this the poker game?"

"Who are you?" he asked in a thick Russian accent. He looked nervous, shifting his weight, but he hadn't pulled a gun.

I took that as a good sign.

"What's happening?" Burns asked into my ear.

I ignored him.

"This has to be the place." Carmen draped herself around the guard. "None of the other boats here look like they can afford us."

"You can't be here," he said. He didn't swat Carmen away, though.

"Look, we're already bought and paid for. I can't go back and tell my boss we didn't deliver," Sasha said.

"Don't you want to have a good time, baby?" Carmen pulled the guard around the corner.

"We're in," I said into the mic.

The luxury of the yacht didn't stop at the door. It looked like the entire inside had been custom designed. The black-and-white theme continued throughout, with white leather and Carrara marble everywhere. The men sat in the middle of the hull at a gorgeous black Armani custom table. Cards, chips, and drinks covered it.

"What is this?" one of the men asked as we poured into the cabin.

"Which one of you is Vlad?" Sasha asked. DC had texted me the name he had overheard. "I have a special birthday message just for Vlad."

For a moment, all the men at the table froze. Then, as if in slow motion, they looked at each other and then at us. I held my breath.

Finally, a distinguished-looking man in a gray suit stood up. He pointed at the other men around the table. Then he smiled big. "Which one of you did this? My comrades love me," he told Sasha. The dancers didn't wait for anyone to change their mind. They engulfed the other Russians. Music quickly blared in the cabin.

With the Russians well occupied, Sheila and I frantically looked for DC. Once we had him safe, I could look for Sam—and Stephanie's body.

"You've come to float my boat." A short Russian with a mustache grabbed my skirt.

I jumped at the touch and squealed when he pinched me. "Did you know the Egyptians created the first navy in 2300 BC?" I asked.

He looked at me strangely.

"Sweetie?" I added tentatively. "Sorry, I need a... pit stop. Can't hold my liquor."

"Did someone put their hands on you?" Burns asked.

It didn't bother me that it bothered him. "Relax. It's handled."

"Psst. Over here." DC's head popped out from in between the white leather cushions.

"Quick, put this on." Sheila pulled out the sparkly gown.

"I am not wearing that," DC said.

"Oh no." I spied Sam Winston emerging from a small room off the main cabin.

"What? What's wrong?" Burns asked.

"It's Sam." He wore a white chef's jacket and hat.

He wasn't working with them. He was cooking for them. "If you want to get out of here in one piece, put on the damn dress." I shoved the dress into DC's face.

"No need to get persnickety." He disappeared into the cushions.

Sam looked around nervously. He pushed away one of the girls. I saw Sasha dosing the drinks and knew it wouldn't be long before Russians started dropping.

"A toast," she said, raising the bottle after filling all the glasses. "What happens on the high seas stays on the high seas."

Sam didn't have a glass. He would be the last man standing if we couldn't get a drink in his hand.

DC popped out of the couch, wearing the dress.

"You look beautiful," Sheila said.

"I look like a fool. Get me out of here."

Sheila and I formed a semicircle around him and scooted toward the door.

Sam stalked the room. He obviously knew something wasn't right, and he wasn't letting it go.

"We're halfway there," I said as much to Burns as DC.

A body dropped in front of me. Then another. When the third guy fell, the rest of them appeared to become alarmed.

"What is going..." Vlad hit the floor next, quickly followed by the last two.

"Everyone freeze or the girl gets it." Sam had Sasha with a gun to her head.

Sheila freaked, pulled the stashed gun from her holster, and pointed it at Sam. "Let her go!"

The other strippers hit the floor.

"We're coming, Kat. Hold on," Burns said into my ear.

"Everyone needs to take a deep cleansing breath," I said.

"Someone needs to tell me what is going on here, or she and I are going to take a ride."

I pulled off my wig. "Sam, we aren't here to hurt anyone."

"Kat? What the... DC? Is that you?"

"Yes, but if you tell anyone I'm wearing this dress, I'll let Sheila shoot you."

Burns and Flynn appeared in the doorway, guns drawn.

"Let Sasha go, Sam. We're just here to talk, I swear," I said.

Sam lowered his gun. Sasha ran to Sheila. Flynn helped Sheila get the rest of the strippers off the boat, leaving Burns, DC, and me alone with Sam.

"Someone want to tell me what you're doing here?" Sam asked.

"We wanted to ask you the same thing," DC said.

"I'm working."

"For the Russian Mafia," Burns said.

"It's not illegal to like good cooking."

"But it is illegal to chop up a dead body," I said.

"Dead body?" He looked surprised.

"The missing morgue girl. The Russians took her. When you saw her picture today, you freaked," DC said.

"These Russians didn't do anything. They're into vodka and food. This was my tryout for their new restaurant."

"Tryout?" I asked.

"I work at the morgue to pay for my culinary classes. I'm graduating."

"Still, when you saw the picture of Stephanie, the missing dead body, you disappeared," I said.

"Stephanie?" Burns turned his attention to me.

"You're right about the Russians. You just have the wrong ones. You want Chentinko."

I was happy Sam had started talking again. It gave me something to focus on besides Burns's relentless glare.

"I saw him meeting with that woman right before she turned up dead," Sam said. "I didn't want to get involved. It's not my job to go poking my nose in other people's troubles. Especially people I work with."

"People you work with?" I asked.

"They were having a heated conversation with Dr. Jaffe."

Chapter 21

"We should go see Jaffe," I said. DC and I stood in the parking lot of the marina with Burns and his crew.

Sheila had made sure all the ladies made it back to Roxy's. We had left Sam working on making it look like the boat had succumbed to the hottest party ever. He would insist that he couldn't believe the Russians didn't remember what had happened—a handy side effect of Sasha's drug—and remind them that they did have an awful lot to drink. Along with reminding them of their other epic antics that he was now constructing. That should have been enough to get him out of trouble.

"We can't just barge in on the Russians," Flynn said.

"No one's barging, and we need to stay away from Chentinko until we know more. Jaffe knows something about Stephanie Jackson. And he didn't kill her. He didn't kill anyone."

Burns stood by the SUV, his hands in his pockets. I figured there was no point in wasting the outfit. I moved closer and ran my hands up his chest.

"I'm not feeling comfortable having this discussion while looking like a reject from a Sailor Moon cartoon. Why doesn't Flynn drive my car back to the McPhee garage, and I'll ride with you and explain everything."

"Good idea. These sequins are causing me to chafe," DC said. He pulled at the hemline of my gown.

On the way to McPhee's, I told Burns how I'd found out about Stephanie Jackson and my theory on Jaffe's connection to her. He didn't show any emotion. He didn't ask any questions. Instead, he listened and, apparently, stewed.

"Jaffe might know something that could help us. Really, unless you're ready to storm Chentinko, it's our only play." I brushed my fingers through his floppy hair. Our eyes locked. His heart beat faster under my hand, but he didn't move a muscle.

"Uh, Boss." Neutron's voice cracked. "I got him. Jaffe's at a nursing home."

"HOT DAMN!" GRAND SAID. "If I'm going investigating, I'm going to have to change. You should change too." She tugged on my bow. "In that place, an outfit like that could cause a medical event with one of the residents."

If we were going to get to Jaffe at a nursing home, we needed backup. Nursing homes didn't let just anyone near their old people. Burns wanted to argue, but after managing Grand these last six months, I'd earned a PhD in geriatric supervision.

"I'll have to find something to go with my hardcore Sherlock hat," Grand said.

Through some miracle of the gods, Grand had found a Sherlock Holmes detective kit at the thrift store when she and Mom had bought china for the lunch with Mrs. Scott. The kit included a brown gingham deerstalker cap, the kind that had a bill on each side. Master Tahkaswami would remind me there was no such thing as cosmic coincidence.

"It's brown. No one looks good in brown," I said. "Use it as an accent and combine it with a blue or a green."

"Green makes me look like an elf," Grand said.

Considering everything we knew about Jaffe, I figured confronting him would be relatively low-risk. He had come unglued at both my mention of him being involved with Stephanie's disappearance and at seeing her likeness on the cake. Maybe he was nervous enough to give up Chentinko in exchange for a way out of the mess he was tangled up in.

Besides, our only other play would be to confront Chentinko. If we were going to do that, the more we armed ourselves with information, the better.

JAFFE WAS AT THE NURSING home, visiting his grandmother. According to Neutron, it was a ritual he undertook every Friday. I knew I needed to look upscale if we were going to convince the tour guide at the home that we were serious about placing Grand there. That would be our cover, which meant I had put back on a power suit and accessorized with pearls.

"Does this thing come with a stepladder?" Grand asked. She tried to jump up into the seat of the McPhee SUV. "Damn newfangled vehicles," she said as Burns boosted her in.

"I like your cape," Grand said, scooting in next to DC. He had switched into his superhero costume in case we ran into Chentinko—or things with Jaffe went sideways.

"I like your hat," he replied.

"It's infusing me with the skills of a great detective." She clutched her matching brown bag, which she'd filled with the rest of the Sherlock detective kit. "You'll get wrinkles if you keep your face that way," Grand said, sizing up Burns once we were rolling and I had made the introductions. "I like the other one better," she told me.

"What other one?" Burns asked.

"The surfer-stud reporter who's got the hots for us," she said. "This one's broody."

"Reid's a hack," he said.

I smiled. Grand hadn't known Burns five minutes and had somehow managed to poke him with the one thing guaranteed to irritate him.

We pulled into the parking lot of Arbor Retreat Retirement Village. The home was a high-end monstrosity, much like the one Grand had been in. A circular driveway mirrored the semicircular configuration of the home. A lobby with a three-story arched atrium more appropriate for a luxury hotel was the centerpiece, with the residential units symmetrically spanning out from it.

"Showtime," I told Grand. "Remember, Burns and I are your grandchildren, looking to help you find bliss in your twilight years. Jaffe's grandmother is on the fourth floor, so we'll have to figure out a way to get up there." Ambrosia Rutledge lived in room 415.

"I think I'm having PTSD flashbacks," Grand said as we approached the entry.

"Comm check," Burns said into his mic.

"Hey, Burns. Isn't this terrific?" DC replied.

"Sorry, Boss," Neutron said.

We'd left Flynn to fit the rest of us in the SUV. That meant DC was playing backup.

"I feel the power," DC said.

"Well, helllloo there." A redhead wearing too much makeup poked her head up from the reception desk. Her voice was two octaves higher than a normal person's.

To the side of the reception area was a common room. Several residents were hanging out, but there was no sign of Jaffe.

"Hi there, gorgeous." An extremely wrinkled man with oxygen tubing protruding from his nose wheeled up to us. Two tanks were mounted on the back of his chair.

"Back off, Casanova. I'm spoken for," Grand said.

"Me too," the man said. "Want to be naughty?" He winked.

"George, what are the rules?" The redhead moved from around the counter and stepped between Grand and George. She was only slightly taller than Grand. She wore a navy suit and clutched a folder.

"Gold digger," George said to the redhead. "She just wants your money, sexy. I'm all about the giving. Come see me." He winked at Grand then rolled back into the common room.

"It's okay, honey. I'm used to it. I'm a magnet," Grand told the redhead.

"Yes, well, I'm sure you would make fast friends if you took up residence here at Heaven's Gate. And who have you brought with you to help you make this important decision?"

"What, you don't think I can make decisions on my own?"

"Hi, I'm Vicki," I said, offering my hand. "And this is my husband, B... B..." I needed a fake name.

"Barkley," Grand said. "And they say I'm the one on the decline. Let's get this show on the road." Grand shuffled forward.

Burns twitched his neck.

"Yes, well, a pleasure to meet you. My name is Margret, and I'll be your guide today." She began her practiced script.

We'd completed the tour of the dining room, rec room, chapel, garden, exercise complex, and treatment rooms and still hadn't seen any sign of Jaffe.

"Chickie, if I'm going to live here, I have to see a room on the fourth floor." Grand laid it out.

"I'm sorry. That's a residential floor. We don't open that for tours."

"I'm afraid my grandmother is very particular," I said.

"The fourth floor is my Frank's and my lucky floor," Grand said.

"I see. I would love to accommodate you, but I'm sure you understand that we have our rules."

"Look, honey, what I understand is that we're about to drop enough money on this place to support a small Guatemalan village.

If I want to see a room on the fourth floor, I'm sure a bright woman like you will figure it out."

Margret blinked her fake eyelashes so fast I thought one of them might fly off and injure us. "Yes, well. Let me get some keys." Margret disappeared back to the reception area.

"Dang. Your granny is a force," DC said.

"Follow me," Margret said. "Like the main floor, each of our residential floors has its own reading room."

"Here, stop here. I think I'm having a spell." Grand had stopped in front of 415.

"Oh my, should I call for a doctor?" Margret went white.

"Grandmother, are you all right?" I asked.

Burns pretended to steady her.

"Water. I need a glass of water."

"I think you'd better get a nurse," I told Margret.

She turned and walked down the hall. Once I was sure she was out of earshot, I knocked on the door.

A stunned look came over Jaffe's face when he opened it. "Waters, what on earth are you doing here?"

"I don't have much time. You can either let us in, or I can explain to the police that you were the last person seen with Stephanie Jackson before she was murdered."

Jaffe's face went white. He quickly opened the door, and the three of us filed in.

"DC, you're on," Burns said into the mic. DC was being dispatched to keep Margret busy.

"Jeffery, who are these people?" A matronly-looking woman in a nightgown sat at the small table in the room.

"You must be Ambrosia. I'm Theodora Waters. Didn't you go to Smith?" Grand sat down next to Dr. Jaffe's grandmother and quickly had her occupied with photos.

Dr. Jaffe began to hyperventilate. He sat on the couch in the small adjacent living room and put his head between his knees while he sucked on an inhaler. "I didn't kill her, I swear."

"How do you know her, and how are you involved with Chentinko?" Burns asked.

"I owe him money. A lot of money. He told me I could either do this job for him, or he'd take one of my hands. I'm a surgeon. I can't lose a hand."

"So how does Stephanie Jackson get involved?" I asked.

"I don't know anything about breaking into houses. That was the job. I was supposed to break into this sex dungeon and steal some laptop. I'd met Stephanie on my last trip to Vegas. We were kind of an item, and she was looking for a thrill. Oh my God, and now she's dead."

He rocked back and forth on the couch and began to cry.

"Keep it together, Dr. Jaffe. How did you know she had been killed?" Burns asked.

"I was the lookout. No one was supposed to be in the house. When Stephanie didn't come out right away, I got nervous, and then I saw that woman in that suit, lugging a giant garbage bag."

"So you called Chentinko?" I asked.

"Yes. If the cops found out who she was, they'd link it to me. Chentinko wasn't going to let that happen. I helped him toss her in the river." He sat up on the couch now, calmer. He'd stopped crying and sniffed. I handed him a tissue.

"Margret's on the move," DC said in our ear.

"We have to go. What about the dead rat?" Burns asked.

"What dead rat?" Jaffe looked puzzled.

"Someone left a dead rat and a threatening note in my locker."

"I suppose Chentinko could have done it on his own. Are you going to tell the police? Chentinko will kill me before he'll let himself be taken in."

"Maybe they can put you into witness protection," I said.

"My career would be ruined. I'd never see my family, my grandmother, again. If we hadn't gone to that stupid barbershop, none of this would have happened."

"What do you mean?" I asked.

"The sex dungeon. That's what it's called. The Barbershop."

I let it roll around in my head for a minute.

"She's almost to you, Boss," Neutron said.

I was missing something. I closed my eyes and replayed the day in my mind. All the pieces were right there. As Master Tahkaswami would say, I only needed to infuse them with my energy.

A knock came on the door.

"You didn't call the cops already, did you?" Jaffe asked.

I continued to replay the day, as I would footage from a pageant.

"She's got a security guard and a nurse with her, Boss," Neutron said.

Finally, I opened my eyes. "Burns, I think I know where the laptop is!" It was a hunch, but I thought it was a good one. If Jaffe hadn't sent the threatening note, someone else at the morgue had.

"Who's on tonight, DC?" I asked.

"You're in luck. It's our favorite weasel."

When Margret showed up, Grand made a miraculous recovery, and Jaffe helped get us out of there smoothly.

We pulled up, and everyone started to get out.

"We don't need everyone to come," Burns said.

"I've got to pee." Grand pushed DC out of her way and held on to his cape as she slid down the high seat to the ground.

"Me too. Plus, I'm hungry," DC said.

"When an old lady says she has to pee, it's time to roll, people." Grand headed toward the entrance.

Burns glared at Neutron.

"Fine. I'll stay in the truck," Neutron said.

DC badged us in. The morgue looked spectacular. It was like walking into a brand-new place. Sam's rouge accent wall glittered against new custom pendant lighting Meg had designed for the space. Everything was set for the open house tomorrow.

"What are you doing here? You can't be here unescorted," Marshall said.

"I have several escorts," I said.

DC threw back his cape.

Burns folded his arms. "I think it's time for your break."

"Right," Marshall said, eyeing Burns.

"Let's get to the evidence room," I said as we watched Marshall leave.

"I'm hitting the bathroom, and I believe I spied a coffee bar. I can see why you like your job so much now," Grand said.

"My stomach's growling. Do you hear that?" DC patted his belly.

"You can't go yet." I took him to the evidence room. The chaotic scene from the early morning had been replaced by neat rows of catalogued merchandise grouped by type, ready to be moved first thing in the morning. The sale was set for the parking lot, where we could catch people coming and going. I spied a gorgeous electric-blue Kate Spade bag I'd have to come steal later. "Point at anything that you couldn't put up for sale. It would be something that could hold something else. Like a bag or container."

"All the stuff he wouldn't let me sell was put back into the cage," DC said, pointing into the room. The evidence room was divided into two sections. As new victims came in, evidence was tightly controlled and processed in a special holding area. The area was separated from the rest of the room by what looked like chicken wire and a locked door. The rest of the room was storage for evidence deemed not needed. Like the Island of Misfit Toys, the stuff here was waiting to be claimed by the family. The cage was piled high with leftovers. "Now, I have to go eat. I'm no fun when my blood sugar is low."

As DC left, Burns opened the lock on the cage, and we started searching. I tossed aside a Crock-Pot, puzzled about why DC hadn't put it into the sale pile. Burns opened a toolbox and lifted the tray out of it. He dumped the contents.

And out fell piles of money.

"What in the world? At least we know now why Dr. Hawthorne was twitchy about the evidence cage," I said. I opened a bread box with blood on the corner of it. I didn't want to know how it had gotten there. More money fell out.

Burns broke a ceramic lamp and kicked aside the pieces and another stack of bills.

We'd cleared almost the entire locker. While we were now surrounded by a hefty sum of money, we still hadn't found the laptop. We were down to the blow-up doll, a few items of lingerie, and a barstool.

"Maybe he traded Chentinko the laptop for the money," Burns said. "Although, that wouldn't explain how he got it or even knew about it."

Burns turned over the barstool. Something inside of it clunked. It had a fake bottom that took a key. "Maybe this is it."

We looked around for something to pry it open with. I grabbed a large knife from a butcher block set in the for-sale section of the room and handed it to him.

Burns struggled to get it open. With one last tug, the bottom of the hidden opening flew off—and revealed not money or the laptop but a collection of porn magazines.

"Damn it!" Burns kicked the barstool over. It landed on top of the blow-up doll. Instead of bouncing off the plastic or squishing into its softness, the barstool landed with a loud thud.

"No way." Burns smiled at me. The doll had a base with weight in the bottom of it to keep it standing upright, so any extra weight from either money or a laptop would have gone unnoticed. He grabbed the knife and gutted the doll.

And there it was. A small laptop computer, lying in the now-deflated belly of the sex doll.

Thinking over the day and Dr. Hawthorne's reactions, I should have known the laptop was in the doll. As Burns picked up the machine, I noticed a large patch in the doll's butt. That must have been how the computer got there.

"Thank you, Katherine. I'll be taking that."

In the doorway stood Dr. Hawthorne. He had a gun to Grand's head.

Chapter 22

"If you hurt her..." I said.

He threw a satchel at us. "Money in the bag, please, and there will be no reason for anything unseemly to happen. I assure you, I have no desire to harm your grandmother. I never wanted to harm anyone."

"Maybe you shouldn't be waving a gun around if you're so committed to not harming people," Grand said.

"How did you know we were here?" I asked as I started loading the cash into the bag.

"Marshall is a very obedient lapdog. He has a standing order to call me if anyone shows up."

Figured. Weasel. Now Grand was being held by a murderer. "Pet services is one of the fastest-growing sectors in the pet industry, growing at twelve percent annually."

Dr. Hawthorne looked confused. I made a mental note to sock Marshall the next time I saw him.

We finished putting the money in the bag, and Dr. Hawthorne led us to the autopsy room. I didn't see Marshall or DC anywhere.

"So what happened?" Burns asked. "Gillian found something on the computer that linked you to something you didn't want to be linked to?"

"Or did she recognize you coming out of Madam Scott's dungeon?" I asked.

"With the morgue's work with the police, I have a lot of exposure to journalists from the paper. She recognized me at Madam Scott's right away. Of course, seeing a madam is not really a crime. While it would have been inconvenient and embarrassing, it wouldn't have mattered much. Blackmail, on the other hand, is illegal and would have landed me in prison."

"You were blackmailing Mrs. Scott's other clients," I said.

"Finding congressmen engaged in kinky extramarital affairs can be a lucrative retirement plan. Ms. Mathers's discovery of my scheme interrupted my returns, however."

"Diversification in retirement planning can be a pain," Grand said.

"What gave me away?" he asked.

"Dr. Jaffe told us the madam's dungeon was named the Barbershop, and the only regular withdrawals in your finances were your overpriced, bimonthly trips to the barbershop," Burns said.

Hawthorne looked startled that Burns had his financial records. "When I first started seeing her, the cover for the place was a barbershop. I never bothered to switch my payments."

"Plus, you were way too twitchy when we mentioned overhauling the evidence room," I said.

"Couldn't have you finding my insurance policy, now could I?"

We hadn't heard from Neutron in a while. I was starting to worry about him.

"You can stick that pension where the sun don't shine," Grand said.

"Are you all right?" I asked her.

"She'd be fine if she'd stop wiggling."

Grand squirmed under Dr. Hawthorne's arm.

"I only need her for insurance. And this, of course," he said, pointing at the laptop. "What I can fetch for this will round out my retirement nicely." He sat Grand in a chair in front of us, keeping the gun aimed at her back, and picked up the phone. "Good evening, Mr. Chentinko. I believe I have something of yours that you'd like returned."

Dr. Hawthorne negotiated a swap with Chentinko. The doctor would give him the laptop in exchange for a new identity and enough money to get him out of the country and set up for his golden years. They arranged to meet at Forest Park.

"I'm afraid I'm in a hurry. You'll have to work faster than that, or I'll have to find a bidder more eager to accommodate my demands," Dr. Hawthorne said into the phone.

Chentinko must have agreed, because Dr. Hawthorne hung up.

"Now, Katherine, if you and Mr. McPhee could please proceed to the walk-in cooler."

"You can't put us in there. We'll freeze," I said.

"You're in a meat locker with a hunk. I'm the one with the gun pointed at me," Grand said.

"I'd imagine one of your associates will be along well before hypothermia sets in."

With his gun, he motioned us into the freezer. I heard a loud clank behind us. Burns pushed on the door, but it wouldn't budge. Dr. Hawthorne must have barred the door.

Burns pulled out his cell phone then shoved it back into his pocket. There was no way he would get a signal in the insulated steel refrigerator.

I rubbed my hands together and blew out a big sigh. I could see my breath. Thankfully, I had chosen one of my winter suits for the trip to the nursing home. It was a bit heavy for the spring weather, but I looked really good in electric blue.

"Someone will be here soon." Burns rubbed his hands up and down my arms.

"We're going to freeze to death surrounded by creepy dead people." The cooler was full of sheet-covered bodies lying on the shelves.

"I'm sure Master Tahkaswami or Kierkegaard or whoever else wouldn't want you thinking negative thoughts." He brought me closer to him. "I don't suppose somewhere in that *Trivial Pursuit*–master brain of yours is a tip on getting out of a walk-in?"

We huddled near the door. Burns had taken the sheets from the bodies and wrapped us under them. Right now, all I could think of was that gun pointed at Grand's head.

"Tell me she's going to be okay," I said.

"I promise you, we'll get her back. There's no reason for him to hurt her until they've made the exchange."

Finally, I heard the door open. We poked our heads out from under our sheet fortress.

"Don't you two look cozy," DC said.

We found Neutron on the ground of the parking lot. He rubbed his head as he started to come to.

"We have to get to Forest Park. Flynn's already on his way." Burns lifted Neutron up and put him into the back of the SUV.

"Sorry, Boss. He surprised me." Neutron opened one of his laptops. He said they had installed a tracker on Dr. Hawthorne's car after Gillian's forensics had gone missing. Now Neutron was using the tracker to find out where the doctor was taking Grand.

It was a good thing too. Forest Park was a massive place. The park was the seventh largest urban park in the country and encompassed over thirteen hundred acres, almost five hundred acres larger than New York's Central Park.

"We'll find her. I promise." He squeezed my hand.

"Got ya. He's at the boathouse," Neutron said.

The boathouse had a deceptive name. The space consisted of two buildings that looked more like tiki huts. One building housed a restaurant, and the other managed the boats. The restaurant was open only during the day or for events. Tonight it was dark and quiet.

We snuck around back. Tables with umbrellas lined the water's edge. The dock sprawled off the back. Paddleboats and rowboats bobbed, tethered to both sides of the dock in little pretend parking places. Stray life jackets littered the metal dock top that glared brightly under the overhanging light.

Dr. Hawthorne stood near the dock with Chentinko and several men with guns. I caught a glimpse of the laptop next to a large envelope on an adjacent table. That must have been how they were making the swap. I didn't see Grand anywhere.

From between the two buildings, Flynn appeared, crouched close to the ground. He looked like something out of an action movie with two large guns slung over his back, ammo belts hanging off his arm, and another gun in his hand. He was almost to the table with the laptop when one of Chentinko's men caught sight of him.

"I wouldn't do that," said someone with a thick accent.

Another man appeared, holding Grand at gunpoint. I squealed and ran out from where we were. Burns, DC, and Neutron followed, brandishing their weapons. Flynn kept moving and grabbed the laptop and envelope.

"Now we have some leverage," Burns said.

"So we meet again, beautiful, my angel," Chentinko said, flashing his eerie grin at me.

"Don't hurt her!" I screamed.

"I will be with you shortly, my love. For now, let the men talk." He made a kissing face at me before turning his attention to Burns. "It seems we both have what the other wants."

"Seems like."

"I will tell you what I will do. We will play a little game. I will be the generous one. You can choose which you take, the old lady or the computer."

"That's mighty big of you, but I think I'll be taking both," Burns said. He and Flynn pointed guns at Chentinko.

"Oh, I'm quite sure that's not going to happen. If your associate doesn't put down the laptop in the next five seconds, I'm going to kill the old lady, and then my men will kill you."

"She's not my grandmother," Burns said.

"There's a blessing," Grand said.

"Five," Chentinko counted.

"He's bluffing," Burns said.

"Flynn, put it down," I yelled.

Chentinko's grin grew. He looked like he enjoyed the game. Not a doubt remained in my mind that Chentinko was going to shoot her.

"Four."

"Someone better do something. I'm not sure he knows all the numbers," Grand said.

Chentinko squeezed Grand a little harder. She winced.

"Burns, what are you doing?" I asked.

"Three."

"Thinking," McPhee said.

"Two."

"Please! Put it down!" I yelled. Tears streamed down my cheeks.

"All right. Put it down, Flynn," Burns said.

"A wise choice," Chentinko said, throwing Grand to the ground. She whimpered.

I scooped in to get her and deposited her behind the building. "Stay here. Don't move."

"It's not like I'm going for a paddleboat ride." She pretended to smoke a cigarette.

Bedlam broke out once Grand and I were out of the way. Flynn had engaged several of Chentinko's men, and Burns had managed to get Chentinko at gunpoint.

Chentinko grinned his evil grin while he and Burns talked.

Then I saw him—Dr. Hawthorne, his gun pointed at Burns. Flynn wouldn't look up. Burns hadn't noticed him.

Dr. Hawthorne stalked closer. He was going to shoot.

I ran toward them and knocked the doctor to the ground. A burning pain tore through my knee, and I felt a fist to my eye. Then came the sound of the gun and a hiccup squeal from me.

When I looked down, Dr. Hawthorne was dead. What happened after that was a big blur. Someone pulled me away.

Chentinko ran to a paddleboat, and Burns and Flynn took one of their own. Bullets flew down the Mississippi as the paddleboats sped along. With a final effort, Burns and Flynn both jumped from their boat to Chentinko's.

The sudden change in weight caused the paddleboat to tip, tossing the laptop into midair. My heart stopped. Burns chased the computer, his face clenched tight with determination. I needed him to catch it. But he was too late. I watched as the laptop landed with a spectacular splat into the river and sank, taking with it both my and Burns's hope for answers. All that remained were bubbles on the water.

My hands wouldn't stop shaking. We sat under the beautiful trees of the park. Music from the outdoor theater played in the background. Grand sat with me. She had a small cut on her arm and some other scrapes but was mostly none the worse for wear.

Burns and Flynn had dragged Chentinko to shore. His grin now gone, replaced with an angry scowl, he sat dripping against an adjacent tree, tied up with one of the ropes from the boat.

"This is not over for us, my love," he said.

I wanted to throw up. I finally had an excuse to use that card Detective Driscol had given me with his contact info, even if I couldn't get any words out.

Burns took over the phone. "Cops are on their way."

A car pulled up near us. I thought one of the detectives would appear. Instead, Claude popped out. He moved slowly, shuffling his feet.

He was dressed in blue slacks and a nice checked button-down with a blue bow tie to match. Grand perked up when she saw him. I assumed she'd called him. He kept his eyes focused on her, moving through the rest of us as though we weren't even there.

"Are you all right?" he asked, stopping in front of her, close but not touching her.

"Mostly."

"I'm terribly sorry about all of this, Theodora."

"It's okay, Claude. It wasn't your fault."

"I hope someday you'll be able to forgive me."

And then Claude Pederski pulled a gun from his pocket, aimed it at Victor Chentinko, and shot him three times in the head.

Epilogue

"**D**on't be a turkey. Release Claude Pederski!"

The shouts came from the crowd in front of the morgue. A week had passed since Claude shot Chentinko. It had also been a week since I had become a killer, even though the shooting was ruled in self-defense. Claude, however, had been arrested for murder.

Apparently, a week was the amount of time the hospital administration thought was respectable before sweeping the whole mess under the rug. They insisted the morgue debut party we had planned would be great publicity, especially now that I was no longer a suspect in the body snatching.

While I was sure some of the people loitering about were waiting to get into the party, the majority appeared to be protesters. Their signs poked up and down above the circling crowd as I approached.

"Judicial frauds jailed our Claude!"

For the first few days following Chentinko's death, a zoo of reporters camped in front of the house. Grand was the star attraction. Everyone wanted the story of the little old couple who had taken on the mob. The more the story got out, the bigger her following. She couldn't go anywhere without being followed by groupies. People left gifts at the house.

"Stand with Grand! Stand with Grand!" shouted the Grand Groupies, all adorned in matching T-shirts and marching in unison, their synchronicity faltering as I pushed past them into the morgue.

Grand's celebrity garnered an offer from an agent about a book deal and a movie. Our living room had once again become Scrapbook Central as she worked on a new crime-themed memory book, this time for Claude, convinced that he had shot Chentinko in a show of devotion. She planned to capitalize on her newfound celebrity to gin up jury sympathy so they'd let him off on self-defense by proxy. Based on the size of the mob I had to push my way through to get to the morgue door, she would have a good shot at it.

The crowd inside the morgue was equally thick. I spied the county commissioner and the new acting mayor of St. Louis hobnobbing with some of the hospital administration near the coffee bar. The remodeled space looked as good as I remembered. Although with everything that had happened here, I couldn't help feeling there was a cloud over it all.

This was the place where someone I trusted had kidnapped my grand and held her at gunpoint. Dr. Hawthorne was also the one who had put the rat in my locker. I thought I had recognized the handwriting on the envelope that day, but I couldn't quite place it at the time. Now I was reconsidering everything.

Moving through the crowd, I waved at Meg and Henry, who were escorting a woman who I assumed was Henry's mother. Neutron and Flynn had saved the day for them. He hacked Ariel Rodriguez's computer and found documentation about her skimming from the store's books. Flynn told her if she didn't leave Henry alone and pay him back all the money she'd taken, her daddy dearest and maybe the police would get a very interesting package.

I looked around and headed toward DC and Neutron, who were standing near the new copy machine.

"Who made these up?" Neutron asked as he looked at a bingo card. "Not being able to pee is not a real cause of death."

"Of course it is. It's in the book on the fifty weirdest ways to die," DC replied.

"Hyperplasia of the prostate," I chimed in, moving in between them and plucking a canapé from Neutron.

DC smiled at me and began a loud clap.

"Here she is, everyone, our own crime-stopping heroine, Ms. Kat Waters."

Some of the onlookers nearby also clapped. I looked at the ground.

"Oh no, you don't. I will not let you continue to feel bad about this," DC said.

"DC's right, Kat. These were bad men. I'm glad they're dead and not you and Burns," Neutron added. He made it sound so simple.

"And you are a badass superwoman," DC finished.

I knew they were right. In the week since the ordeal, Neutron had filled me in on Chentinko and the Red Mafia, one of the most dreaded mob families in the world because of how savagely they murdered their terrified victims. I'd learned how Chentinko had been shipped here from New York and how much he hated St. Louis. His whole scheme to lean on Mrs. Scott had started as a way to impress his bosses into giving him a ticket out of here. Instead, it had all gone horribly wrong. A couple of weeks ago, the head of the Red Mafia, Simon "The Mole" Mogilevich, came to town. This was a huge deal, apparently. He hadn't been seen in public for years, but supposedly he was here now, cleaning up Chentinko's mess.

"So are you officially out of hiding, or is this just a quickie reprieve?" DC asked, eyeing me up and down.

Since the shooting, I hadn't moved much from my bed. He'd come to see me a few times, but I hadn't ventured out from the apartment.

"I'm not in hiding."

"Uh-huh, and Neutron's going to be a contestant on *Dancing with the Stars*," DC said.

"Hey, I hacked someone famous. I could get third-tier celebrity status. You've never seen me salsa." Neutron imitated some fancy footwork.

I appreciated his attempts at cheering me up. "I'm not sure yet. I'm trying to stay in the moment," I said and dipped a chip in Neutron's dip.

"Still not sleeping, huh?" he asked.

I shook my head. Since the shooting, nightmares had haunted my dreams. Visions of gunfire intertwined with the sights of Stephanie Jackson's dead, mangled body, Chentinko's cruel, evil grin, and Dr. Hawthorne's last gasp. I contemplated the irony that Chentinko and Dr. Hawthorne were both now lying in the morgue somewhere.

Mostly I had just lain under the covers, trying to process everything. Or not process it, trying instead to compartmentalize it all so I could stuff it in a mental box where it belonged, never to be opened. Screw Master Tahkaswami.

"That settles it. I'm bringing over the Serenity Slumber machine. It has a hundred forty-two settings and is guaranteed to bring you a night of uninterrupted tranquility."

"Does it play crickets?" Neutron asked. "I always found crickets soothing."

"You're a good friend, DC. No Kimi today?" I asked. With Fletcher's help, DC was being credited as instrumental in bringing the killers to justice. That had brought Kimi around, and the lovebirds were supposedly once again living in domestic harmony.

"You know she wouldn't be caught dead near here. Kimi could catch a virus just *looking* at the building. She's at home trying out a new herbal pet-grooming system. Our pet therapist suggested it might help with their bond."

"Give her my hellos. I need to mingle," I said, pointing toward my mom.

"Katherine, what on earth are you wearing?" Mom asked as I approached her and Charles Montgomery, who I'd guessed was there to support his godson, Dr. Jaffe.

I hadn't bothered to dress in anything formal. Until she said something, I didn't even remember what I had put on this morning. I looked at my jeans and sweater. "Eh, whatever," I said.

"I think you look as lovely as always," Mr. Montgomery said, shaking my hand. "Jeffery is around here somewhere. I'm sure he'd love to say hello."

Dr. Jaffe had been put on probation and sentenced to mandatory Gambler's Anonymous meetings, but they hadn't taken away his medical license. The generous donation Mr. Montgomery and Teradyne Defense had made to both the medical board and the police fund probably hadn't hurt. Plus, Jaffe had fully cooperated. He led the cops to where Stephanie Jackson's body had been dumped. After a few hours of dredging, they'd pulled her to the surface, along with several other bodies I was sure would be connected to Chentinko.

Following the shooting, I met Detective Lambert in interrogation. For some reason, they let Burns go right away. This time, he corroborated my story, so they didn't hold me long. The cop at the scene ruled the shooting self-defense. It helped that Mr. and Mrs. Scott had appeared midway through my conversation with the detectives to confess their role in it all.

None of us mentioned the laptop.

I'd asked Jaffe directly, but he didn't know what his uncle wanted with the laptop. That secret sank to the bottom of the Mississippi with the machine, but I didn't think it was a coincidence that Mr. Montgomery was now keeping my mom close.

"This place looks truly amazing," Mr. Montgomery said.

"Yes, Katherine, you've certainly put your talents to good use here. Maybe you should consider turning your career aspirations to the decorating field," she said.

I gave myself points for not rolling my eyes at her. "Thank you, Mother. It's very nice to see you again, Mr. Montgomery. If you'll excuse me, duty calls," I said and pointed at the crowd.

I moved through the main cube area and toward the refreshments.

A hand lightly gripped my arm. I flinched instinctively.

"There you are, Stretch." Fletcher dropped his hand and took a pull from a soda bottle. He looked around us, taking in everything and everyone in the room. "Good turnout. I think the Cause-of-Death bingo was an especially nice touch."

"Everyone does seem to love bingo." I looked around too. It was a decent crowd. "Good turnout if you count the protestors, anyway. You've created a monster." I smiled at him.

In exchange for downplaying any possible connection to my dad, we gave Fletcher the exclusive on Grand's story. He ran a three-part series on her heroism in the face of danger. I was mostly spared attention, except as a way to explain the missing body from the morgue. Burns was a minor footnote, mentioned only as providing security for us. After Fletcher obtained the exclusive, the circus of reporters went away. Then when the first story ran, the groupies appeared.

Fletcher grinned and grabbed some appetizers from a passing waiter. He handed me a couple. "Where is our geriatric demon, anyway? I don't think I've spotted her yet."

"She's with her people, holding vigil at the prison."

"Claude still not talking?"

I shook my head. Eventually, the detectives had made it to the park and tried to make sense of the scene. They took Claude into custody. He hadn't said anything since then, not a single word—not to me, not to the cops, and not to Grand. The last thing he'd said was a week ago when he gave the apology to Grand, right before he murdered Chentinko.

"It's only been a week," Fletcher said. "He'll come around. Now that your mobster stalker is no longer in the picture, we can have that date you owe me."

In exchange for his help getting a story about Meg's lighting published on the society page, I'd agreed to have dinner with Fletcher. Meg was now a local celebrity, her Megathon lamps in demand at every high-end boutique, including the one with that rude man who had insulted her. Too bad his store wouldn't be getting any.

"'In the picture' is such a poor choice of words for a prolific writer like you, given my ordeal," I said.

Fletcher winced. The police had found hundreds of creepy stalker pictures of me, and Jaffe said that Chentinko had been following me for weeks before Stephanie Jackson's murder. He also told Jaffe that I had something of his that would fix the situation if he failed to get the laptop. He said we were fated to be together and that I was his "angel of deliverance."

Of course, I had no idea what I could have had that belonged to Chentinko, and he never told Jaffe. I had an inkling that it was related to my dad, but with the laptop turned into fish food, I might never know.

"You take your time. I'm not in a hurry. One of *my* mom's rules is that good things are worth waiting for," Fletcher said before inhaling a shrimp puff.

I didn't want to contemplate his idea of good things. Instead, I made my excuses for moving on.

I moved through the crowd, searching. In the Hall of Famous Autopsies, I found my target. Burns stood in front of a beautifully framed portrait of Gillian Mathers. Meg and Henry had added her heroic story to the exhibit.

"They did a great job," I said.

He didn't turn toward me but nodded.

"Her story belongs up there. She died trying to save more girls. She did good," I added.

"You did good," he said.

I blushed.

"Thanks to your tenacity, the St. Louis prostitute serial killings are a solved case, and I now know why Gillian was killed. You should feel proud."

I did feel proud. Proud that I hadn't given up. Not on the prostitutes, not on Stephanie Jackson, and not on my dad. Proud for saving Burns. But...

"But that's the thing," I said. "It seems all settled, but it's not. Not for me with some cryptic set of missile launch codes still out there. Not for you with a mysterious code word still unexplained."

"No," Burns said. "Not totally settled. But Stephanie Jackson's parents can finally lay her to rest. You and Jaffe aren't living in fear of being murdered by the crazy Chentinko. The county got rid of a corrupt coroner. Your grand's a celebrity. That ain't nothing." He stood resolute, hands on his hips, eyes on Gillian's picture.

"True, not nothing," I said.

"In fact, it deserves a toast." He turned toward me. "Let's find something."

These achievements did deserve to be celebrated, and Burns was probably the only other person who could fully understand that. He smiled that devilish grin of his and ran his hand lightly down my arm before grabbing my hand. "Not settled," he repeated, rubbing his thumb over the pulse point on my wrist. He pulled me lightly though the corridor.

"Heard you're off probation," he said as we walked toward the break room, where the refreshment table was.

"Yup. Full reinstatement."

"You going to stay?"

I smiled. In the week since the shooting, I hadn't been able to make decisions about anything. "Maybe. Probably, maybe."

"Always definitive with the decisions. That's my girl." As we stepped into the room, he pulled a brochure from his pocket and handed it to me. It was for the Forensic Science program at the university.

"What's this for?" I asked.

"Jaffe said you needed to study."

He had. He told us at the police station that he didn't feel bad about having Duff call in the false report about me taking the body for Chentinko because he didn't think I liked my job very much. He said that if I would apply myself, however, I could be really great at my job. I apparently had a knack with puzzles, families, and dead people. That was why he was always so hard on me, always asking me those weird questions, not because of my supposed mob ties but because he thought I was wasting my potential.

It was odd to think that I might actually have found something I was good at.

"I like the work here," I said as I surveyed the food. "Dead people always have something important to say."

"What about your parents' disapproval?" he asked, filling a plate.

"Children are supposed to cause their parents unwarranted stress," I said, smiling.

"They have a scholarship," Burns said with a grin as I opened the pamphlet. His smile faded as he looked up at me. "I want you to know, in case you were unsure, I never would have let anything happen to your grand. Flynn had Chentinko in his sights the whole time and wouldn't have hesitated to drop the bastard if he even flinched wrong."

"Yeah, I figured."

"I just kept thinking that with enough time, we could find a way to have both your grand and the laptop."

"What will you do now?" I asked. "Wasn't that laptop your only lead?"

"I'm not sure, but something will turn up. Every time I've hit a dead end, the universe has given me something. Last time, I got you," he said, tugging one of my curls.

I put the pamphlet in my bag.

"How are you really doing?" He looked at me more intently now, a flash of concern pinching at his temples.

"I'm only able to sleep if Grand's in the bed with me."

"It will fade, Kat. Give yourself some space. And for what it's worth, I don't believe you're a mob princess."

"I guess I don't either. And that's something too," I said. I picked up a drink and raised my glass in a toast. "In all of this, in all of my indecision, that's the one thing I feel certain of. Clarke Waters did not work for the mob. I don't care what the missile launch codes say." I took a big swig. "You think little old Claude works for Simon 'The Mole'?" It made sense that they would have Chentinko killed to shut him up. It was laughable to think of Claude as their chosen hit man.

"No," Burns said with a chuckle, "but I'm not sure I buy that little old Claude went mental either or shot Chentinko in some fit of revenge for your grand."

"Me either, but that's one more thing that doesn't fit. One more screwed-up thing in this whole mess."

"I noticed your mom has mysteriously been hired by none other than Charles Montgomery."

"She's now head of event planning for his charitable foundation. Isn't that convenient and interesting?"

"Hmm." He nodded. "Speaking of events..." He eyed me over his glass.

I'd seen that look before.

"You having any more dinners with Fletcher Reid?"

"Why? Would you care?"

"Maybe."

I grinned. "Then maybe it's only a one-time thing. Honestly, with things with Dad and now Claude, I almost feel like I'm being disloyal whenever I'm with him."

"Good," he said with a smirk.

We finished eating, and Burns left. I'd had enough of social interaction and headed out past the protesters into the parking lot. I just wanted to climb back under my covers. The ring of my phone startled me. I didn't recognize the number.

"Hello," I said, curious.

"Hello, Katherine."

Another Russian accent. Great. "Who is this?"

"You can call me Simon."

I knew only one Simon who was Russian—The Mole. My heart raced.

"How did you get this number?"

"You'll find that I'm very resourceful. I thought it was time for us to get to know each other better. First, I thought I should apologize for the unfortunate series of events. You never should have been involved in such a distasteful matter. Victor was unwell."

"Thank you. Yes, he was."

"But I understand he will no longer be a worry for you."

Panic swept through me as I tried to decipher his meaning. I wondered whether he'd had Victor killed or if perhaps Claude had worked for him.

"I wish we could be introduced under different circumstances, but unfortunately, you have something of mine that I need."

"The laptop did a giant belly flop into the Mississippi."

"I'm aware of the outcome of your last business transaction. It is regrettable, but I'm not concerned with the laptop. We have other systems that will cover things."

So another system did exist. But if that wasn't what he wanted, I wondered what on earth he did want.

"It's beautiful out this time of year, isn't it? Perhaps we can take a walk on the riverfront together very soon. I'll be back in touch. Goodbye, Katherine."

And with that, he hung up.

About the Author

The owner of a boutique chocolate factory in Atlanta, MJ O'Neill loves to write lighthearted, romantic mysteries with a sweet twist. She has a degree in business communications from North Carolina State University. Through creative endeavors in her IT career, she has written everything from technical manuals to corporate blogs, and as a certified project manager, MJ is sure everyone's life needs a project plan!

MJ has recently survived transplanting from the Midwest, where she was raised, and is now soaking up the Southern hospitality of Atlanta, Georgia. When she's not spinning a sweet yarn or creating delicious confections, she spends time with her husband, Brian, their kids, who range in age from 24 to 7, a hyperactive cocker spaniel named Divo (after the band), a princess tabby cat named Twilight (before the book stole her name), and a collection of stray fish. The whole gang can be found tooling around the back roads of the South in their RV, where MJ uses the downtime to hatch her next sweet plot.

Read more at www.mjoneillauthor.com.

About the Publisher

Dear Reader,

We hope you enjoyed this book. Please consider leaving a review on your favorite book site.

Visit https://RedAdeptPublishing.com to see our entire catalogue.

Don't forget to subscribe to our monthly newsletter to be notified of future releases and special sales.